THE FARTHING GIRL

DAISY CARTER

Copyright © 2024 Daisy Carter
All rights reserved.

This story is a work of fiction. The characters, names, places, events, and incidents in it are entirely the work of the author's imagination or used in a fictitious manner. Any resemblance or similarity to actual persons, living or dead, events or places is entirely coincidental. No part of this work may be reproduced, stored in a retrieval system, or transmitted, in any form or by any means, without the prior permission of the author and the publisher.

CHAPTER 1

*S*outh Wales - Mid 1800s

THE MIST ROLLED across the moors, drifting ever closer to Castleford Hall and carrying with it a faint salty tang from the coast. Like wraiths in the dead of night, its blanketing whiteness muffled the cattle lowing and shrouded familiar landmarks, making them unrecognisable. It was the sort of mist that could disorient an unwary traveller and send them stumbling to their doom—the sort of mist a superstitious person might say was the harbinger of troubled times ahead.

* * *

KATIE WIGGLED her toes in front of the fire in the kitchen, watching the steam rise from her woollen stockings. Her boots pinched and had a hole that let in water, but she hadn't wanted to tell Grandpapa. It wasn't that they couldn't afford to be replaced or mended at the cobblers, just that it would entail a trip to Pembrey Minster, which was what they always did with Mama. But not anymore.

Beryl Pertwee, the family's cook, was bustling between the sink and the large scrubbed wooden table, preparing dinner. "Time for some new ones, is it?" She nodded towards the abandoned boots Katie had kicked off. "They're getting too small anyway."

"They only pinch a little bit. And my feet are wet because I went through the stream to take some windfall apples to the ponies on the moor. I'll stuff them with newspaper to stretch them." A memory of hot chocolate and buttered crumpets at the tearoom after her mama had taken them all into town for new boots the previous autumn came back to her. She reached hastily for her book to block it out.

"You're growing fast. The cobbler will mend them and they'll do for Polly when she's bigger. I suppose you'll need a couple of new winter dresses soon as well."

"I suppose so." She wondered who would do the myriad of things a mother was meant to do with her daughters now. Would she and Polly get a governess? And what about the boys, Wilbur and Tim? How would they fare now that Papa was gone? *Now that we're orphans.* Katie felt restless, as though she needed to do something to push her worrisome thoughts away.

"Do you want me to help you get dinner ready, Mrs Pertwee?"

"No, cariad. You enjoy a few minutes with your book." She used the affectionate term often with Katie and her siblings, and her eyes twinkled. "It will be noisy enough once the little 'uns come downstairs. That is if the new maid remembers to bring them. Half the time, Susan's head is in the clouds, daydreaming about the butcher's boy."

A few minutes later, the sound of brisk footsteps in the hallway rang out. "Are you bringing the poached salmon through to the dining room, Mrs Pertwee, or do I have to do it myself?" Norman Cavendish's moustache quivered with irritation as he stood with his hands behind his back in the kitchen doorway, disdainfully eyeing the cavernous room with its workaday furniture.

"Now?" Mrs Pertwee shot a flustered glance at the clock on the dresser. "It's not time to eat yet, Master Norman."

"Not time?" He sounded indignant. "I rang for dinner some twenty minutes ago. Don't tell me the servants' bells have stopped working. This wretched place is falling apart." Norman stepped into the room and glared up at the board where a brass bell for each room in Castleford Hall was neatly labelled.

Katie looked up guiltily from her book, still sitting in the shadows of the inglenook fireplace. It had felt nice being lost in a story about two waifs running away from a miserly old crone who lived in a shack in the forest. Now that she was nine years old, she had her pick of books in the library, but it was the fairy tales she turned to at the moment. The faint scent of Mama's violet perfume on the pages comforted her. "Sorry, Uncle Norman." She slipped the book behind her onto the chair and quickly stood up, shoving her boots on again. "I heard the bell when Mrs Pertwee was in the garden picking fresh herbs, and I forgot to tell her."

"I should have guessed." He strode across the

room and peered through the kitchen window at the gathering dusk, then frowned as he caught sight of her book. Perhaps if you spent more time tending to your chores instead of with your nose buried in those childish stories, you would have realised dinner should be served now. Amelia and I have been sitting in the dining room waiting."

"But it's too early for dinner, Master Norman." Beryl Pertwee glanced at the clock again, puzzled. "Your father likes it served at seven o'clock sharp. Unless he's out on the moors, in which case I plate it up so he can—"

"That's as maybe," he interrupted, "but when we're staying as guests, it would be polite to pay attention to what I want. Papa has let things get completely out of hand, I can see." Norman wasn't interested in the details of how Sir William Cavendish lived, that much was clear.

"Well," Beryl lowered her voice sympathetically, and Katie felt the familiar leaden weight of sadness in her chest. "Things have been difficult since...you know."

"Since Grace and Edgar died?"

Katie edged closer to the cook, noticing how her uncle was staring at the smudges of chocolate and cinnamon on her apron from baking earlier in the day. It had been a few months since the shocking event that had left her, Wilbur, Polly, and Tim orphaned, and Beryl Pertwee had become something of a second mother to them since. Most people spoke gently about it, if at all, but Uncle Norman took no such care.

"Yes. Sir William has been a true rock for the little 'uns, even though it's hard for him as well to have lost his daughter. He spends a lot of time in his study and often says it hardly matters if dinner is a few minutes late."

Norman pulled a face. "I don't agree. It's times like this that rules and discipline become even more important, Mrs Pertwee. Papa might think Grace's children need mollycoddling, but a firm hand is what will get them through this. Goodness only knows what was on Edgar's mind, taking Grace for a day out on the paddle steamer. It was a ridiculous idea if you ask me, and a waste of money."

"It was a surprise treat for her birthday. Edgar confided to me how he wanted them to enjoy a few nights in the big smoke and a trip on the Thames on the paddle steamer." Beryl pursed her lips and added a knob of butter with a pinch of chopped parsley to the potatoes. "Sir William tells me you owned the steamboat," she muttered. There was an edge of accusation to her comment.

Katie gasped and stared at her uncle.

"Partly. An ill-advised investment, as it turned out. It was just a passing interest I had, but I don't see a big future for them. I focus my time on the rest of the business now."

"You…you were there when Mama and Papa had the accident?" Katie felt as though she had been punched with all the air driven from her lungs.

"Of course not. It's a minor detail that I invested some money in it…nothing a child needs to know." He shrugged as though the tragedy that had shattered life at Castleford Hall was an inconvenience. "Anyway, Amelia is hungry and we can't wait for Papa to finish whatever he's doing in his study. He leaned over the table and peered at the salmon suspiciously.

"Freshly caught this week by one of the gamekeepers from the neighbouring estate." Beryl slid the platter away from him with a challenging stare. She might be getting a bit slower with age, but she knew there was nothing wrong with her cooking. "And I expect it's a sight better than what you and Mrs Cavendish are used to eating in London."

"I doubt it."

The old cook bridled at the insult. "Perhaps you don't want dinner after all, then?"

"Bring it through immediately." He reluctantly attempted a smile. "You know Papa and I don't always get along. He's been worse than ever since the funerals."

"Yes, it's a shame you couldn't attend your sister's funeral. And Edgar's. The whole town turned out. At least some folks cared enough to show their respects." The saucepan lid clattered as Beryl put it on the side of the range with more force than necessary.

"Half-sister," Norman corrected, tugging at his cuffs, looking slightly contrite. "I had some business matters which kept me in London."

Katie wondered why her uncle was so rude. He had only been at Castleford Hall for two days and had found fault with every meal, not to mention grumbling about dandelions growing on the croquet lawn and insisting that there was no need to have a stable full of horses now that only Grandpapa lived here with her and her siblings. *Does he mean to offend everyone? And Aunt Amelia is no better.* She gulped as he gave her a beady look, hoping her thoughts weren't written on her face. "I'll tell the others to wash their hands. They're in the nursery. Susan, the new maid, is still getting used to things."

"Oh, certainly not." He looked alarmed. Amelia has a delicate disposition; she would rather you eat in the kitchen."

A sense of injustice grew in Katie's chest. "Why are you so horrid?" she blurted out, hot tears pricking behind her eyes. "Grandpa always likes us eating with him. And you haven't even said you're sorry Mama and Papa are…are gone."

"Well, of course I'm sorry," he blustered, backing towards the door. "That goes without saying." He drew himself taller. "All these emotional outbursts are exactly why it's best you children eat supper in the kitchen. Besides, your grandfather and I have important things to discuss."

"I'll bring the food through now if you'd like to tell Sir William."

"Thank you, Mrs Pertwee. And, for goodness sake, keep the children out of the way. The last thing I need is for my dear wife to get a headache from all the noise."

"We're not noisy. Grandpa says we stop the house feeling like a mausoleum." Katie couldn't help but defend herself. "He says this is our home, no matter that Mama isn't here and that you don't even like it at Castleford, anyway."

"Hush, child," Beryl said hastily, resting her hand on Katie's shoulder. " I'm sure your grandfather just meant that they prefer living in London. Castleford Hall is home to all of you, including your uncle and aunt."

"Not forgetting our son, Maxwell," Norman added firmly. "I'm sure one day in the future, we might consider returning to live here, but for now, my business and Maxwell's schooling make London a necessity." He glanced through the window again, where ribbons of mist were starting to shroud the garden and moorland beyond, grimacing slightly. "Although I always forget how remote it is here."

The brass bell for the dining room suddenly jiggled, ringing out with a sharpness that signalled Amelia's annoyance from afar.

"Anyway, we must dine now, Mrs Pertwee. And keep the children away from us, if you please." He strode away, muttering about his family home falling into wrack and ruin and being overrun with unruly orphans, not caring that Katie heard every word.

"Yes, sir." Beryl scurried to the pantry to fetch the salad she had made earlier. Usually, she would have cooked a hearty game stew, given that the early autumn evenings were chilly, but Amelia had made it known she preferred fish, as the rich meat might give her indigestion.

Katie put the salmon platter on a tray and added the dish of herb butter Beryl had made to go with fresh bread and lightly pickled cucumber salad. "How long are they staying?" she asked quietly.

"A few more days." The cook suppressed a sigh. "I always find myself at sixes and sevens when Mrs Cavendish has all these strange requests. What's wrong with good plain food?"

"You're a wonderful cook," Katie said, too polite to mention the incident of the burnt marmalade when Beryl had fallen asleep when she'd supped too much sherry to ease her arthritis.

"How she expects me to find some of those fancy ingredients at a moment's notice, I've no idea." The cook's cheeks flushed with indignation. "Mr Houghton at the greengrocers laughed in my face when I asked for truffles. Told me I'd have to wait two weeks for him to sail to France, find a pig to sniff them out, and then sail back again. A pig...if you please!"

Katie bit her lip so as not to smile, but when she caught Mrs Pertwee's eye, they both dissolved into laughter. Beryl had been the family cook since before she was born, but her loyalty was always tested when Uncle Norman returned for one of his infrequent visits. "Maybe Aunt Amelia will want to leave early if the weather takes a turn for the worst. It's a shame for Grandpa, though. I think he likes having more company."

"I won't be encouraging them to stay a day longer than necessary." Beryl picked up the tray and nodded for Katie to follow behind with the tureen of potatoes. "Mind you, your uncle doesn't care one jot about what would please your grandfather," she muttered darkly with a sniff of disapproval. She sailed on ahead along the dark hallway, still talking to herself. "He was always a peculiar boy…never one to like the animals on the farm. And then so jealous when Sir William remarried and had another child. I used to see him leaning over Grace in her cot in the nursery with such a strange look in his eyes—"

"He didn't like Mama? Even though she was his sister…I mean, half-sister." Katie walked faster, trying to keep up.

"Oh, that's not what I meant, dear." Beryl pressed her lips together as though she'd revealed too much. "Your uncle and mama were just rather different, that's all. Now, you run along and fetch the little 'uns as soon as we've put this food in the dining room.

I've got a nice bit of cold ham, and I'll fry up some bubble and squeak."

Katie's stomach rumbled. Leftover fried potato and cabbage with ham was one of their favourite meals, and the prospect of eating in the comfortable kitchen sounded like a much better idea than being in the company of her overbearing uncle and trying not to do anything to annoy Aunt Amelia. As for her cousin Maxwell, she had barely seen him all day, but she felt rather sorry for him.

At least her parents had loved each other, she thought. If only they hadn't drowned trying to escape that awful fire on the steamboat.

If only Mama and Papa were still here with us.

CHAPTER 2

"Is it apple pie for pudding?" Five-year-old Polly pushed her dark auburn hair out of her eyes and fidgeted in her seat, peering around the kitchen. "Please say it's apple pie, Mrs Pertwee."

"Of course, it's going to be apple pie." Wilbur, who had just turned six, always liked to seize an opportunity to boss his younger sister around. "If you're hoping for a chocolate sponge, it's wishful thinking. If anyone gets the posh pudding, it will be Uncle Norman."

"It might not be," Polly shot back.

Katie smiled to herself. She was four years older than Polly and could already tell that her sister was going to be high-spirited. She had discovered her dressed in Wilbur's trousers the other day, rolled up because they were too long, and trying to slide down the bannister because Wilbur had bet she wouldn't be brave enough to attempt it. She winced at the thought of what Uncle Norman and Aunt Amelia would make of that sort of behaviour, but to be honest, since they had been orphaned, Katie figured that anything which brought laughter into the house could only be a good thing. Little Tim had been sitting at the bottom of the sweeping staircase with a pile of cushions on the floor, looking very serious as he waited to catch Polly at the bottom. And Susan, the new maid who was meant to be keeping them out of mischief, had just looked on helplessly.

"It is apple pie, as it happens," Beryl said. "It's been a good harvest this year, and we'll have more than enough to see us through the winter."

Katie cleared the plates away and fetched some bowls from the dresser, passing them around the table.

"Have we got cream as well?" Wilbur was already trotting towards the pantry with a hopeful expression.

"Yes, but mind that you don't use it all. Mrs

Cavendish said she would very much like egg custard at luncheon tomorrow, and I might not have time to get more from the farm."

There was a moment's silence as they all gazed in admiration at the apple pie in the centre of the table. The pastry crust was the perfect shade of golden brown, topped with crunchy sugar, and the room filled with the delicious aroma of cinnamon and nutmeg. Katie served the first portion, and everyone sniffed appreciatively and leaned slightly closer, watching a curl of steam rise from the pie dish. She poured some thick cream over the top, and Wilbur grinned. "That looks like a boy's portion. You should have less, Polly; otherwise, you'll be grumbling you've got a tummy ache later because you ate too much."

"That's not true," Polly said hotly. "Make sure I have the same amount as Wilbur, please, Katie. He had the biggest slice of cheese at lunchtime and more bubble and squeak than me just now, and it's not fair."

"What about me?" Tim piped up. "Susan said I should go first because I'm the littlest."

Polly turned and gave four-year-old Tim a withering look. "Don't be silly, she was talking about choosing a book to read when we were in the nursery, not having pudding, and she only said that because you're babyish and you take the longest to choose."

Tim's chin began to tremble, and his brown eyes filled with tears. "You're mean, Polly Anderson," he cried. "Mama wouldn't let you say that. She told me my reading was getting better every day."

"Yes, but Mama isn't here anymore, and neither is Papa." Polly hid her sadness with anger. "You have to do what I say, Tim, because I'm older than you, and we don't have parents anymore."

Katie cast a worried look in Beryl's direction. As the eldest, she knew she should keep her siblings in order now, but it was hard once they all started arguing. She took a deep breath.

"Now then, Polly, that's not very nice for little Tim, is it?" She hastily spooned out some more apple pie and passed the jug of cream to her younger sister. "You help yourself, and if you want a little bit extra just this once, I can go to the farm early in the morning and fetch more cream if we need it."

Polly's cheeks flushed red, and she looked guiltily at Tim before sliding the bowl around the table to him. "I'm sorry, Tim. You're right, you are getting better at reading. I'll help you with the words you find difficult," she added stoutly.

"That's more like it, children." Beryl Pertwee was used to the outbursts, knowing that it was only because they were adjusting to their new circumstances. She patted Katie's hand with a sympathetic smile. "You're doing a grand job looking after the little 'uns."

"I worry about doing the wrong thing. Uncle Norman makes it sound as though we have no manners at all."

Beryl rolled her eyes. "Ignore him," she muttered. "He goes out of his way to find fault."

"Will we have a governess, do you think? Or go to the little school in Pembrey Minster? I liked it best when Mama taught us in the nursery."

"That's for your grandfather to decide, and I'm sure now that summer is over, he will." The cook smiled brightly at them all. "What you all have to remember, children, is to stick together. You might encounter difficult times as you get older, it's only natural. But when you look out for each other, instead of arguing, it makes things easier." She hesitated. "It's what your ma and pa would have wanted. They were very proud of all four of you and always said how important it was to be a close family."

A worrying thought suddenly occurred to Katie. "You don't think Grandpa will send us to live in London with Uncle Norman and Aunt Amelia, do you, Mrs Pertwee?"

Beryl looked surprised and then chuckled. "I think there's more chance of us having snow in July than that happening, my dear. Master Norman has a very pleasant life in London, I'm sure. I think he would find it quite a shock to the system to have four more children in his care, especially as young Maxwell is so quiet."

The kitchen door creaked open, and Katie was surprised to see her cousin hovering uncertainly on the threshold of the room.

"Come in, Max, we were just talking about you. I mean, Mrs Pertwee was just saying how polite and well-mannered you are," she added hastily.

"Papa said he needs to talk to Grandpa about some business matters. I've finished all my studies for the day, and it always looks so cosy in here." He stood awkwardly, not quite knowing whether he was welcome or not.

"I was just about to make hot chocolate," Katie said. "Sit down with us for a little while and have a mug." She quickly drew another chair closer to the table.

"How about some apple pie, Max?" Wilbur grinned at him and served a generous portion into his own bowl he'd just scraped clean without waiting for an answer, and then slid it across the table.

"Wilbur! Why didn't you get him a clean bowl?" Polly wrinkled her nose with disgust. "Are you too lazy to walk to the dresser and back again?"

Max pulled the bowl towards him and picked up a spoon as he sat down. "I don't mind in the slightest. We are cousins, after all." He tucked in with evident pleasure. "This is very tasty, Mrs Pertwee. Mama doesn't allow us to have food like this in London very often. She says it's what the poor people eat because pastry is so filling."

"Really? Well, I wouldn't exactly describe us as poor," the cook said, her eyes twinkling with amusement. "But we do eat good hearty food here. It's what folk need if they're going to spend a day working hard outside on the land or walking the moors."

Katie brought the saucepan of velvety hot chocolate to the table and ladled it into five mugs.

"You must get very lonely," Polly suddenly blurted out, staring at Max. "I don't think I would like it if I didn't have any brothers and sisters."

"Polly, hush." Katie looked at him apologetically. "She does rather speak whatever's on her mind," she said quietly as the younger ones started talking noisily about whether they would be able to go scrumping in the orchard for a few more apples the following day instead of doing book learning in the nursery.

Max gave a small shrug. "Out of the mouths of babes. She has a point. I have always been rather envious of you having each other. Mama doesn't seem to like children very much. Now that I'm eleven, they want to send me away to a boarding school for young gentlemen. I suppose at least I shall make some friends there."

Without thinking, Katie reached across and squeezed Max's hand, feeling sorry for him. "I know we can be noisy and squabble a lot, but we do like each other," she said, glancing affectionately at her siblings. "And you too, Max. Mama always used to say that she wished you could come and stay at Castleford Hall more often because you always used to enjoy riding the horses and helping on the farm with us. Do you remember?"

Max put his spoon down and leaned back in his chair, grinning. "I do, Katie. We used to have so much fun before Papa got it into his head that having a son roll up his sleeves and help with chores on the farm wasn't suitable for someone of his standing. Remember when we thought it would be a grand idea to muck out the barn, and I tripped over the wheelbarrow and fell in the midden? It was steaming and I stank for hours."

Katie giggled at the memory. "You were covered in straw and dung, and Aunt Amelia nearly fainted when I brought you back home for a bath. And what about that time when we packed a picnic and went down to the river and caught two brown trout?"

"We cooked them over a campfire, and it was the tastiest food I've ever eaten, but Papa said that sort of thing was for common folk and made me stay in the library for the rest of my visit." He sighed with a hint of regret. "Thinking about it, some of my best memories are from times staying here. I'm so sorry about what happened to your parents. I wish I could do something to help, but once I'm away at school, we probably won't visit much anymore."

Even though they looked so different because Max had the same sandy-coloured hair as his father, while Katie and her siblings all had dark hair and olive skin, taking after Mama's side of the family, she felt a surge of affection for her half-cousin. He was the only one from that side of the family who had expressed any sort of sympathy for the fact they had been orphaned under such terrible circumstances. She reached across and squeezed his hand again. "Just don't forget about us, Max. Come and visit whenever you can. Once you're a little bit older, you'll be able to come without your parents. I'm sure they would want you to visit Grandpa often, even if they don't really approve of me and the little ones."

"Katie's right, cariad," Beryl chimed in. "We like having you to stay, and it's important for you to spend time with your family."

"Cariad?" Max looked confused.

"It sort of means sweetheart," Polly explained. "It means Mrs Pertwee likes you." She nodded and gave him a kind smile. "You don't have to be lonely anymore, Max. We'll be your friends. Mama always said it wasn't your fault your papa thinks he's better than us."

"Oh, lawks," Beryl muttered.

There was a shocked silence around the table for a second, then Max burst out laughing. "Oh, Polly...you're going to turn into a proper firecracker, I can tell. And you, Katie. I know it's hard that you've lost your parents, but you have each other, and Grandpa will look after you."

The ponderous chimes from the grandfather clock echoed along the hallway, and Beryl clapped her hands. "Right, that's enough chattering. Bedtime, everybody. We've all had a busy day, and there's plenty more to do tomorrow. You can fetch the last of the apples from the orchard for me, and if you're well-behaved, Sir William might let you ride over the moors with Maxwell, Katie. Make the most of being able to take the horses out before the weather turns."

"Shall I put the children to bed, or do you want Susan to do it?"

"You do it. Susan is busy making sure all the fires are stoked up and fetching more logs. Your aunt feels the cold and doesn't do well putting up with a little bit of hardship."

"Goodnight, everyone." Max wandered off to head back to the library, and Katie spent the next few minutes putting the dirty crockery in the scullery to be washed, then chivvying the little ones out of the kitchen. This was the time of day she missed Mama most keenly. Bedtime used to be fun, with stories in the parlour while Papa worked on his sketches of new ideas for pieces of furniture, and Mama would read to them in front of the fire.

"Do we have to go to bed now?" Polly demanded crossly with a pout. "We haven't even said good night to Grandpa." She tugged Katie's hand, trying to steer her towards the dining room.

"You heard what Max said. Uncle Norman has important things to talk to Grandpa about. They won't want us interrupting."

Polly huffed with frustration, and Tim plugged his thumb into his mouth, a sure sign that he was exhausted.

"You can sleep in bed with me tonight if you like," Katie suggested.

She and Polly already shared the same bedroom, but she knew her little sister found it more comforting snuggling under the same patchwork quilt as Katie.

They started walking up the wide staircase. For some reason, fewer lamps were lit, and the oil paintings of distant relatives loomed over them in the shadows.

"I don't like them," Polly whispered, glancing nervously up at the wall. "It feels like they're watching us."

Katie drew her closer, inwardly agreeing, as they walked past the painting of a dark-haired gentleman with a hooked nose and piercing blue eyes. "They're just pictures," she said, shooing them up the stairs a little bit faster. "You don't notice them in the daytime."

"Is Grandpa trying to save money? Is that why we've had to stop having so many lamps burning?" Wilbur raised his eyebrows as though it was a puzzle to be solved. "Perhaps we're going to become destitute after what's happened," he added casually.

"What does destitute mean?" Polly nudged him. "Use words I understand."

"Paupers…thrown out on the street," Wilbur explained with relish, enjoying scaring her.

Her eyes rounded. "We have to leave Castleford?"

"Stop putting ideas into their heads," Katie said sharply, frowned at him. "You know Grandpa owns one of the biggest estates in the area."

Wilbur shrugged. "He doesn't work like Papa used to. Not since he had influenza. Maybe I'll have to do an apprenticeship as soon as I'm old enough."

"And you, Katie," Tim mumbled around his thumb, looking up at her. "Maybe you'll become a washerwoman."

Katie laughed as they scampered ahead of her

along the upstairs hallway towards their bedrooms. "I don't mind working if that's what Grandpa wants us to do, but I hope it's something a little more interesting than taking in washing. Now, get ready for bed before Mrs Pertwee gets cross because we're dawdling."

She threw open the double doors between the bedroom where she and Polly slept and the boys' room next door. Since losing their parents, she liked being able to listen out in case Tim or Wilbur had a nightmare, so she could comfort them. In many ways, Tim was still too young to understand properly what had happened, but she had heard Wilbur crying out in his sleep several times. She wondered whether she did it as well and pushed the thought aside. She had to stay strong for her siblings. Look to the future instead of wishing Papa had never suggested the birthday treat for Mama.

But is Grandpa keeping things from us?

Wilbur's question about money was unsettling. She knew they lived a more privileged life than many of the locals and had seen the large families crammed into the cottages on the estate. But several times recently, Sir William had mumbled about needing to make economies and that they must cut their cloth to suit their changed circumstances. She wasn't exactly sure what he meant, but she noticed Beryl had started ordering cheaper cuts of meat from the butchers as well.

By the time they were all in their nightclothes, Tim could hardly keep his eyes open. Katie tucked him in and brushed a lock of hair off his forehead. It was still soft and babyish, and he hadn't quite lost his plump toddler cheeks.

"I like cousin Max," Wilbur said sleepily from his bed near the window. "Mainly because he's not much like Uncle Norman and Aunt Amelia."

Katie turned down the oil lamp, leaving just a faint flickering light in case Tim woke up and was afraid of the dark.

"Good night. Don't let the bedbugs bite." She grinned at Wilbur, whose eyelids were also growing heavy. "We'll make sure Max has a nice day riding on the moors tomorrow, and maybe he'll ask his parents if he can visit more often."

Back in their bedroom, Polly was still sitting up in bed, hugging the stuffed felt teddy bear Mama had made for her last Christmas. Its ears were looking a little bit ragged already, and she made a mental note to mend them the following day before they got any worse. "Do you want me to read you a story, Polly?" she asked softly.

THE FARTHING GIRL

Polly shook her head and hugged the bear tighter. "Are you sure we're never going to see Mama and Papa again?" Her voice cracked with emotion.

"Yes. I'm sorry, but we have to get used to it." An ache of longing filled her chest. "Why don't we take some flowers for the grave this week."

Her sister nodded, still looking glum. "I miss them so much. What if we have to leave Castleford Hall? What if Grandpa gets sick, and we don't have anybody to look after us?" Tears pooled in Polly's eyes, quivering on her eyelashes before rolling down her cheeks. "I'm scared. I overheard someone in the village saying our family is cursed. Is it true, Katie? Is that why we're orphans?"

"Oh, Polly, you never told me that." Katie sat on the edge of the bed and gave her sister a hug, wiping the tears away with the edge of her shawl. "Of course, it's not true. I've never heard anyone say that before. It's probably just a silly rumour or someone who's jealous of our family."

"But what if it is true? What if more bad things happen to us?" Polly hiccupped, breathless with alarm, and rubbed her knuckles in her eyes where more tears were gathering.

"We can ask Grandpa about it if you think that will help, but I promise it's nonsense." She pushed away her own misgivings and gave Polly a cheerful smile, passing her a book to look at. "You read that for a moment, and I'll go and fetch you a cup of warm milk and honey from the kitchen. You know that helps you sleep."

Polly opened the pages and nodded, already looking more cheerful. That was the good thing about her younger sister, Katie thought as she retraced her steps along the upstairs hallway. Polly sometimes had mercurial moods, but she never stayed downhearted for long.

Standing at the top of the stairs, looking down into the gloomy hallway below, Katie was shocked at the sudden sound of raised voices as an argument erupted.

"What's to say Katie won't turn out to be exactly like her mother?" It was Uncle Norman, and he sounded angry. "I saw with my own eyes this afternoon that she's already becoming rude and opinionated. We know where she gets that from."

Katie was torn. Part of her wanted to run back to the bedroom and block out the harsh words. But another part of her wanted to hear more. She still didn't really know what had happened the day her parents had died. She crept down the stairs, drawn like a moth to a flame, hoping that despite his heartless demeanour, Uncle Norman might let slip some more details that would satisfy her craving to know more. It had been enough of a shock to discover that her uncle had invested in the paddle steamer her parents had perished on.

What she couldn't understand was why he hadn't been able to save them.

CHAPTER 3

"What a very unkind thing to say about a young girl who has lost both her parents." Sir William's tone was sharp, and Katie felt a surge of love for him.

"We're not asking for much." Aunt Amelia sounded more conciliatory, and Katie crept closer, making sure to stay in the shadows in case someone suddenly burst through the door into the hallway and caught her listening. "You probably don't understand how expensive everything is in London, Sir William. Living here in the middle of nowhere, with an easy life, might make it difficult for you to appreciate how much Norman does for his family to give Maxwell and me the life we deserve."

The sound of slow footsteps crossing the dining

room made Katie hold her breath, but then she realised it was just Grandpa. He always liked to walk back and forth when he had a lot on his mind.

"I find your comment rather patronising, Amelia. Just because I inherited Castleford Hall, and it has been passed down from one generation to the next in the Cavendish family, doesn't mean that I haven't worked hard during my life. I like to think my days in Parliament made a difference to the working class with the laws I helped change. Do you have any idea how much the upkeep of a house like this is? And how many nights I've lain awake worrying about keeping the estate workers employed through bad harvests and challenging times."

"But you have to understand, Papa," Norman interrupted briskly. "I have certain standards to maintain in London. It's expensive running a house with servants in Portland Place, but I have the reputation of the Cavendish name to uphold. How would it look if I could no longer afford to entertain business acquaintances at the finest eating establishments or take dear Amelia to opening nights at the theatre? Do you want us to look like some sort of penny-pinching paupers after it's taken me so long to establish myself as an important person in London society?"

"And what about darling Maxwell?" Amelia added with a wheedling tone. "It would be cheaper to have a private tutor for him, but Norman and I are so busy attending important social events we decided it would be better for him to go to a boarding school. You must understand that comes at a price."

Katie heard her aunt's voice hitch with emotion, followed by a few dainty sobs as she cried into her lace handkerchief. She wondered whether the tears were genuine or just designed to make Grandpa feel guilty.

"Poor...poor Maxwell," Amelia sniffed. "He's always felt second best compared to Grace's four children."

"Amelia is right, Papa," Norman grumbled resentfully. "You've always favoured Grace and her family for as long as I can remember. You held me to much higher standards, and you can't deny it."

"How can you say that? It's simply not true." Katie could hear Grandpa was starting to sound distressed, and she was tempted to march into the dining room and tell them to leave him alone. But she couldn't. She had to think about what was right for the little ones, and it was clear Uncle Norman disliked them all.

What if he makes life more difficult for us? It was a

worrying thought. She didn't know her uncle very well, and it was hard to gauge his reactions when he didn't seem to have much loyalty towards his own flesh and blood.

"You had every opportunity a young man could ask for, Norman. The finest education. A year travelling around Europe followed by introductions to influential people in London. That's how you met Amelia. If you haven't managed to make the most of those introductions, I can't be held accountable for that. You've made some poor business decisions, by the sounds of it. There was the warehouse near the docks where you lost your stock because of a rat infestation. And the paddle steamer...but I can't bear to talk about that."

"That's just the nature of business, Papa and none of the failures were my fault. The point is, you gave Grace and Edgar as much money as they ever needed." His footsteps sounded sharp as he strode across the dining room, and Katie heard a clink of glass. She could imagine the ruby-coloured port and the heavy cut-glass tumbler winking in the candlelight before he gulped it down.

"You're behaving like a sulky child. I certainly never gave them more money than you've had from me over the years." Sir William was starting to sound weary and irritated now.

"I don't believe that for one minute," Norman sneered. "Who knows what you did for her when we were in London? You always let Grace get away with whatever she wanted, even marrying beneath her to a man with no prospects."

"She loved him. Besides, Edgar was a very fine furniture maker," William shot back.

"Dabbling in making rustic pieces that nobody wanted to buy, you mean? The man was scarcely more than a ham-fisted carpenter, even though you try to paint him as something more gentlemanly. You could hardly say that he was successful at business."

"Tell your father the other thing you're worried about," Amelia said from just the other side of the door.

There was a long pause, and Katie tiptoed across the hallway. Perhaps now they were going to talk about exactly why Mama and Papa hadn't been rescued from the paddle steamer.

"We need to discuss your will, Papa," Norman said bluntly. "You're not getting any younger, and you had bad influenza again last winter. I'm only saying this because I'm concerned about you. I would hate for there to be any problems in the future, so you should let me help you with legal matters to do with Castleford Hall."

Sir William was seized by a coughing fit, and Katie wondered whether the stress of the argument might make him ill again. Her stomach clenched at the thought of it. Uncle Norman hadn't bothered to visit when Grandpa had been ill, and it was Mama who had nursed him back to full health again with help from the village doctor and herbal tinctures from the old woman who lived on the moor.

"I suppose you're worried I might leave the place to Katie and the other three children, are you?" William muttered eventually, between coughs.

"You surely wouldn't?" Amelia sounded horrified. "That would be preposterous. Norman is your rightful heir, and then Maxwell."

"Exactly." Norman's voice was rough with alarm. "Comments like these are why I'm worried you're not capable of managing Castleford's financial matters anymore."

Katie peeped through a small gap in the doorway and saw her uncle doing his best to summon a reassuring smile. "It's a lot for you to manage at your age, Papa. Why don't you at least let me take care of a few things for you? We can hire a proper solicitor in

London, and I can do the accounts. It's like you said a few minutes ago, it takes a lot to run this place."

Sir William shook his head stubbornly. "You don't need to write me off so soon, Norman. I have a good many years left in me yet, and I'm perfectly capable of managing Castleford. When I decide that I'm not, I might think about involving you." A glint of mischief came into his eyes that only Katie could see as he turned away from his son. "Who knows, by the time I need help, young Wilbur might become my right-hand man. He's already showing a fine head for figures and is as bright as a button."

Katie pressed her hand to her mouth at the sight of Norman's cheeks turning brick-red with outrage. "I simply won't allow it, Papa. You probably think you're being amusing, but your attitude is causing a lot of distress to me and Amelia."

"Then perhaps you should show some respect. I am still the head of this family."

Norman took a deep breath. "Father, I'm begging you to give us some more money. It's only right. Grace's children won't make anything of themselves, so think of it as investing in the future of Castleford Hall. There are new business opportunities aplenty in London, but how can I take advantage of them if you keep the family money tied up in this place? Surely you want me to do well?"

"I'll think about it. I need to look into the estate's finances now that the harvest is over. I don't want to raise the rent for our tenants. Times are hard."

"So you care more about the yokels here than your own son?"

"Oh, Norman, that's enough. All this arguing is exhausting. I think I'm going to take coffee in my study now."

"But what about the money? We need to know." Amelia was becoming hysterical and pressed her handkerchief to her eyes again. "Tell him, Norman," she sobbed. "We must have the money; otherwise, we risk social embarrassment. It's not as if the other children need it. They're so rude and practically as wild as the homeless urchins littering the streets of London, the way they charge about the farm and onto the moors. It's clear Grace brought them up very badly."

William turned and faced her, his expression darkening immediately. "How dare you speak ill of the dead in my house. I won't hear another word of it." He snatched up his walking stick and started heading straight toward the door Katie was hiding behind.

She spun around and sprinted back up the stairs and along the landing as the argument raged on below her. Hot tears pricked the back of her eyes.

How can Uncle Norman speak so cruelly about his own sister and four helpless children who have been left orphaned?

She felt sick at the thought of a rift in the family right when it was more important than ever for people to be kind to each other.

As she let herself back into her bedroom, Katie was relieved to see that Polly was fast asleep. She didn't think she could bear to explain why she had returned without the warm milk when she could hardly trust herself to speak without bursting into tears.

She turned the lamp off so that just a small candle in the corner of the room flickered to provide a faint glow of light and slipped between the sheets, pulling the patchwork quilt up to her chin. No sooner had she closed her eyes than a host of troubling questions filled her mind.

Why has everything gone so wrong? Uncle Norman only seems to care about himself. And Grandpa must be worried about money, otherwise he would have agreed to give more to Norman and Amelia. Was it always like this and I never realised? Did Mama and Papa protect us from such worries?

She tossed and turned, then pressed her hands over her ears, trying to shut out the sound of the ongoing argument, but there was no end to it.

Doors slammed. Scurrying feet echoed along the corridors, and she squeezed her eyes tightly closed, praying desperately for sleep to come.

Just as she started to feel as though she might drift off, something rattled against the window, snapping her awake again. She slipped out of bed, taking care not to wake Polly up and carefully opened the window.

Max's pale face was below her. He was holding a couple of small pebbles in his hand, and he glanced nervously over his shoulder. "Sorry to wake you. My parents have had a terrible argument with Grandpa," he whispered urgently. "Papa has woken the stable boy to hitch up the carriage now, and we're leaving tonight."

"Oh no. When will we see you again?" She leaned further out of the window, wishing she could give him a hug because he looked so upset.

"I don't know. Perhaps it will all blow over, and we might visit at Christmas, but I didn't want to leave without saying goodbye."

"Write to us," she called. She could hear voices around the side of the house by the stables. Uncle Norman must have dragged Jacob, the stable lad, from his bed to prepare the carriage.

"Don't think badly of me because of anything Mama and Papa have said, Katie. They've had a few money worries, but they don't know I know about it. Papa isn't always this thoughtless. He was shocked to hear about your parents. I expect he'll write to Grandpa, and everything will be better soon."

"I hope so. Safe travels." She smiled down at Max and waved as he hurried away. She wasn't sure about Grandpa; she had never heard him so angry. But Uncle Norman was now his only remaining offspring, so they would have to make up, surely? "Enjoy your new school, and we'll see you soon," she called just before Max disappeared around the corner.

A moment later, she saw the carriage rumbling down the drive into the darkness. Sir William walked slowly after it a little way, carrying a lantern. His shoulders drooped, and he shook his head, his sense of distress palpable even from that distance. He cut a lonely figure, and Katie closed the window quietly again, not wanting him to know that she had seen him looking so sad.

* * *

Katie carefully slipped into bed again. Polly's eyes flickered open for a moment, but she wasn't properly awake, just enough to sigh softly and roll over before falling fast asleep again a few seconds later.

But sleep was elusive for her. She lay on her back, looking at the familiar shadows on the ceiling, turning over everything that had happened in her mind. She would miss Max and dearly hoped that he would make new friends at the boarding school. She couldn't imagine what it must be like being sent away by your parents instead of living at home. In fact, it seemed absurd. She vowed she would never do the same if she was fortunate enough to get married and have a family of her own one day.

Outside, the wind picked up. The noise of it soughing through the pine trees outside their bedroom window made her think of the sea. She closed her eyes, letting it gently soothe her, and had a hazy memory of holding Mama's hand, looking out at white-tipped waves. *Is it a real memory or wishful thinking?* During her short life so far, she had no recollection of being anywhere other than Castleford Hall and the nearby villages and Pembrey Minster. But if she concentrated, she could almost feel the warm sun on her cheeks and sand between her toes again and the way her petticoat was damp at the bottom from paddling in the sea. She smiled to herself as she slowly drifted off to sleep, hoping that she would meet her parents again in her dreams that night.

SUDDENLY, Katie's eyes flew open with a start. She lifted her head and saw that there was only a stump of the candle left, and the feeble flame was hardly giving out any light. A shaft of moonlight created a silvery path across the bedroom floor, and she sat up cautiously, wondering what had woken her. Judging by the position of the moon, which had moved across the sky so she could see it from her bed now, she must have been asleep for several hours.

The rumble of a deep voice downstairs made the hairs on her arms prickle.

Had Uncle Norman returned? It didn't sound like him, and she was gripped with an overwhelming need to know who it was.

She wrapped her shawl around her shoulders and tiptoed along the upstairs landing again, feeling a strange sense of déjà vu. The corridor to the kitchen was in darkness, meaning Mrs Pertwee had long since gone to bed. She heard more talking and realised the only light was a soft yellow glow coming from beneath the door of Grandpa's study, other than one solitary lamp on the mantle in the entrance hall.

Keeping her back against the wall, Katie felt her way slowly down the stairs, grateful to be familiar with every step. She felt a momentary pang of guilt for eavesdropping. The vicar had said at a recent Sunday service that it was a sin to listen to conversations not intended to be heard by children, glowering at all the youngsters in the congregation.

But too many times since Mama and Papa's death, Katie had felt frustrated as murmured conversations were abruptly ended as soon as she appeared. Villagers and acquaintances had shaken their heads sympathetically before whispering about the family behind their hands. Everyone was so polite, but it made it feel like Mama and Papa never existed.

She squared her shoulders. *I have to know what's going on.*

If Grandpa was struggling, or the future of Castleford Hall was in any doubt, she was sure Mama would have wanted her to know.

She edged closer to Grandpa's study, but unfortunately, this time, the door was firmly closed, so she couldn't peep through the gap as she'd done earlier. She tucked her long hair aside and pressed her ear to the smooth wood, holding her breath to hear what she could of the conversation. Her bare feet felt cold on the tiled floor, and there was a slight draught around her ankles as if a window had been left open somewhere, but she didn't care.

"I've given it plenty of thought...it's for the future security of my family," Grandpa said firmly. It sounded as though they had been talking for a while.

"Don't you think you're overreacting, Sir William?" the visitor replied.

"It's for the best. Who knows what fate has in store for any of us in the future? At least by doing this, I can rest easier at night. It's all arranged, and now I need to make it formal."

"It is highly irregular," the visitor remarked. He sounded doubtful.

"I don't care. I've already suffered enough loss, and you know as well as I do there are certain people who would love nothing more than to see the Cavendish family fail."

"Don't take this the wrong way, but do you think your imagination might be playing tricks on you, Sir William? You're up here living in the middle of nowhere by the moors with just a handful of servants and the children to keep you company. So much solitude after a great tragedy can do strange things to the mind."

"Don't treat me like a fool. This is to protect them from—" Another fit of coughing muffled Grandpa's voice and try as she might, Katie couldn't hear his next few words. She huffed with annoyance.

Protect us from who? Is it some sort of danger? She leaned closer to the door, feeling the smooth grain against her cheek.

"If you insist, I will, of course, always follow your wishes."

There was a rustle of paper and a sound that Katie recognised as Grandpa opened the ink pot he kept on his desk next to his quill pen. *Is he writing something?* A moment later, she heard more rustling, which she knew must be him blotting the ink, then she smelt a faint whiff of the musk scent he favoured for his red sealing wax.

"There's nothing more to do," the visitor said a moment later, with an air of finality. "I just pray that it will never need to see the light of day. I will keep it in my possession so that you don't need to give it any more thought."

A chair scraped, and footsteps hastened towards the door, much to Katie's horror. For the second time that night, she hitched up her cotton nightgown and sprinted back across the hall and up the stairs.

This time, she wasn't quite quick enough to get all the way along the landing to her bedroom, so she knelt behind the bannisters.

The visitor swept out of Sir William's study and paused. He gazed around the entrance hall, pulling on his gloves, then slowly lifted his head, looking directly at her.

Her heart hammered under her ribs, and she stifled a gasp. In the flickering lamplight, he looked almost cadaverous, with his hooked nose, sunken cheeks and dark eyes. His greatcoat hung off his thin shoulders.

"Do you want me to light your way out?" Sir William asked, still in his study.

"No. I can see perfectly well." The stranger's gaze was still locked on her, but he didn't smile. Instead, he tipped his hat and turned on his heel, striding to the heavy front door and closing it silently behind him. She shivered. Something about his demeanour made her wonder whether he had known she was listening at the door the whole while. But who was he? And what was so urgent that he had to visit

Grandpa in the dead of night, under cover of darkness?

She ran back to her bedroom and hurried to the window. The man was riding a dappled grey horse, and his greatcoat billowed out behind him as he galloped away, lit only by the pale white moon overhead. He didn't go down the long drive to the imposing stone gateway but took a narrow track that most people didn't know about, which led straight out onto the moors.

Who is he?

She cupped her hands against the glass to get a better view, but all she could see was a faint, ghostly outline of the horse and rider against distant trees before he vanished into the mist. The wind rattled in the chimney, and a ragged cloud covered the moon, plunging the land into darkness again.

CHAPTER 4

Six Years Later.

"So, which of you can list the dates of the Tudor monarchs in order?"

A groan went up from Polly, and Tim wriggled in his chair, hardly pausing from the sketch of a robin he was doing to think about the answer.

Fiona Murray shuffled the papers on the desk in front of her absentmindedly, glancing towards the door as though she was needed somewhere else. Katie sat up straighter. She could rattle off the dates easily but knew that it was the younger children that Fiona really wanted to hear an answer from.

"Polly? Do you remember them?"

"Are we going to do some arithmetic after this, Miss Murray?" Wilbur suggested hopefully.

"Well, let me see." She peered at her timetable and dragged the back of her hand wearily across her forehead. "Maybe later. We still have half an hour more allocated to history, and it doesn't do to hop from one subject to another."

Katie noticed the young woman had dark circles under her eyes, and her hair was coming loose from its usual neat coil on the nape of her neck. Fiona Murray had been their governess for two years now and seemed to like the job. Miss Clatworthy, their previous governess, had only lasted a year, claiming that Castleford Hall was too remote for her liking and that the empty moors made her scared when the mist rolled in and blanketed the house. Katie suspected a dalliance with a travelling salesman who was heading back to her native county of Yorkshire might also have had something to do with it. Not to mention the time Polly and Tim had released a mouse during a particularly dull geography lesson, which ran up her dress onto her head, sending her shrieking all the way to Grandpa's study, where she declared the Anderson children were an abomination. By contrast, Miss Murray was local, so had no fear of the moors. She walked from the village every day, and although she was very sweet, Katie hadn't dared to tell Grandpa that the younger children found her rather uninspiring.

"Are you feeling unwell, Miss Murray?" Katie asked, giving her a kind smile. "You seem a little distracted."

"Oh no, it's nothing," the governess replied hastily. She cleared her throat and patted a stray lock of her lank brown hair back into place. "Perhaps we've had enough history for today. What would you like to learn instead?"

Katie gazed longingly through the window. It was a beautiful summer day outside, and bees drifted lazily along the lavender border that edged the rose garden. She could see old Mr Dryden trudging along the path towards the kitchen garden, pushing his wooden wheelbarrow in front of him. As the only gardener for the estate, he was fighting a losing battle against the weeds, but he did his best and cheerfully provided Mrs Pertwee with what fruit and vegetables he could.

"Perhaps whatever it is, we could do it under the silver birch trees at the end of the croquet lawn?" She jumped up and walked to the window looking across to the trees. Their silvery bark looked pretty against the blue sky, and the leaves rustled in the summer breeze. The croquet lawn was little more than rough grass now. She smiled as she remembered Papa showing her how to hold the wooden mallet and knock balls through hoops...back before everything had changed.

Miss Murray pursed her lips. "I don't think your grandfather would approve of that, Katie." Her gaze flickered towards Polly and Tim, who were whispering about something behind their hands. "The little ones do seem to get terribly distracted outside. I promised Sir William that they would know all the Kings and Queens of England by the end of summer."

Katie nodded, understanding the governess's dilemma. To be honest, she thought Polly and Tim would be distracted wherever they were. They usually took all their lessons in the library, but it seemed a shame to waste the lovely weather sitting inside.

"What about some more times tables?" Wilbur ignored Polly's disappointed sigh. "It's important to learn arithmetic, Polly," he explained with exaggerated patience. "Well, maybe not for a girl, but if I want to become a bank manager when I'm older, I need to know how to do accounts and all sorts, don't

I, Miss Murray?" he asked, looking at the governess for agreement. "Or how about some algebra instead? That would be fun."

"It's so boring," Polly grumbled. "Why can't we go for a ride over the moors or go fishing in the river for tiddlers? That's fun, not sitting inside learning about monarchs."

The young woman looked slightly flustered. "I'm not sure algebra is my strongest subject, Wilbur. Maybe that's best tackled another day." She glanced towards the door again and jumped when the grandfather clock chimed.

"Are you sure there's nothing troubling you?" Katie asked again.

Much to her dismay, Miss Murray sniffed and hastily pulled a cotton handkerchief from her pocket, blinking back tears. "I'm sorry, Miss Anderson. I feel terrible that my mind isn't as sharp as it usually is, but it's because my ma isn't well. We had to call Doctor Frogwell out to her last night, and…" she gulped and dabbed her eyes. "He said she doesn't have much longer."

Katie felt terrible that she hadn't realised. Miss Murray had mentioned a few months ago that her elderly mother was struggling to walk after slipping over on icy cobbles when they'd had a late frost, but she hadn't mentioned it since, so Katie had assumed she was better. "You must go home to be with her, Fiona. What about food? Do you want to take a basket of supplies? We want to help you however we can."

"That's a kind suggestion, but I can't leave until the proper time." The young governess looked embarrassed and blew her nose. "My parents rely on me for my wage, you see."

Katie heard her grandfather walking across the entrance hall from his study. "Let me ask Grandpa. I'm sure he will agree that it's more important for you to be home with your mama at this time." She hurried away, noticing afresh how anxious the poor woman looked.

Sir William's expression was sympathetic when he came back to the library with her. "Fiona, my dear. I didn't know your mama was still ailing. Katie has just told me you had to call Doctor Frogwell out."

"Yes, Sir. But it doesn't mean I can't do my work."

"Nonsense, I won't hear of it. Go straight home and don't come back until you feel ready, and not a moment before." He pulled some money out of his pocket and pressed it into Fiona's hand. "Take this to buy whatever medicine your mother needs, and tell the doctor I'll pay his bill."

Tears filled the governess's eyes. "Thank you, Sir." She bobbed a curtsey and hastily put her bonnet on, needing no second bidding.

"We'll be thinking of your ma," Katie said. "Send a message if there's anything you need."

"God bless you all for being so kind."

Once she had bustled away, Tim grinned at Wilbur. "No algebra today, then."

"Does this mean we don't need to do any schoolwork until Miss Murray comes back, Grandpa?" Polly clasped her hands together, giving him a winsome smile. "It's only a few weeks until the summer holidays…hardly worth doing anymore until September, don't you think?"

Sir William chuckled and hobbled back towards his study. "Nice try, Polly, but I'm sure Katie will be able to step into Miss Murray's shoes and take the lessons."

"Do you mean that, Grandpa?" Katie's heart jumped with happiness. "I've been meaning to ask you if I could train to become a teacher when I'm older."

He nodded with a twinkle in his eyes. "I think you would make a fine teacher, Katie. Consider this the start of your training. If you can keep those three scamps in order and instil some knowledge when exciting alternatives like helping out during the harvest are beckoning, you'll be able to teach anyone." He paused in the doorway for a moment, and a shadow crossed his eyes. "Besides, it's good to have something like tutoring you can rely on to earn a few coins," he added, almost to himself. "You never know when you might need it, especially with financial hardships coming when least expected."

Before Katie had a chance to ask what he meant, a squawk of annoyance from the kitchen distracted them all.

"What's wrong with Mrs Pertwee?" Tim asked.

"I've no idea, but it's time for our morning break. Let's go and see if she needs any help and have some lemonade."

"And some of those shortbread biscuits I baked yesterday." Polly skipped ahead of them all through the hall, pausing only to curtsey to the tall mahogany statue of a noble hunter in the corner of the hallway, which one of Grandpa's ancestors had brought back from India. There was a rumour that the Cavendish family's superstition was that bad luck would befall anyone who disrespected the hunter, which used to make them all shiver with fear when Mama told them about it one snowy Christmas Eve.

"If you want a cup of tea, you'll have to make it yourselves." Mrs Pertwee looked flustered as she emerged from the pantry, holding a plate with a small piece of cold roast beef on it. "I'm going to have to think of something different to cook for luncheon and dinner tonight. Norbert, the delivery boy from Pembrey Minster hasn't turned up. He was meant to come yesterday, and he does run late occasionally, but there's no sign of him. That means I'm without my supplies from the butcher and the grocer."

"That's strange. He's usually fairly reliable." Katie crossed the kitchen and opened the door to look out. A sudden thought occurred to her. "I overheard him after church talking to Doctor Frogwell about wanting to work on the coast where they land the fish off the boats. Perhaps that's what he's done, and Mr Houghton hasn't found anyone else to replace him yet."

Beryl shook her head with a tut of disappointment. "You'd think they would make some sort of arrangement for Sir William. Everybody knows his health isn't as good as it used to be, and we don't have the number of servants a place like Castleford Hall should."

"Why don't we go for you?" The allure of an outing to Pembrey Minster in the sunshine was almost irresistible. "Did you see Fiona had to rush home to be with her mama? I'm sure Grandpa won't mind if we don't do any more lessons today."

A cough in the doorway made Katie spin around, and she smiled guiltily as she saw her grandfather standing there. "Did I hear myself mentioned?" he asked, raising his eyebrows.

As he limped closer, the bright sunshine streamed through the kitchen windows, and she noticed that his hair was almost white and his shirt collar gaped slightly, making him look frail. He still had the upright bearing of a man who took his responsibilities to the estate and his position in society seriously, but these days, more often than not, it was with the help of his silver-topped walking stick.

Grandpa is getting old. How much longer will we have him as the head of our family? The stark thought filled Katie with sudden dread for the future, and she fussed over Tim's fringe that was sticking up in its usual haphazard way, hoping that nobody had noticed.

"I was just saying to Mrs Pertwee that we can take the horse and cart into town to collect provisions," she said brightly. "The delivery boy hasn't been."

Sir William eyed them all doubtfully. "I'm not sure if that's a good idea."

"Oh, go on, Grandpa," Polly cried, "let us have a day out. We hardly ever go to Pembrey anymore. It's nice being at home, but we used to visit more often when Mama was still alive."

He glanced towards Beryl, who nodded encouragingly. "It would be doing me a good turn, Sir William. And Katie should probably speak to the dressmaker about some new gowns. The girls can't go on wearing those that are too short, flapping around their ankles and patched up; it's not ladylike."

Sir William relented and smiled indulgently, pulling some money out of his pocket and handing it to Katie. "Very well, but you're not to go alone, the four of you. Ask Jacob to hitch up the horse and cart and go with you."

"Are you sure? Won't he be busy bringing in the hay before it rains?"

"The weather is set fair for the next few days. I've heard rumours that there's unrest brewing in some of the local towns over changes in working laws."

"Uprisings?" Beryl tutted again, but this time with alarm. "I thought we'd seen the last of that when the Swing Riots were quelled."

"Yes, and the Poor Laws were meant to end all sorts of social inequalities." William tapped his walking stick on the flagstones. "Quite right, too. A gentleman with land and assets owes a great deal to his workers. They should be treated fairly. But when I visited the bank last month, there were whispers of more unrest."

"I doubt that sort of thing would affect us here, would it, Grandpa?" Wilbur asked. "I read in the newspaper that some of the millworkers in the northern towns have threatened to march against the mill owners, but surely somewhere as rural as this wouldn't be affected?"

Katie was surprised to see genuine worry on their grandfather's face. "You're too young to remember when unrest spread across the whole country, Wilbur. It only takes a few ill-placed comments by people who wish to foment trouble, and these things have a way of spreading in the most unpredictable fashion."

Wilbur folded his arms. "I'll make sure the girls are safe. And Jacob will be with us."

"It's only a trip to Pembrey, Grandpa, we've done

it plenty of times before." Katie looked at him pleadingly. The thought of a day away from Castleford Hall, feeling as free as a bird for a few hours, was so tempting. They had become more isolated since their parents had died, especially now that Grandpa was less sociable.

"Katie's right. And Wilbur's tall for his age, Sir William. It will do them all good to mingle with a few folks other than us," Beryl said firmly. She had already fetched two wicker baskets from the pantry and produced a list from her apron pocket, handing it to her. "Mind you get everything, and don't waste any money on unnecessary treats. We have to be frugal, remember."

"Mr Houghton's son always turns bright red whenever he sees Katie," Polly said, giggling and doing a twirl, holding her dress out as if she was about to do a waltz. "I reckon he's sweet on her, Grandpa. I'm sure I'll be able to work my charm too, persuade him to put a twist of mint humbugs in the basket for being such good customers."

"Trust you to have the poor shopkeepers wrapped around your little finger," Tim said, rolling his eyes and pushing Polly aside so he could pick up one of the baskets. "You know I don't like mint humbugs. Can't you persuade him to give us some fudge instead?"

Sir William chuckled as a cheerful squabble about the best sorts of sweets they could look forward to broke out. Katie hoped it wouldn't spoil their chances of a day out.

"I do admit things have been a little bit dull at Castleford Hall recently, especially as it's so long since Max and his parents visited," he said, drawing her aside. "I know you miss not having your mama for outings like this, so use a little bit of that money to take them to Mrs Bright's tea room for hot chocolate and cake like you used to when dear Grace was still alive."

"We would like that very much, Grandpa." She gave him a hug, and his whiskers tickled her ear. "I hope things never change," she added, hugging him again. "And shall I get some linctus from the apothecary for your cough? I should have got better by now."

"It's nothing. Doctor Frogwell said I'm fighting fit for a gentleman of my age."

"I'll get some anyway. And once the rosehips ripen, I'll make more rosehip syrup."

"You're a good girl, Katie. Now, I meant what I said about staying alert to trouble," he added quietly.

"I don't want to alarm the younger ones, but do keep an eye out and make sure Jacob stays with you."

As she ran upstairs to fetch their bonnets, leaving the boys to go to the stables and ask Jacob to hitch up the cart, Polly hurried after her.

"Jacob will be happy Grandpa's asked him to escort us today," she said with a mischievous grin. "I'll make sure Wilbur sits in the back with Tim. You know he's as blind as a bat when it comes to noticing things like that."

"Like what?" Katie picked up her favourite green bonnet and tied the ribbons.

"That Jacob's sweet on you."

Katie rolled her eyes and handed her younger sister a shawl. "First, it's Bobby Houghton, then Jacob. I think you've been reading too many penny dreadfuls filling your head with romantic nonsense." She turned away to hide her blush. Jacob Bedingfield, their stable boy and handyman, had grown into a strapping young man, and her heart fluttered sometimes when he smiled at her in that lazy way he had that was just the right side of respectful.

"Grandpa will want you to start attending dances soon to meet a suitable young man to marry." Polly draped her shawl around her shoulders and grew serious again. "Who will look after me and the boys then?"

"That's years away." Katie linked arms with her sister and they descended the wide stairs together. "I'm only fifteen."

"Nearly sixteen."

Katie wrinkled her nose at the thought of the stuffy young gentlemen she had seen at the occasional social gathering Grandpa still attended at neighbouring estates and grand homes. They all seemed so false with their easy charm, and great wealth. She knew that as Sir William's granddaughter, she would have to marry into a suitable family, but she felt torn between two different worlds. The Cavendish money seemed to be dwindling fast from whispered conversations she'd overheard. She didn't belong with the elegant young ladies who graced balls with a new gown for every occasion. But she also didn't belong to the humble working-class families who relied on people like Sir William for their employment.

"Maybe I shall marry an adventurer," she declared, more to shock Polly than anything.

"Just make sure you don't leave me behind to look after the boys. Wilbur would bore me to tears talking about arithmetic, and I don't think Tim will ever grow out of putting creatures in my boots. It was a slug this morning…wretched boy." She rushed ahead to get the baskets from Mrs Pertwee and Katie smiled to herself.

Marriage was a long way off, but when the time came, she hoped they would still live together. Her rambunctious siblings might test her patience almost daily, but she couldn't imagine life without them.

CHAPTER 5

"Everybody ready? Is that comfortable for you, Miss Katie?" Jacob grinned at them all as he picked up the reins and clicked his tongue, telling the horse to walk on. "'Tis a nice day for a ride into Pembrey. I've been meaning to go myself, to get a new whetstone for sharpening the scythe."

"We're all very, very comfortable, thank you, Jacob," Polly said, nudging Katie, who was sitting next to her. "Aren't we," she added, fluttering her eyelashes.

"If you don't behave, I'll leave you at home," Katie muttered. Everyone was in high spirits at the unexpected day out, and she hoped the younger ones would behave well for her.

The sturdy piebald cob trotted along briskly in

front of their cart, and Katie turned around to wave at Grandpa, who was standing on the terrace in front of his study. The view of Castleford Hall from the long driveway was always her favourite, and seeing it against the clear blue sky reminded her how fortunate she was to have been raised there. It wasn't as grand as many of the homes of the landed gentry in the area, but the red brick building had a pleasing symmetry with two small wings on either side of the main frontage, and the mullion windows in the oldest section sparkled in the sunshine. From afar it still looked like a well-kept family home; it was only as visitors drew closer that they saw the signs that Sir William did not have as many servants as a place that size needed. But Katie didn't care. It was home, and it held all the precious memories of times with Mama and Papa. It didn't matter to her that the croquet lawn was full of weeds or that some of the rooms were closed off and no longer used. Grandpa still made sure there was plenty of laughter in the house, and that was what mattered more than anything.

"The moors are looking good," Jacob said, gesturing toward the wide-open landscape beyond the farm buildings. "There should be plenty of pheasants for the pot in a couple of months."

"That will make Beryl happy." Katie looked across the landscape. It would soon be awash with purple once the heather flowered, and the gypsies would arrive to harvest what they needed for selling lucky heather from their gaily painted wagons as they travelled from town to town.

"I saw the hares up there last week," Tim said from behind them, where he and Wilbur were perched on the extra seat, "and plenty of buzzards and red kites."

"Let's hope Grandpa is right and that the fine weather continues. He'll be pleased to have a good harvest this year."

"That he will," Jacob agreed. He lowered his voice slightly and smiled at her. "I hope you'll be bringing harvest teas out to the field, Katie. It's thirsty work cutting the corn for the thresher."

She felt slightly flustered, suddenly aware of how close they were sitting on the wooden cart seat. Jacob was three years older than her, and his dark brown eyes had a way of lingering slightly longer than they needed to when he looked at her. He raised one eyebrow, and she coughed to cover her embarrassment.

"Of course, we always like doing the harvest teas, Jacob, you know that. Polly has promised she will help, and I expect Tim will want to join in to rescue any baby animals that might be left behind when the corn is cut."

Jacob nodded, but she detected a hint of disappointment by the way his mouth tightened momentarily. Clearly, he had been hoping it would only be her taking the basket of pies and cold flagons of ale out to the men as they worked. She had heard of many a young girl being kissed for the first time under the hot August skies during harvest. Part of her wondered what it would be like to be held in his strong, tanned arms, but she had her reputation to think of.

Katie let the chatter of the others wash over her as she admired the view. As the moors gave way to more sheltered land, the hedgerows were dotted with nodding white oxeye daisies and tall pink spires of rose bay willow herb. The farmland was lusher and more fertile the closer they got to the small market town that was their destination, and she enjoyed waving at a few acquaintances as they tended their gardens and did outside chores.

"It seems busier than usual," Wilbur remarked as Jacob guided their horse and cart into Pembrey Minster a little while later, before jumping down to hitch the reins outside the tavern on the western corner of the town square.

"Fresh coffee! Beans new off the ship and roasted this week!" A rotund man with red cheeks beckoned them to his stall, and Katie shook her head.

"Strawberries, Miss?" A woman in a patched dress with a tight bodice sashayed forward, carrying a tray of punnets that certainly looked tempting. "Look at 'em!" she urged. "They were still growin' in the fields 'afore sunrise. You won't get finer than these juicy delights, and we won't be back again until next week."

"Can we, Katie?" Tim couldn't tear his eyes away. "Mr Dryden said the strawberries at home are past their best now."

"Why don't you try one, Sir?" The woman gave Jacob a provocative smile and dangled one of the red berries by its stalk. "Sweet and tempting…just how you like, I expect," she added with a saucy wink.

"Maybe on our way back after we've done our errands." He grinned, enjoying her attention. "I'll be sure to keep a lookout for you, don't you worry."

The sound of costermongers shouting their wares mingled with a hum of conversation between all the people going about their business in the busy market town. Smart carriages pulled by gleaming pairs of horses trotted past at a fast clip, followed by more ponderous cob horses pulling carts laden with all manner of goods. The drayman had stopped outside the tavern and cursed colourfully as he hefted barrels of ale onto the cobbles and shooed toothless beggars away who pleaded for a sup of free beer to improve their day. Elegant ladies swept past with lace handkerchiefs pressed to their noses, trailed by scurrying maids carrying their purchases. Governesses herded gaggles of children and scruffy families hungrily bartering for bruised vegetables. But, as she surveyed the scene, Katie realised there seemed to be more men than usual, huddled on street corners, glancing expectantly towards each other every now and again as though they were waiting for something.

"I don't recognise a lot of them," she said, wondering if there was some sort of event taking place that they didn't know about.

Some of them milled aimlessly through the narrow alleys and strolled slowly past shop windows, pausing to look at goods displayed inside. They didn't look like the usual shoppers she was used to seeing.

A young boy with tatty trousers and grubby bare feet rushed forward. "I'll look after your cart for a penny. Ain't nobody as attentive as me. Don't let Percy do it; he's partial to having a snooze."

Wilbur gave the lad a coin. "Do you know why it's so busy?" he asked.

A crafty look came into the boy's eyes, and he tapped the side of his snub nose. "Of course I do, Master Anderson," he said nonchalantly. "Nothing gets past Fred Murphy."

Polly huffed impatiently. "Fred, everyone knows you love to be the first to gossip. Are you going to tell us, or what? I suppose you'll do it for a couple of mint humbugs when we return, but it will be too late then. We want to know now."

He gave Polly a gap-toothed grin and stuck his thumbs in his waistcoat, walking with a swagger. "Humbugs is our usual arrangement, Polly. Don't disappoint me."

Katie smiled at him. She knew he was only a year younger than Polly, but he was small for his age. "We'll see you right, Fred. But it is curious why there are so many people in Pembrey today. It's not even market day."

The young boy glanced furtively over his shoulder and edged closer to her. "Folk are saying it's them fancy boats from France as have moored up off the coast, and the sailors are visiting the local towns."

Katie looked around the cobbled square, noticing that some of the men did look as though they were dressed differently. They wore jaunty neckerchiefs tied around their necks, and their swarthy dark features set them apart. "French, you say? I hope they will enjoy visiting Pembrey if that's who they are."

Fred screwed up his face. "Hold tight to your reticule, Miss Anderson. My granny says the Frenchmen only have one thing on their minds, and it ain't polite to repeat in front of a lady…whatever she means by that."

Katie chuckled as she strolled away. Wilbur stuck his hands in his trouser pockets and walked next to her. "You won't expect me and Tim to be with you all the time today, will you? Sitting in the dressmakers while you and Polly choose new fabric is the last thing we want to do."

"I agree, but you know Grandpa said we should stick together."

Wilbur turned and beckoned to Jacob, hoping for an ally. "We don't really need to be with the girls all day, do we? I know it's busy in town, but everyone seems to be in good spirits. I think Grandpa's concerns about trouble brewing are unwarranted."

"I'm inclined to agree. I have got a few errands of

my own that need taking care of. Perhaps we should agree to meet back at the tea room in an hour." Katie followed Jacob's gaze as he watched two attractive young women walk past on the far side of the square. They were wearing low-cut dresses, and their lips were painted vermilion red. They paused outside the Traveller's Rest Tavern, then hastened inside. It was only then that she noticed a tatty poster stuck to the door. It looked as though there was some sort of performance happening, and she wondered whether the women were part of the travelling troupe or ladies of ill repute who would ply drinks to the men and perform bawdy dances with high kicks revealing frilly petticoats for a handsome fee. Either way, he seemed rather interested.

"We'll be okay," Polly said impatiently. "We're only going to our usual shops, Katie. It's not as if anything bad could happen at the grocers. Let the boys go and do their boring errands. Tim and Wilbur want to look around that second hand bookshop, which always makes me sneeze, it's so dusty."

"Very well." She gave the boys a stern look. "We'll meet at Mrs Bright's tearoom in one hour, and make sure you're not late, or you'll give me indigestion." Jacob had already started strolling away. "Join us if you like," she called after him. "Unless you have other things planned, in which case we'll see you back here."

He tipped his hat and jingled the coins in his pocket. "Mind you stay out of trouble, or Sir William will have words with all of us."

Katie linked arms with Polly, and they turned down West Street. If anyone was likely to get into trouble, it was Jacob, she thought privately. He was a good-looking young man, and this was the first time she'd seen how he liked to turn on the charm and flash his dazzling smile at susceptible young ladies. She hoped he would remember Grandpa expected the Castleford Hall servants to behave with propriety.

* * *

"Give my apologies to Mrs Pertwee." Mr Houghton shook his head and folded his arms across his waistcoat, settling in for a chat now that he had packed their order into their wicker basket. There was salt-cured smoked bacon for Grandpa, a selection of dried fruits along with flour and sugar for baking, a bundle of scented candles for the bedrooms, along with tea leaves, rice, and more spices. They had already stocked up on cheese from the dairy shop next door and ham from the butchers in St George's Street. "Young Norbert has been wittering on about working in yon' harbour for months, but I never thought he'd actually do it. Bobby's been flat out trying to keep up with double the amount of work."

"It must have been a shock to learn that he ran away in the night."

Mrs Houghton bustled through the curtain that separated the storeroom from the shop and popped the last item in the basket. "There you are, dear. More of that polish for the silver than Beryl likes." She rolled her eyes. "I kept telling Eli that Norbert's head was turned by those sailors that travelled through town last year."

"Maybe he'll realise it was nicer working for you and come back soon," Polly suggested helpfully. She eyed the rows of glass jars behind the counter that contained an array of sweets.

"What'll it be?" Eli Houghton smiled and reached for the nearest one. "Humbugs like usual?"

Polly hesitated. "Maybe fudge this time, please. That's what Tim likes best."

"Very thoughtful of you." He smiled at them both. "You've done well since the accident, Katie. Your ma would be proud that you're raising the little 'uns with such polite manners." His eyes misted over. "Poor Sir William. He's never been the same since. Master Norman never had the same kindness towards us working class folk as his sister—" He broke off as his wife nudged him.

"Why not choose something else as well, Polly," Mrs Houghton said brightly. "These lemon drop sweets are nice. I'll pop a twist of them in your basket, and remember to apologise to Mrs Pertwee and Sir William. We'll make sure your usual deliveries resume next week, even if we have to ride out to Castleford Hall ourselves, won't we, Eli."

"Definitely," he said, nodding firmly. "'Tis an honour to have served Sir William all these years, and we won't be slacking when it comes to finding a new delivery boy, you can tell him."

Katie talked with them for a few more minutes, then bade them goodbye. Polly had already wandered off with one of the baskets and was standing outside. The dressmakers had been closed, so they still had plenty of time until they were due at the tearoom.

"Let's go down Dillwyn Lane, Katie. I can hear singing. It sounds like there's a gathering."

"I'm not sure if that's a good idea." It was in the opposite direction from Mrs Bright's tearoom and she glanced back the way they had come, where the streets now seemed surprisingly empty. "You know what Grandpa said."

Polly's face fell with disappointment. "I think there's a band playing. Come on, Katie, you never let me do anything fun anymore, not since Mama died." She tugged at her sleeve. "Look! There are people holding banners...let's follow them." Without waiting for an answer, Polly darted away, wriggling between two costermonger's barrows.

"Wait!" A sense of panic flooded through Katie as she saw Polly run from her, gaily swinging the basket. She was heading straight towards a throng of people she didn't recognise. "Come back." She looked around again, hoping to spot Wilbur and Tim or Jacob, but they were nowhere to be seen.

There was nothing for it but to follow her sister and hope for the best. Katie hurried after her, suddenly uneasy that something felt different about Pembrey Minster. While they had been in the grocers, the streets had filled with more strangers, and the air crackled with something she didn't quite understand.

CHAPTER 6

"I expect I'm just being silly. It's only because of what Grandpa said," Katie muttered to herself as she pushed through the throng in Dillwyn Lane. If it hadn't been for Sir William's worried warnings, she would just have assumed the town was busy because it was a sunny day and there were folk visiting from away.

Her basket was heavy, so she slowed her pace to catch her breath. With the sun shining down on the cobblestone streets that were bustling with the hum of merchants and townsfolk, she felt hot and paused in the shade of a doorway for a moment, standing on tiptoes to see if she could catch sight of Polly's straw bonnet.

The scent of warm bread from the bakery

mingled with the sweet smell of roses wafting towards her from the flower-seller's stall. She looked this way, and that, but a niggling sense of unease was making it hard to concentrate.

"Move out of my way, ducky." A woman clutching a bundle of filthy rags glared at her. "This is my doorway, and I need to rest my feet."

Katie stumbled slightly as she moved aside, shocked to see a tiny hand emerge from the rags accompanied by a wailing cry. The woman pulled down her dress, not caring who glimpsed her scrawny chest, and sank wearily onto the stone step. As the baby suckled, she swigged some gin and glared at her.

"Think I'm only fit for the gutter, do you? Maybe a toff like you should spend a day in my shoes before looking down your nose at me." She looked down at her worn leather boots that gaped where the stitching had rotted, revealing her toes. "Not as I can call 'em shoes, really." A defiant look came into her eyes. "You might disapprove, but I'll do anything to stay out of Monkton Workhouse. I'd rather scavenge for scraps and perish in midwinter than go there."

"Oh no, I'm not disapproving of you in the slightest. Sorry if it appears that way. Would you like a currant bun?" Katie rummaged in her basket.

"Don't want yer charity," the woman slurred. "Unless it's a bottle of gin…don't s'pose you've got some of that for a poor unfortunate?" She barely finished speaking before her head slowly drooped, and she fell into a doze.

Katie realised she'd lost precious minutes during their exchange. Even though the woman's comment about being a toff stung, she pushed it from her mind. Finding Polly was all that mattered for the time being, and she would come back and give the woman some food later.

"Have you seen a young girl?" she asked the flower seller. "Eleven years old, wearing a blue dress and straw bonnet."

"No, miss, but it's been so busy today that I've hardly had time to think."

"Polly." She shouted. "Polly, where are you?" People turned to stare, but she didn't care.

"Try looking down towards the park," an old man said, taking pity on her. "It's a squash, what with so many people heading there. I'd escort you myself, but I don't want to get involved."

"Involved in what?" Katie sighed. The old man had already hobbled away. *What's going on?* She shivered as she allowed herself to be swept along with the crowd. Something about the hum of chatter had changed, and the atmosphere felt different. A subtle tension simmered beneath the surface like a storm cloud waiting to burst.

Suddenly, she glimpsed a flash of Polly's bonnet. She was just ahead of her.

"Excuse me." She barged past two young men, no longer worried that they might think her impolite. "Polly! There you are. I've been worried sick about you." Her tone was sharp with fear.

Polly pouted. "Don't fuss, Katie. You're behaving as if we're in the centre of London town, not little old Pembrey." She pointed ahead. "Look, there are people with banners. I think they're marching about something."

Katie clutched Polly's hand. "We need to turn back. It's nearly time we should be at the tearoom, and the boys might be worried about us." She didn't want to point out to her little sister that a cold sense of foreboding was making her feel panic-stricken.

Polly twisted to look behind them, but a solid wall of people blocked their way. "I don't think we'll be able to. We may as well carry on and see what it's about, then we can slip away through the back lanes to get to Mrs Bright's.

Katie nodded, but her attention was elsewhere. As the lane opened into the small park, she spotted a small group of men gathered near the iron gates. They were rough-looking, with threadbare coats and caps pulled low over their eyes.

"Stand on an orange crate so we can see you better," somebody yelled. The wooden crate was passed forward over people's heads, and the tallest of the men sprang onto it. He raised a clenched fist, and a hush fell over the crowd. "We've accepted our fate for too long, thinking we were powerless, but today that changes," he said forcefully.

A roar of approval went up from the crowd.

"Too right!" a woman shrieked. She waved her tatty shawl in the air. "They keep us downtrodden, but together, we're strong enough to demand what's rightfully ours."

"Better pay. A roof over our heads. Is that too much to ask?" someone else yelled.

The man on the crate had a thick, black beard, and his eyes gleamed with fervour as people started chanting for change.

"... treated like dogs, we are!" the man's voice boomed. "While the rich sit in their grand houses, eating fancy food and living in luxury, our children starve. How long must we suffer this injustice?"

A fresh roar of agreement echoed around them, and for the first time, Polly looked alarmed. "What do they mean, Katie? We look after Mrs Pertwee and the families on the estate."

"Hush." Katie saw a man carrying a sturdy stick turn to stare at them. His gaze raked up and down, taking in their clothes, which clearly showed they were more well-to-do than many of the people around them. Her stomach lurched as more people turned to stare. There was something dangerous in the air, something that made her heart beat faster with terror.

"...the time for talking is over...now we need to show them we mean business."

"We should go," Katie whispered, tugging at Polly's hand. "Come on, Polly." But it was too late. The crowd was still growing as people were drawn in by the fervour of the speaker's words. What had started as a small knot of discontent was quickly swelling into something more formidable. Katie tried to pull Polly away, but they were stuck, being pushed further into the throng towards the front.

"The rich take and take while we have nothing!" another voice cried out. An old woman this time, her voice shrill with anger. "We toil from dawn to dusk, and for what? Pennies. Barely enough to feed our families, and me so crippled with arthritis now I can hardly walk, but my old master doesn't care."

More voices joined in, and soon the air was filled with chants of "Unfair!" and "Justice!" Katie's heart pounded in her chest as she looked around, searching for a way out. But the crowd was pressing in on all sides, and because most of them were taller than her, she couldn't see which way they could escape.

"Katie, what's happening?" Polly asked, her voice trembling. Her earlier excitement had been replaced by dismay. "Is this the unrest Grandpa meant?"

"I don't know," Katie replied, trying to keep her voice steady. "But we need to get out of here."

The crowd was becoming a living, breathing entity, moving as one with a dangerous energy that crackled in the air. The chants grew louder and more frenzied as people began to surge towards one of the grand houses that overlooked the park. Katie could see the owners peeking out from the upstairs window, their faces pale, etched with a mixture of alarm and disdain. She knew they were safe behind their thick walls and heavy doors, but out here, in the open, it was a different story.

Suddenly, a stone flew through the air, striking a window with a sharp crack. The glass shattered, and a cheer went up from the crowd. Katie gasped, her grip on Polly tightening. This was no longer just a protest; it was turning into a riot like the ones Mrs Pertwee had described in hushed tones.

"We have to get out of here," Katie shouted over the noise, but her voice was lost in the roar of the crowd. She could feel the panic rising in her chest. Polly was crying now, her small frame shaking with terror, and Katie's heart ached with the need to protect her sister. Everything was spiralling out of control, and she wished they had heeded Grandpa's words earlier that morning.

"Down with the toffs!" The thickset leader of the mob suddenly pointed directly towards her and Polly. "There they are…toffs like them. The landed gentry mingling among us and laughing in our faces at our suffering."

The crowds parted, leaving Katie and Polly standing alone at the centre of a circle of people.

"That's them! The Cavendish family brats."

Katie gasped. The accusation came from a young man she recognised from the hardware shop where Papa used to buy tools for his furniture making.

"Look at 'em in their finery, thinking they're better than us," he sneered. His eyes were cold, and his face was twisted with resentment.

Katie knew she couldn't stand silently. "That's

not true, Bryn, and you know it. Grandpa has done a lot for this community over the years."

"Your uncle treated us like we meant nothing." The old tailor from Lombardy Lane pushed his way forward to stand in front of her. "He always used to have us make his suits until he swanned off to London."

"I can't help that." Katie tried to appease the old man. "Times have been harder for Grandpa since Mama and Papa died," she added quietly.

A burst of laughter went up from strangers she didn't recognise. "The poor little rich girl is pleading poverty. Did you ever hear anything so insulting?"

"She ain't got no idea." A scowling man strode towards them, shaking his fist. His eyes were glazed from drink, and Katie recoiled. "Thrown out of my home and kicked out of my job at the mill I was, simply for enjoying a tipple of ale. Now my wife has left me, and it's all down to rich people like you."

"W…we're not rich," Polly stammered. "Grandpa has worked hard all his life, and we're orphans."

"Orphans who live on a grand country estate," someone snorted disparagingly.

"Enough talking…let's show 'em what strife really looks like." The man shook his fist again, and another group of men surged behind him, armed with makeshift weapons—sticks, stones, anything they could find. "Let's storm the posh houses," someone yelled. "That will get their attention…and take these well-to-do brats with us…maybe the gentry will listen then."

"Katie, I'm scared!" Polly sobbed. Her face was white and she flinched as someone plucked at her shawl.

"I know, Polly, I know," Katie said, her voice choked with fear. "Just hold on to my hand and don't let go, no matter what." A sense of dread filled her as she realized they were being swept along at the very centre of the uprising. She had a horrifying vision that if the constable arrived, they might be arrested and thrown into jail.

But as the crowd surged again, Katie's worst fears were realized. A man stumbled into them, knocking Katie off balance. Her grip on Polly loosened, and she felt her sister's hand slip from hers. Desperation surged through her, and she fought to keep hold, but the force of the crowd was too strong.

"Polly!" Katie screamed, her voice lost in the din. She turned frantically, searching for her sister, but all she could see were bodies pressed together, faces contorted with anger and fear.

The world around her blurred as panic overtook

her. She couldn't lose Polly. She had to act fast. A second later, through the chaos, she caught a glimpse of Polly's pale face. Katie lunged forward, pushing through the mass of bodies with every ounce of strength she had, and grabbed her hand again.

"This way…follow me." She lowered her head and dragged her sister behind her, forcing her way through a section of the crowd that had thinned slightly, finally plunging into a dark, cobbled alleyway she had never seen before.

"I think some things were knocked out of my basket." Polly was still crying, and even though every cell in her body was screaming out to carry on running, Katie stopped.

"It doesn't matter." She pulled her sister into a hug and rubbed her back. "I still have a few coins left. We can replace what was lost." She even managed a weak smile as Polly wiped her tears away with the back of her hand. "It's a miracle we still have the baskets, to be honest—" Her relief was short-lived as the drunken man from a few moments earlier staggered into the alleyway after them.

"They're here," he yelled. His shout sounded unnaturally loud as it echoed off the walls. "Don't let 'em get away…" Three more thugs jostled their way after him.

"I like the figure of the older girl," one of them slurred. "And it looks like we're all alone with nobody to come to their aid." His cruel laugh made Katie's blood run cold.

"Go away," she yelled at them. Katie snatched up her basket again and bundled Polly in front of her. "Run…run as fast as you can." The alleyway was so dark after the bright sunshine in the park that she could barely see where they were going, but as they followed the dog-leg, between two crooked buildings, for one blessed moment, Katie thought they were safe.

Suddenly, an arm shot out and dragged Polly into the shadows…then a tall figure emerged and pushed Katie into the shadows as well. She took a deep breath to scream, and a hand was clamped over her mouth.

"Hush…" a deep voice said. "Keep still and quiet, and they will pass by without knowing you're here."

Katie could feel Polly trembling as they huddled together. She stared up into the face of her captor, just as a shaft of sunlight filtered through the narrow gap, and was surprised to see warm blue eyes that crinkled at the edges as he smiled. His mouth was partially covered by a loose scarf, and he tugged it down, revealing white teeth against his tanned skin. He had a smattering of freckles and looked apologetic as he took his hand away from her mouth.

"Sorry. I didn't mean to frighten you, but I knew your natural instinct would be to scream out."

"What do you expect, grabbing me like that?" The shock had made her angry instead of grateful for being saved, and she drew herself up to her full height, glaring at him. "Who are you, anyway? How do I know you're not one of them?"

"I'm just a visitor coming into town for a few supplies, that's all." He grinned easily, not in the least offended by her reaction. "I never knew Pembrey would be this lively. Is it always like this?"

Polly edged out from behind her, eyeing him warily. "Why did you help us?"

"I don't like to see young ladies being taken advantage of by drunken thugs." He leaned out from their hiding spot, looking in both directions. "They've gone now, and I expect whatever shenanigans they thought they were stirring up will soon blow over."

"Are you sure you're not part of it? I've not seen you around these parts before." Katie wanted to trust him, but part of her held back. She guessed he was three or four years older than her, and his blue cotton shirt made his eyes look even bluer as he stepped into a pool of sunlight.

"Like I said…I'm just visiting."

"And where are you from?" Katie knew she was pressing him for details, but somehow it felt important to know.

"Over yonder." He gestured vaguely south.

"You didn't tell me your name—"

"Katie! There you are." Jacob's sharp shout made her jump. He strode down the alleyway towards them and raked a hand through his hair. "Don't tell me you got caught up in all that trouble? I was only in the tavern for half an hour, and when I went to find you at the tearoom, I heard those protestors saying they were chasing after two wealthy girls."

"Were you meant to be chaperoning them?" The young man stepped protectively next to Katie. "If so, you shouldn't have been in the tavern. Anyone could see trouble was brewing."

"And who are you?" Jacob scowled, not liking the criticism. "Has this stranger been bothering you, Katie? Just say the word, and I'll sort him out." He started rolling up his sleeves and clenched his hands into fists, squaring up for a fight.

"Actually, he saved us." She stepped forward to stand between them.

"I don't like the look of him." Jacob's eyes glittered with anger, and he suddenly threw his arm around her shoulder, jutting his chin out jealously. "Whoever you are…if you've laid a finger on her and done anything to besmirch her honour, I'll make you pay."

The young man lifted his hands and smiled casually. "That's not how I was raised."

Rather than feeling flattered by Jacob's attempt to take back control of the situation, Katie suddenly felt annoyed. He was behaving as though her rescuer was in the wrong, which wasn't fair. She shrugged away from Jacob and shook hands with the young man. "Thank you for your kindness. It won't be forgotten. Please tell me your name and where I can find you again. I'd like to give you a small gift for saving us. We were terrified, and those thugs had trouble on their minds, for sure."

"There's no need. The pleasure was all mine, Miss Anderson." The young man lifted his cap and grinned as he hurried away.

"Wait. How did you know my name?" she called after him.

He turned and shrugged with another grin. "I must have heard the protestors mention it. I hope we'll meet again one day."

"I hope so too—"

"You shouldn't be talking to him," Jacob interrupted gruffly, steering them in the opposite direction. "He looks like a wrong 'un if you ask me."

Katie could tell he was still angry and that it was compounded by embarrassment that he hadn't looked after her and Polly as he was meant to have done.

"Still, I would like to have thanked him properly."

"What's the point? Give him no heed, Katie, he's just some stranger who you'll never see again." Jacob frowned, still clearly jealous. "We'd better find the boys and get home. It's best you don't mention any of this to Sir William. He'll only worry, and there was no harm done."

Katie looked over her shoulder again, hoping to see the young man, and her heart fluttered as she saw him still watching them intently. Something in his expression made her think he knew more than he was letting on…or that perhaps it wasn't a coincidence that he knew who she was. He gave her a small nod, and they shared a conspiratorial smile, making her heart flutter again.

CHAPTER 7

Four Years Later.

KATIE SWUNG her bonnet from her hand, enjoying the summer breeze blowing through her dark hair. She glanced around to make sure nobody was watching them.

"I'm sure Grandpa won't mind us visiting his grave without putting our bonnets on." Polly was carrying a bunch of flowers they had picked from the increasingly wild garden behind the house. She had larkspur, roses, and colourful snapdragons. They had already walked out on the moors earlier, and Katie had tucked tiny sprigs of vetch in the top buttonhole of her dress. They were all Grandpa's favourites and reminded her of him. She needed that sense of closeness.

"I still can't believe we were standing with the vicar watching him being buried just two weeks ago." She blinked back her tears, trying to remember all the happy memories instead.

"I suppose we have to keep in mind what Doctor Frogwell said, that we were lucky to have him for so long."

"Grandpa did have a stubborn streak, which helped," Katie said with a wry smile.

"Exactly. Many of the villagers thought he wouldn't survive the last few winters, especially as his lungs were damaged when he had influenza."

"I put it down to wanting to make sure he could be with us for as long as possible." Katie felt a surge of gratitude for their kindhearted grandfather. She didn't know how they would have managed without him after losing their parents. "That, plus Mrs Pertwee's special rosehip syrup."

"You mean the one she used to give him every evening with a nip of brandy in it," Polly chuckled. "Grandpa always said the ladies in the village who belonged to the Temperance Society were forever nagging him to stop enjoying a nightcap, but Mrs

Pertwee said it was for medicinal purposes, so it didn't count."

They walked together into the family graveyard at the edge of the Castleford Hall estate. Even though other areas of the gardens had become overgrown, Mr Dryden always made a special point of keeping this part tidy. He scythed the grass regularly and deadheaded the roses, so there were always plenty of attractive blooms during the summer. The azaleas were a blaze of pink and purple at the moment, and some early butterflies danced between the flowers.

"I do miss Grandpa so much," Katie said quietly as they walked to the new grave. It was too soon for the headstone to be in position because the stonemason hadn't finished carving it, but she quite liked the plain wooden cross that was there for the time being and thought that Grandpa would have approved of its simplicity. He wasn't a man given to grand gestures, but tradition dictated that he would have a marble headstone soon.

"At least he has been laid to rest next to Mama. I find that gives me some comfort," Polly said, looking unusually serious.

"You're right." Katie looked at the three graves side by side, feeling melancholy. *Mama, Papa, and*

Grandpa. The three people who meant so much to us. And now we're alone, just the four of us.

They laid the flowers in front of the wooden cross, and both stood back, their heads bowed in quiet contemplation for a couple of moments. Just beyond the boundary, a skylark rose up into the clear blue sky, and the lilting song washed over them, feeling like a fitting tribute. Grandpa had always loved listening to the wild bird song in the grounds of Castleford Hall and the moors beyond. A song thrush started chirping in a nearby ash tree, followed by two collared doves cooing at each other.

"We thought we would find you here." Wilbur and Tim walked towards them. Tim was carrying two fishing rods, and Wilbur had five plump brown trout hanging from a stick over his shoulder. "We had a successful couple of hours at the pools under the willow trees. The fish were rising for the flies."

"Beryl will be pleased. Fresh trout for supper. We've been for a walk. It was too nice to stay in the house, and I couldn't settle to anything," Katie admitted. She knew the boys would understand.

"Is there any news about when Uncle Norman might return?" Tim shook his head in puzzlement. "I still find it very strange that he only came to Castleford for the day of the funeral, don't you, Katie? It seems disrespectful that he got the very first train back to London and didn't even spend one night at home."

Katie shrugged as they started walking back towards the house. "I've long since given up trying to understand Uncle Norman. If you think about it, he and Aunt Amelia have barely visited since they moved to London. I thought maybe they would come back more frequently after Mama and Papa died. It's obvious, looking back, that he didn't get on with Mama because he resented Grandpa remarrying and having another child, even though Grandpa ended up widowed early both times."

"I suppose their lives are in London," Wilbur added. "Uncle Norman made no secret of the fact that he thinks Castleford Hall is an exceedingly dull place to live. It's a pity they kept cousin Max away, too."

"I suppose that trouble with the protests in Pembrey a few years ago didn't help either. When Grandpa wrote to Uncle Norman about those marches, it probably only convinced him even more that London was a better place to live." Her thoughts drifted back to that terrifying day four years ago when she and Polly had got swept up in the violence. An image of their handsome rescuer slid into her mind, and she let out a small sigh of regret. Despite making some discreet enquiries, she never had discovered his name...or anything more about him, much to her disappointment. There was something about his bright blue eyes and broad smile that filled her with longing now and again, making her heart flutter.

"...Katie?" Polly's quizzical tone snapped her back to the present from her pleasant daydreams. "I said, what do you think will happen now that Grandpa isn't here with us anymore?" She picked up a stick and swung it through the long grass, looking pensive. "Even saying that doesn't feel right."

Katie shivered in spite of the warm sunshine on their backs. It was exactly the same question that had been gnawing at her day and night since Sir William's short illness and unexpectedly rapid decline. Several times, she'd had the impression that their grandfather might discuss his will with her when he started to talk about the future in hoarse gasps as he struggled to breathe. But when he became bedbound, it didn't feel right to bring it up.

Don't worry, Katie...I've made sure everything will be fine for you and Polly and the boys after I've gone. Those were the only words on the matter she had been able to glean. When she asked quietly what he meant, he had already drifted off into a slumber, and in the end, his passing had happened so quickly she was none the wiser.

"I honestly don't know anything other than Grandpa told me not to worry. He said he's taken care of things for us."

"I doubt if Uncle Norman will want to live here." Wilbur whistled cheerfully as they approached the back door to the kitchen. "I suppose he'll visit now and again to make sure things are in order, and our lives won't change much."

Beryl clapped her hands with delight when they all trooped into the kitchen. "Bless you, boys. I was already wondering what we would have for supper. I should have known you wouldn't let me down. I'll make buttered new potatoes, and Mr Dryden can pick some spring greens to go with the trout. How does that sound?"

"Delicious, as always." Wilbur grabbed a tin bucket and carefully slid the fish off the stick. "I'll gut them for you."

"Do we have any rhubarb?" Katie rolled up her sleeves. "I'll make a tart for pudding. And I should bake some apple cakes to take to the almshouse for the old folk. They've all been so kind with their well wishes since Grandpa died."

A shadow fell on the flagstones from the entrance. It was Jacob, and he came in without asking, lounging against the dresser. "I thought I heard you all coming across the garden. Have you got time to make a thirsty worker a cup of tea?" He winked at Katie in a slightly impertinent manner, which made her pleased Wilbur was still nearby.

"Have you finished mending the belt on the threshing machine?" Wilbur asked. His hands were red with fish guts.

"I'll get to it shortly, there's no hurry." Jacob's tone was dismissive. "I take my orders from Katie, now," he added with a grin just for her. "Now that she's the mistress of Castleford Hall." He folded his arms as though he had all the time in the world, not caring that Beryl tutted as she bustled past with a bowl of muddy potatoes to scrub. "'Tis just a formality reading Sir William's will, is it, Katie? It will all be left to you four, I expect."

"We don't know." She didn't want to discuss such important matters with one of their workers, but then she reminded herself she had known Jacob for years. He was probably just making polite conversation. "We have to wait and see what Uncle Norman says."

"But you're nineteen years old now, almost twenty." He arched one eyebrow, his gaze lingering on her womanly curves for a beat too long. "And Wilbur is sixteen. Everyone knows your uncle can't stand being here. You're plenty old enough to manage the estate yourself, Katie…with a bit of help from me," he added airily.

How does Jacob manage to be so impertinent but charming at the same time? Katie managed not to roll her eyes.

"You're still as full of yourself as ever," Polly grumbled good-naturedly as she reached past him to fetch mugs from the dresser and pour tea out for everyone. "Anyone would think you'd been promoted to estate manager."

"Now that's a good idea. Someone has to make sure your sister has the right sort of guidance," Jacob said, missing the subtle dig. "There will be all sorts of charlatans trying to worm their way into your affections now, Katie, you mark my words. A woman with an inheritance like this could get into trouble without a guiding hand."

"I'm sure Miss Anderson will have all the guidance she needs from Sir William's bank manager and solicitor when the time comes," Beryl Pertwee said crisply. She had no time for Jacob's flattery. "Take your tea outside and help Mr Dryden. He's run off his feet with the garden at this time of year."

Jacob pushed away from the dresser, scowling slightly at the older woman. He wasn't used to being told what to do, and Katie realised she would need to manage him with a firm hand. His easy-going nature was edging towards insolence now that there was no fear of being reprimanded by Sir William. "Can you come to the stables for a moment, Katie? I need to show you what's left of last year's hay to see if we should keep it."

She hesitated. Usually, Grandpa would have decided such matters, but now it would fall to her, so she had better get used to it. "Of course. I can make the cakes in a minute."

As she and Jacob strolled towards the stable block, Katie felt her worries ease slightly in the sunshine.

"I expect it will be hard running the place without Sir William." Jacob gave her a kind smile. "Even from his sickbed, he always knew exactly what was happening on the estate. He was a good employer, and I'm grateful he took a chance on me all those years ago."

She wondered if she had misjudged him. Perhaps Jacob had her best interests at heart after all. "It just feels so strange without him. I thought Uncle Norman would stay after the funeral, but he said he had urgent business in London to attend to."

"He's a strange 'un, that's for sure." Jacob glanced around the empty barnyard, then suddenly slid his arm around Katie's waist, pulling her to his chest.

"What are you—" She was speechless and tried to turn away, but his grip tightened.

"You need me now more than ever," he muttered, with a glow of ardour in his eyes. "I meant what I said about folks sniffing around once they think you're rich, Katie. You can't trust outsiders to do right by you."

"Jacob, let me go." She pressed her hands to his chest and pushed. "Don't be so silly."

"I'm the person who cares the most for you," he growled. His arm felt like an iron band across her back, and he lowered his head towards her.

She realised with horror that he was going to kiss her whether she wanted it or not. Panic gave her unexpected strength, and she shoved him away, stumbling backwards, tearing the lace trim on her dress in the process. "I'm the mistress of the house, you should treat me with respect." Her voice sounded shrill and panicky to her ears, but instead of bringing Jacob to his senses, it seemed to anger him.

"We don't know that for sure yet," he sneered. "Things might change when you least expect them to," he added rather mysteriously.

"What do you mean? Do you know something I don't?"

He shrugged insolently with a small smile that didn't reach his eyes. "How would I know? I'm just the stable hand…a nobody."

"Jacob, don't say that." Katie felt wrong-footed. He was their employee, but she'd thought he was a friend as well. But trying to kiss her risked damaging her reputation. "I like you, but not in that way. Surely, you understand that I have to preserve my modesty."

"It didn't seem that way when you were chasing after that stranger in the alleyway, begging to know his name."

Katie gasped at the insinuation, then folded her arms. "It was to thank him for saving Polly and me from those thugs. You're being ridiculous if you imagine it was anything more. Not to mention it was years ago!"

"Maybe, but tongues wag in Pembrey. It doesn't take much for a rumour to spread."

"There is no rumour." She sighed with exasperation, wondering why Jacob was so jealous of the encounter so long ago. "I have chores to do in the house. Do you want to show me the hay or not?"

"No, not now. You'd better run along and play at being a toff again." Jacob stomped away, throwing one last comment over his shoulder. "Anyway, there are plenty of pretty young ladies in the village who would be happy to have my attention, Katie. If you think being the mistress of Castleford Hall puts you a cut above folk like me who worked loyally for Sir William all these years, so be it. But don't expect us to rush to help you when times change."

She watched him stride away, feeling bemused. It was true that she used to have romantic daydreams about Jacob when she was younger, but she had to be sensible. Such a dalliance would be a disaster. Grandpa would have expected her to marry someone with good prospects, although she wasn't sure how she would meet such a gentleman now that she had nobody to chaperone her to dances or introduce her to anyone suitable.

With a shake of her head and a small sigh, Katie hurried back to the kitchen, pausing only to pick some dill and chives in the garden to go with the trout. Her thoughts turned to the uprising in

Pembrey again. Things had calmed down in the town after a few days of trouble, but Mrs Pertwee was still convinced it wouldn't take much to spark unrest again.

Who was the young man in the alleyway? And why was he there? The questions would forever remain unanswered. And now she would have to make amends with Jacob. The last thing she wanted was for them to fall out. She couldn't afford to lose his friendship. She picked a sprig of lavender for her pillow, hoping it might help her sleep better after so many nights of tossing and turning with worry lately.

Maybe Jacob's jealousy was sparked by recognising that she had felt an unusual connection to the blue-eyed stranger. Katie held the lavender to her nose and breathed in the fragrant aromatic scent before mentally giving herself a shake. There was no time for fanciful thoughts about a person she had only met once and would never see again.

"I have to plan for the future," she muttered to herself. "If only we knew what Grandpa's will says for me, Polly, and the boys."

She decided she would ride into Pembrey the following morning and visit the bank manager. She had no idea who Sir William's solicitor was and assumed it must be someone in London if Uncle Norman had taken over managing his affairs, which was what he had pushed for. Once she knew there was some sort of provision for their future, she would feel more settled. But waiting passively was not what Mama would have advised, she was sure. Instead of waiting for Uncle Norman to write to them, she would take matters into her own hands and ask for a meeting with him.

CHAPTER 8

By the time supper was almost ready to be served, dusk was already falling outside. Katie sat on the wooden bench in the kitchen garden, watching the sky turn from blue to soft hues of pink, listening to the bats squeak as they flittered and swooped under the barn eaves. Fat moths batted against the window behind her, drawn by the lamplight inside, and the heady smell of night-scented stock filled the air. It was a perfect early summer evening. The only thing missing was the faint waft of cigar smoke that would normally have signalled Sir William strolling on the terrace, coming to find her for a chat.

"Are you coming inside before Tim eats your share of the food?" Polly skipped impatiently down the steps to join her, thinking she might be missing out. "What are you doing? Come and save me from the boys squabbling about whether we should write and invite Max to come and stay."

Katie stood up and shook the creases out of her skirt. "I think we should. He's old enough to make his own decisions now. I think it's strange we haven't heard from him."

The repetitive clip-clop of horses trotting in the lane caught their attention, and much to their surprise, a carriage bowled up the drive, pulled by two gleaming black horses. The familiar silhouette of a man leaning forward to look out of the window made her stomach drop.

"It's Uncle Norman." She stared at Polly, momentarily lost for words. "Why has he come without sending a note first? He never does that."

"That was when Grandpa was still alive." Polly shot her a rueful look. "He probably thinks we don't deserve the same consideration. Don't worry, the guest bedrooms are still made up and aired from when we got them ready for the day of the funeral."

"I was planning to send him a letter tomorrow asking for a meeting about the will, so it saves me a job." They hurried into the kitchen to tell Wilbur and Tim the news.

"Lawks! How am I going to stretch five trout between all of us and two more visitors?" Mrs Pertwee hobbled around the table, grabbing extra plates and looking flustered. "I doubt Mistress Amelia will enjoy such plain fare...maybe I can make devilled eggs for her instead."

Wilbur put his hand on her shoulder. "They can't expect a three-course dinner if they turn up with no warning. I expect they ate at one of the roadside taverns on their way. They might not even be staying the night, so let's not panic."

"True enough, Master Wilbur." The old cook peered into the shiny surface of one of her copper pans and adjusted her mobcap, which had slipped a little on her grey hair. "I don't know why I get in a flap every time they visit." She took a calming breath. "Sir William used to joke that I was like a cat jumping on hot coals. How I wish he was still alive." Her eyes misted with tears at the memory, and she dabbed them away with the corner of her apron.

"Let's go and greet them," Katie said decisively. It felt like an important gesture, rather than her uncle finding them all hiding in the kitchen as if they were servants.

* * *

"This is a lovely surprise," Katie said, opting for diplomacy instead of the truth and ignoring the butterflies in her stomach.

They all stood at the bottom of the steps as a coachman she had never seen before held the carriage door open. Norman stepped down and extended his hand to assist Amelia.

"And it's nice that you have come to Castleford Hall as well, Aunt Amelia." Katie stepped forward and peered into the depths of the carriage, hoping to see Max waiting patiently to join them, but it was empty.

"How is Cousin Max?" Wilbur asked. "It was such a shame he couldn't come to Grandpa's funeral. We miss him."

Amelia looked around with a disapproving expression as her gaze fell on the weeds sprouting in the gravel carriage sweep and the dishevelled state of the flower beds nearby that were blooming in a riot of disorganised colour. "We managed to secure him a good position in Her Majesty's British Army for a few years."

"Max has become an officer in the army?" Katie couldn't hide her surprise.

"Goodness me, of course not. He will serve as a Captain, and it won't be long until he's a Major or

Lieutenant Colonel, or higher, I expect, once he has proven himself. Naturally, we impressed upon the recruiting officer that the Cavendish family name had a history in the military, and I'm sure they will treat dear Maxwell accordingly and with great respect."

"That must have cost a pretty penny, paying for a commission," Tim blurted out without thinking.

Katie saw Uncle Norman's eyes narrow with irritation. "That's none of your business, Tim. Now, Polly, please show Amelia up to our bedroom and carry her bag, and Katie, if you could kindly inform Mrs Pertwee that I would like coffee and port served in the library as soon as possible. Once Amelia has had a chance to freshen up from the journey, I would like you all to come to the study for a meeting." He pulled an ornately engraved gold pocket watch from his waistcoat and opened it, pursing his lips. "Let's convene at half past eight. That will give me time to sort a couple of things out."

"Are you sure we shouldn't have our cousin Max here if this is to discuss the future of Castleford Hall?"

Norman frowned again. "I have already written to Max to discuss matters. As Amelia said, he will only serve in the army for a short while, until he helps me with the business. There are some things I'm planning to start soon."

"In London, you mean?" Katie couldn't understand why he sounded as though he didn't want to share any details.

"Are you always this persistent?" Amelia snapped, opening her fan and fluttering it in front of her face. "Spare a thought for the fact that your uncle and I are tired from travelling, Katie, instead of peppering us with irrelevant questions. Max's future is no concern of yours. He has a glittering career ahead of him, and that's all that matters."

Polly and Katie exchanged worried glances as they helped carry their aunt and uncle's belongings inside. Wilbur and Tim rushed away to light fires, mindful that even though it was summer, some of the rooms could be chilly in the evenings.

A LITTLE WHILE LATER, even though Norman and Amelia weren't joining them for supper, Katie could barely eat a morsel as she sat at the large wooden table in the kitchen with her siblings.

"I tell you, the whole atmosphere of Castleford Hall changes when those two arrive," Beryl grumbled under her breath. "Lord knows, it will probably be ten times worse without Sir William here to keep Master Norman in check."

"I'm just grateful that they never stay very long." Katie pushed her plate away. Tim and Wilbur eyed the food she had left, and she nodded to indicate they could eat it. There was no point wasting Mrs Pertwee's delicious cooking, but her appetite had deserted her.

"What do you think the meeting is about?" Polly helped herself to a generous portion of rhubarb tart and poured cream over the top.

"Grandpa's will, I hope."

The ticking of the grandfather clock in the hallway felt as though it was counting down the minutes to bad news in Katie's mind. She couldn't shake the feeling that Uncle Wilbur was enjoying keeping them waiting, but she didn't want the others to know.

"As long as you stick together, everything will be fine. Of course, things will be different, but Castleford Hall has weathered many changes." Beryl Pertwee sounded unnaturally bright, as if she was trying to convince herself. "Your grandfather was a well-to-do man, even though we've had to be careful with the pennies recently."

Where the evening had dragged earlier, by the

time Katie had cleared the table, she realised it was half past eight, so they all hurried into the study. A fire crackled merrily in the hearth, and her heart felt heavy at the memory of so many hours spent there with Sir William, listening to him read or talk about what was happening on the farm.

"Should we fetch more chairs?" Wilbur looked around the room. Uncle Norman was sitting in the large leather chair behind Sir William's polished walnut desk, and Aunt Amelia was standing next to him, resting her hand daintily on his shoulder.

"No need for that, you can stand. The meeting won't take long." Norman smoothed his moustache, then steepled his fingers together, looking at them with a curiously detached expression.

"This doesn't seem right," Katie murmured.

"What doesn't?"

"You sitting in Grandpa's chair." She lifted her chin, deciding she should speak her mind. "This is his study and always will be. Perhaps it would be better to use another room as your study."

"Nonsense," Norman snapped. "There's no need for such maudlin sentimentality." He leaned back in his chair and reached for the glass of port. It had spilt on the wood and left a small ring-shaped mark.

"Grandpapa is barely cold in his grave, and you're

taking over without any regard for what he would have wanted."

"I'll thank you to mind your manners and remember who you're speaking to." His eyes glittered with anger, and Katie sensed Tim's shock next to her. She had always suspected Uncle Norman didn't care much for them, but this was the first time she had seen such naked hostility.

"I'm sorry," she murmured, knowing she needed to keep the peace. "It's hard not having him here anymore. Especially after losing Mama and Papa as well." She squared her shoulders and linked her hands in front of her apron, trying to stay deferential as she knew that was what their uncle expected. "What's harder still is not knowing what the future holds for the four of us now. I was going to send a letter asking if we might be told what Grandpa's will says about us and Castleford Hall."

"I'm old enough to help Katie manage the farm," Wilbur said hastily.

"And I don't intend to start courting yet," she added. "I would rather spend my time doing my best to look after Grandpa's legacy while you're in London."

"That won't be necessary. Amelia and I are going to remain in Castleford Hall for the foreseeable future. The rest of our luggage is arriving tomorrow. We intend to make this our home now."

Her siblings gasped. "Oh…y…yes, of course." Once again, Katie felt wrong-footed as she struggled to make sense of the shifting sands under their feet and so many changes. "But, we…we thought you didn't enjoy living on the moors, away from all the things you enjoy in London."

"Everyone says you don't like being here," Tim mumbled while Polly nodded next to him.

"I've never known such impertinence." Norman jumped up from his seat with such speed that they all stepped back in alarm. His cheeks had turned blotchy and red, and he snatched up a thick document, waving it in their faces. "This is Papa's will, and thankfully, he finally did the right thing. I have inherited everything he owned."

Katie was stunned into silence. It wasn't that she had expected anything different; her shock was more due to the look of jubilant excitement on her uncle's face.

"So…there was no mention of us as his grandchildren?" she asked, trying to gather her scattered thoughts.

"Of course not," Amelia snapped as though she was asking something ridiculous. "The Castleford

Hall estate and all of Sir William's money and assets are quite rightly going to his son. Sir William's second wife, your grandmother, was nothing but a flibbertigibbet who married above her station, which is why your mother turned out to become so irresponsible. From everything Norman has told me, Grace expected to be cosseted by your grandfather all her life, which is why she married someone equally as feckless. A man with no prospects."

"You can't speak about our parents like that," Wilbur cried angrily. "At least they loved Grandpa and cared for him. You only ever come to Castleford when you want something, or for your own benefit."

Katie put a restraining hand on Wilbur's arm and frowned at him, signalling that he had gone too far. "I understand that you and Mama didn't always get along, Uncle Norman, but all that is in the past now."

"Quite. It's time for a change."

"It will certainly feel rather different having you both living here with us, but I'm sure we will all adapt very soon. Can I read the will, please?"

"It's far beyond your capabilities," Norman snapped, tucking it away in the top drawer of the large desk and turning the key in the lock. "I wouldn't expect you to understand such a complicated legal document. Suffice to say, my solicitor in

London has confirmed that everything is correct and I am the sole beneficiary."

"I see." There was nothing more to say, but Katie decided she would still secretly visit the bank manager in Pembrey next time she was there to see if he would tell her who Grandpa's solicitor was.

"You sound as though you don't believe us." Amelia looked at her coldly. "Anyway, we have decided that Castleford Hall needs a clean sweep. Things have been allowed to drag along in a most unsatisfactory fashion these last few years, so Norman and I are going to give the estate a much-needed fresh start."

"Things have been working perfectly fine," Wilbur said, still simmering with anger.

"What sort of changes are you thinking of?" Katie knew she had to stay calm. "Mr Dryden and Jacob are doing their best with the farm and the grounds, but we don't have as many workers as we used to. Grandpa has always been good about letting our tenants stay on in their cottages because he disapproved of people being thrown out of their homes after years of loyal service. It's harder to get labour these days as some of the village men have decided to travel to bigger towns to work in these new manufactories."

THE FARTHING GIRL

"I know all that." Norman was starting to sound impatient. "The fresh start we are referring to concerns the four of you, not the farm. Even though I'm not obligated to look after my half-sister's children and make up for her mess, I will do so anyway."

"And we will do our best to help however we can on the estate," Katie replied, ignoring his heartless taunt.

"I've decided it's best for you to leave Castleford Hall," he added casually.

"What?" Polly gasped

Tim scowled. "Leave our home?"

"You can't do that...we've lived here our whole lives."

The clamour of her siblings' shocked replies echoed around the study, and Katie felt panic rising in her chest. She stepped up to the desk and reached out to grab Uncle Norman's hands and plead with him. "Don't send us away, please, I beg of you. The others are right. This is the only place we know. It's our home. The place where we have our only memories of Mama and Papa, not to mention Grandpa."

Norman shook his head, removing his hands hastily from her grasp, looking uncomfortable. "You're all panicking about nothing. If you would just quieten down and let me finish speaking, you will understand that I only have your best interests at heart."

"Well, go on then, tell us." Polly's expression was mutinous, but Katie could tell by the tremor in her voice that she was close to tears.

"Your uncle has decided that it would be good for you to live in London for a couple of years," Amelia explained impassively, not looking at all bothered by how upset they were. "You will stay in our home in Portland Place, where we have hired a governess to continue your education."

"But, what if we don't want to go to London?" Tim still sounded disgruntled. "Grandpa said we didn't need to continue with any more book learning." He loved nothing more than being out in the countryside fishing and helping on the farm, and Katie knew he would hate being hemmed in by all those buildings.

"It's all decided." Norman paced back and forth with his hands behind his back. "I've given it a lot of thought, and that's why I went back to London following Papa's funeral to make all the necessary arrangements. Your upbringing has been rather haphazard, and it's time to put that right. I don't really approve of how Grace raised you, but now that I'm head of the family, I think she would have wanted this for you. It's a fresh start for all of us and an opportunity to better yourselves rather than being stuck here like some country yokels with no prospects and no chance of making the right sort of connections."

"Will we be alone in London, other than having a governess?" Katie knew she sounded suspicious, but there was so much that didn't make sense.

"Not all the time." Amelia shook her head with a tinkling laugh at her naivety. "Your uncle and I will travel back to London regularly and chaperone you to some dances and plays at the theatre and such like. It's important that you marry well, girls, and Wilbur and Tim will need to decide what careers they wish to follow, with our help."

She turned to the others and gave them a tentative smile. "Perhaps it will be good for us. Mama and Papa often said they would take us to visit London when we were older, and Grandpa always told us we should keep an open mind."

"As long as we can come back and visit regularly." Tim still looked unconvinced. "We're not born and bred to be somewhere like that. The countryside is in our blood. Besides, I already know I want to be a furniture maker like Papa."

"It will only be for a couple of years." She glanced at Uncle Norman, and he nodded in confirmation.

"Good, that's all agreed then." Amelia fanned herself, looking worn out by it all.

"Yes, run along and pack your bags," Norman said briskly. "The coachman will have the carriage ready shortly."

Katie's mouth gaped open. "We're leaving tonight?"

"Of course. What did you think?"

"But we need to say goodbye to everyone and let them know when we'll be back. Mr Dryden will wonder where we are. And Jacob…and all our friends in the village."

Norman sighed impatiently. "The tickets are already booked for the steam train that leaves at the crack of dawn tomorrow morning." He gave a pitying shake of his head and chuckled. "I can see you have a lot to learn about how the world works beyond Castleford. You'll be back before you know it, but London awaits, Katie! An exciting new start for you all. Why would you want to delay it a moment longer?"

Doubts still rattled through her mind, but Polly shrugged and linked arms with her. "Uncle Norman is right, Katie. If the train tickets are booked, and we'll be coming home regularly, we may as well leave now."

Amelia opened the study door and shooed them away. "Pack lightly," she called after them. "One bag each will be plenty, and I'll take you to my dressmaker when I visit in a few weeks."

Katie pushed her misgivings aside, not wanting to appear ungrateful. Everything was happening much faster than she would have liked, but Polly was already bounding up the stairs, eager for their next adventure, and Wilbur was telling Tim they would be able to visit Hyde Park and see fascinating artefacts in the British Museum.

It won't be for long. Castleford Hall will always be our home. The thought comforted her as she hurried after Polly, wondering about what to pack in her carpetbag.

CHAPTER 9

"What's the meaning of sending them away at the dead of night?" Beryl Pertwee looked indignant, her jowl wobbling as she bustled around them all in the spacious entrance hallway.

"Do stop being so dramatic," Amelia snapped, glaring at the cook with ill-concealed disdain. "It's not your place to question your new master's decision. Sending them to London is done out of the kindness of his heart, might I add." She shivered and tightened her beautiful silk shawl despite the generous fire crackling in the hearth in the corner of the room.

Katie was about to say that she had better get used to the draughty house and dress more sensibly, especially in the winter when they could be snowed in for weeks at a time, but pressed her lips together instead, thinking better of it. Her aunt was quick to take offence, and they needed to stay on Uncle Norman's good side now that they relied on him.

"But it's not right. The poor things should be allowed a few more nights in their own beds to get accustomed to the idea of moving so far away." Beryl's voice cracked with emotion. "When will I see you again, my cariads?" She pulled Polly into an embrace, not caring that Amelia would disapprove.

"The coachman has the carriage ready," Norman said, striding into the hall from the study. "Let's not dilly-dally. You don't want to miss the train."

"I thought you said it's not going until daybreak?" Wilbur tipped his head, giving his uncle a cool look. "It feels as though you can't wait to get rid of us."

Norman laughed in an attempt at joviality, but it sounded false to Katie. "You know how rough the lanes can be around her. And all it takes is one inconsiderate farmer blocking the way as his cows meander in for milking. It's better to get to the station during the night. The waiting room is quite comfortable, and the night porter will be there, I checked."

A thought suddenly occurred to Katie and she

lowered her voice, stepping away from the others and closer to him. "I feel a bit embarrassed saying this, Uncle Norman, but what about money for food? We don't have any money of our own because Grandpa always gave us what we needed for shopping in Pembrey."

Amelia looked at her sharply. "You had supper already, didn't you? And the governess has been instructed to meet you off the train in London."

"We can't travel penniless. The train might break down." She felt bad begging for money, then remembered that Norman and Amelia had never wanted for anything. She knew Grandpa had showered them with money and help, even though Norman jealously tried to insinuate that it was Mama who had been treated unfairly as Sir William's favourite. It was only right that she and her siblings should have a few coins to help them settle into this new life that had been thrust upon them.

Norman drew Amelia aside and whispered something to her, and Katie desperately tried to catch what was being said.

"...spoiling them…"

"...nothing else for it…if it gets them on their way…"

She decided to play her trump card - one that she

knew would tap into Uncle Norman's snobbery. "It wouldn't be right for members of the Cavendish family to have to beg strangers on the train for pennies to eat if there's a delay."

He spun around and glared at her. "You're not to use the Cavendish family name. Your father was Edgar Anderson, and Anderson is what you should be called, not that it counts for much. Your father came from humble beginnings and has no relations remaining."

She shrugged, feigning innocence. "I thought you wanted us to better ourselves? Surely I can call myself Katie Cavendish now that you are our only close family and effectively our guardian, Uncle Norman."

Wilbur nodded solemnly, joining in. "Don't worry, we'll be very polite so that we show the family name in good light."

Polly held her hands out and adopted a feeble tone, with drooping shoulders, mimicking the poor wretches they always tried to help when they saw them begging in Pembrey Minster. "Can yer lend us a few coins to fill out bellies with some food, kind sir...'tis a terrible time for the Cavendish family, but I can't let my siblings starve."

"That's enough, Polly," Katie murmured. She gave

her uncle a polite smile. "We don't need much and appreciate your generosity in letting us stay at Portland Place. But truly...we don't have a penny to our names. How will we manage?"

"Sir William wouldn't send them away without a shilling to their name," Beryl said, looking wildly around the hallway. "I'll fill a bag with silver trinkets for them to sell sooner than let the poor moppets travel to London town without some money in case of emergencies."

"Oh, for goodness sake," Norman blustered angrily. "Get into the carriage, and I'll bring you a pouch of coins. The coachman must be wondering what the delay is. You need to hurry up so he can get to the stables to feed and water the horses in good time."

He stormed away, followed by Amelia, both muttering urgently as though there were still more plans to make.

"How will I manage here without you all?" Beryl lamented, tears flowing down her wrinkled cheeks. "I think of you as practically my own children since that terrible time we lost your ma and pa." She scurried between them, dispensing more hugs.

"Uncle Norman said we'll come home often."

"I hope so, otherwise, I've a good mind to follow you to London." Beryl sniffed. "I bet the cook at Portland Place won't know how to make your favourite meals." A new upsetting thought made her eyes fill with tears again. "They haven't even given me enough time to pack a basket of food for your journey."

Katie glanced towards Wilbur, feeling slightly helpless.

"Now then, Mrs Pertwee," he said kindly. "I'll make sure we come home at the end of summer. And then it won't be many weeks until Christmas, and we'll all be together again. Maybe even with Max if he's not overseas with his regiment."

Her eyes lit up. "Harvest festival…yes. Make sure you come home for that. And Mr Dryden will cut down a big fir tree to decorate for the festive season, and we'll have a lovely time. Maybe you could put in a word for me to travel back with you now and again. Master Norman seems to have plenty of money to pay for train tickets." She followed them down the steps to the awaiting carriage, already looking more cheerful.

"In you get." The coachman jerked his head brusquely towards the open carriage door. He grabbed their bags and threw them up into the storage area behind his seat, making the horses fidget in their harness.

"Goodness, it's so dark tonight." Beryl eyed the coachman suspiciously. "Do you know your way to the station? I haven't seen you in these parts before."

"How do you think I brought Mr and Mrs Cavendish here?" He gestured for them all to hurry up.

"There's no need to take that tone with me." Beryl pulled herself up to her full height, even though she barely reached his shoulder. "Make sure you look after my dearest ones, or there'll be trouble."

The coachman smirked as he started to close the carriage door. "Trouble? I answer to Mr Cavendish, not a doddery old crone who thinks working for Sir William lends her some sort of status."

"I...I beg your pardon—" Beryl looked shocked.

Katie slid forward on her seat. "Don't speak to Mrs Pertwee like that. I don't know who you are, but my uncle won't stand for such insolence. That's not how we behave towards our loyal servants."

He laughed out loud. "My, my...what a shock you're going to have soon—"

"Giddings, I told you not to speak to them," Norman said sharply as he hurried down the steps. He nodded curtly to Beryl. "Go inside and prepare hot milk for Amelia, please. She's coming down with a headache."

"Yes, Mr Cavendish." Mrs Pertwee bobbed a curtsey, then fluttered her handkerchief to say one final farewell and looked rather forlorn as she hobbled up the steps and disappeared into the house.

"Are you ready to leave?" he asked the driver.

"Yes, Sir. I was just putting that nosy old woman in her place."

"You know what I said," Norman hissed. "Be discreet, and it will soon be done. I'm making it worth your while," he added in a low mutter.

"What does he mean?" Tim whispered.

Katie suddenly remembered something. "Uncle Norman, I forgot Mama's hair combs. Polly and I only wear them for special occasions and I left them in the dressing table drawer. I'd better run upstairs and get them."

He hastily stood in the carriage doorway, blocking her way. "There's no time, Katie. Giddings needs to set off now. Otherwise, you might miss the train, and I don't want you staying in lodgings without a chaperone. Your aunt will bring them next time we come to Portland Place. Do you want this or not?" He held up a bulging pouch of money, dangling it in the light from the house as if bribing her to do his bidding.

"Sorry…yes. Thank you, that's very kind."

He gave her a thin smile. "Very good. Keep your wits about you. Giddings will take you safely to your destination, and remember to be polite."

Katie felt as though she should say something to mark the occasion and try and mend bridges between them. "Mama always spoke fondly of you, Uncle Norman. I know you were both very different, but we are part of the same family. Just because Grandpa has gone doesn't mean we should forget that."

He looked momentarily taken aback. "I've waited a very long time for my rightful place in society."

"And we shall all enjoy Castleford Hall together. Two years away will be hard for us, but this is where our hearts lie."

Norman shuffled his feet, glancing back at the imposing facade of the house. "Don't cling to the past," he murmured, almost to himself. "A fresh start…it's what I deserve."

"Goodbye—" Katie's words were cut off as he dropped the pouch into her lap and then slammed the carriage door shut. "Onward, Giddings, and don't spare the horses," he called.

"As you wish, Mr Cavendish. And you're sure about...?" The coachman sounded doubtful as his question trailed off.

"Yes." Norman clambered up the steps at the front of the carriage, and she heard the two men talking in low voices. "...you should be there well before dawn...Mr Smethurst is expecting them."

The coachman said something else she couldn't catch, then laughed as he slapped the reins over the horses' backs, urging them into a fast trot. She leaned forward for one last look at their home, feeling a hollow ache of sadness in her chest at the familiar shadowy outline of the house and the dark swell of the moors beyond. The carriage bowled down the long drive, lurching slightly as the horses slowed to turn onto the lane. The last thing she saw was Aunt Amelia and Uncle Norman silhouetted in the window of Grandpa's study, watching them leave.

Goodbye, Castleford Hall...until we're home again.

She sank back in her seat with a sigh. So much had changed, and she couldn't shake the feeling that this was just the start of something even more momentous.

CHAPTER 10

The four of them sat in silence for the first few miles, each lost in their own thoughts. Katie rested her chin on her hand, leaning against the carriage window. After recent bright nights when the full moon had cast a silvery glow over the moors, it felt darker than usual. Clouds scudded across the sky, hinting that rain might arrive soon. Every now and again, she glimpsed the waning crescent moon, a thin sliver high in the sky surrounded by faint pinpricks of stars. It reminded her of Mrs Tryton, the old woman who lived at the edge of the village, who could often be seen gathering herbs by moonlight for her potions and balms.

Katie shivered as the memory of one of their conversations came back to her. She had gone to visit her to collect some cough syrup for Grandpa on a cold autumn night the previous year when the scent of woodsmoke and damp leaves filled the air.

The wizened old woman had gripped her arm with surprising strength to take her into her overgrown cottage garden, pointing up at the sickle-shaped moon low over the horizon. "You see, it's a time to surrender to whatever has happened that is beyond our control," she had said, nodding to make sure she understood.

"What does that mean?" Katie wondered if it meant letting go of the lingering sadness she still felt about being an orphan.

The old woman had smiled, glancing up at her with age-old wisdom in her kind brown eyes. "Listen to what the moon wants to tell you, Miss Katie, for she won't let you down. Whenever you see the waning crescent, it shows an ending is coming. Some will be big, some so small you barely notice, but don't fear them, child. Without endings, there can be no new beginnings."

Looking back now, the moment seemed prescient. Had the old woman known they would be leaving Castleford?

"I don't know what's got into this coachman, he's whipping those horses as if we're being chased by the devil," Wilbur grumbled, breaking into her thoughts. He winced as the carriage lurched, throwing him against the sharp edge of the seat.

"Perhaps that's why Aunt Amelia always looks so sour when she arrives," Polly mused with a mischievous smile. "He's not used to these winding country roads."

Wilbur thumped on the roof, and they heard the coachman call to the horses, mercifully slowing down slightly.

"What are you most looking forward to about being in London?" Polly lifted the lantern and hooked it overhead so they could see each other better. The light it gave out was feeble but better than nothing.

"I'm going to see if Uncle Norman will agree for me to take up a furniture making apprenticeship," Tim said immediately. "I don't care if he thinks it's not a suitable profession. People liked the furniture Papa made, and when I used to help him in his workshop, Papa said I had a talent for it. I've had enough of book learning, so I hope the governess won't mind me missing lessons."

Polly nodded. "And you, Wilbur?"

He folded his arms, thinking. "If I could study accounting, it would make the time in London pass faster. Then, I can prove to Uncle Norman that I can do the accounts for the estate."

"Chance would be a fine thing." Katie huffed with annoyance. "Did you see how fast he put the will away without letting us read it? He treats us like simpletons."

"All the more reason to show him we're not," Wilbur said firmly.

"I'm looking forward to attending balls and meeting lots of exciting new acquaintances." Polly patted her hair and sighed wistfully with romance on her mind. "I always feared that Katie and I would have no way of coming out, but perhaps Amelia will surprise us, and we'll be like the daughters she never had."

"That's what she hinted at." Katie didn't warm to her aunt and wasn't particularly bothered about attending stuffy social occasions where they would have to be on their best behaviour, but she knew Polly would adore the glittering evenings in their new gowns and couldn't help but be pleased for her.

"What about you, Katie? Will you enjoy mingling with all those handsome young men?" Polly nudged her and arched one eyebrow. "Perhaps you're still holding a flame for the kindhearted stranger who saved us all those years ago?"

Wilbur looked startled at the suggestion.

"Don't worry, she's only teasing," Katie said hastily. She fingered the pouch of coins, holding it up in the meagre lamplight.

"Ooh, open it up and tell us how much is in there." Polly leaned forward eagerly, as did the boys. "I hope he's been generous. Maybe we'll have enough for a new gown. It might be a while until Aunt Amelia takes us to her dressmaker, and we weren't given the chance to pack a banded trunk." She pouted. "We'll look like country bumpkins compared to our neighbours."

The coachman had slowed the horses to a walk as they wound their way up a long hill hemmed in by tall banks, so Katie decided it wouldn't harm to open the pouch. Truth be told, she was itching to know how much Uncle Norman had given them as much as the others were. She spread her shawl out over her knees, undid the leather cord, and started tipping the contents out.

"We're rich—" Polly's excited exclamation faltered, and Wilbur grabbed the lantern to hold it closer so they could see more clearly.

"It's…it's just a handful of rubbish." Katie could hardly get the words out, she was so shocked.

"Where's the money?" Tim riffled his fingers

THE FARTHING GIRL

through the nails and scrap metal pieces - the sort of detritus that looked like it had been swept off the floor of a blacksmith's workshop. "I don't understand."

Katie shook the pouch again, wondering if her eyes were deceiving her, and one last item fell out. It was a scrap of paper folded around something.

"It must be a note. Read it, Katie." Wilbur frowned, and the swinging lantern in his hand cast strange shadows on his face.

With trembling fingers, she unfolded the paper to reveal a single farthing.

"The smallest amount of money possible," she murmured, feeling sick as she held it up to the light.

"What about the note, what does it say?" Polly looked shaken.

She took a deep breath, wondering how much worse their situation was about to become, then read out the short message.

"Dear Katie,

You and your siblings have benefited from Papa's generosity for far too long, for no other reason than his irrational favouritism towards your mother, Grace.

I have no intention of continuing with this unfairness.

Money is earned, which is why you all need to be taught this lesson.

Keep this farthing coin and look at it often to remind yourself that you are not a true Cavendish, no matter what you wish. You carry the stain of being Papa's second family and an illegitimate one at that.

What you never knew and your mother decided not to tell you is that Sir William never married again. Your grandmother was merely a mistress. He should never have taken up with her after my mother died.

From this moment, I am cutting you, Wilbur, Polly, and Tim off.

You are no longer part of the Cavendish family or Castleford Hall. Do not attempt to wheedle your way back or claim foul play otherwise, my solicitor will deal with you with the full weight of the law.

Yours,

Norman Cavendish"

Everyone gave a collective gasp, and Katie felt as though the ground was shifting under her feet. The very essence of truth she had grown up with had just been shattered into a thousand pieces.

"That…that can't be right," Wilbur said hoarsely.

"He's lying, just so he can have Grandpa's inheritance all for himself and then hand it on to Max."

The carriage had reached the top of the hill just as the clouds parted, allowing a faint light from the moon to light up the landscape. Katie peered through the window, realising that they had been so busy talking about the future for the last half hour that she hadn't paid any attention to what was outside.

"Do you recognise this lane?" She wiped the window with the corner of her shawl. "This isn't the way to Llancarn Station."

"How do you know?" Polly leaned forward, trying to see out.

"I went there with Papa once. He was sending a piece of furniture someone commissioned to Cheltenham."

"Maybe the coachman has taken a wrong turn." Tim was starting to look worried. "But he made a point of saying to Mrs Pertwee he knew the way."

They trundled past a farm entrance, and a dog howled in the distance. An icy trickle of fear ran down Katie's back. "This is the back lane to Lower Knighton."

"Don't be silly, you must have made a mistake." Polly reached over to slide the window open so they could speak to the coachman, but it was jammed shut.

"Think about what Uncle Norman just told us in his note. He has no intention of sending us to London." She could hear her voice rising with panic and took a deep breath to calm herself. She had to think logically about what to do. "We'll have to tell Giddings he must take us back to Castleford Hall."

In the distance, the countryside gave way to cottages on the outskirts of Lower Kington, shown only by candles flickering in the windows.

"But why…why has Giddings brought us this way?" Wilbur sounded angry, and he grabbed the handle of the carriage door. "I'll tell him he must stop immediately and explain what's going on." He rattled the handle, then clambered past Tim to put his shoulder to the door, but it wouldn't budge.

"It's locked, isn't it." A sense of calmness and clarity came over Katie as everything fell into place. "When Uncle Norman told Giddings that Mr Smethurst was expecting us, I couldn't think where I'd heard that name, but it rang a bell."

"It's the station master, surely?"

Katie hesitated, scarcely able to believe what she was about to say. "The last time I heard that name, it was from one of the poor women begging under the arches in Pembrey Minster. She pleaded for a few coins and said if she couldn't find shelter for the night, she was afraid she might get sent to Monkton Workhouse in Lower Kington."

"You think that's where Giddings is taking us?" Wilbur looked at her in disbelief. "Uncle Norman wouldn't dare!"

"The beggar woman told me the owner, Mr Smethurst, prowls around the haunts of the poor unfortunate homeless folk at night, forcing them into his wagon and taking them to the workhouse… never to be seen again."

"So all that talk of Aunt Amelia taking us to her London dressmaker for new gowns and having a new governess was all just a ploy to get us away from Castleford?" Polly grabbed hold of her arm with a look of sheer terror. "Make Giddings stop the carriage, Katie. He'll listen to you."

"How can I? We're locked in, and I expect he's being paid handsomely to deliver us to the workhouse. It's Uncle Norman's way of making sure we never bother him again."

"I can't sit here and do nothing." Wilbur rattled the handle again but to no avail.

"Unlock this door!" Polly screamed. She drummed her fists on the carriage roof.

"I've been given my orders," the coachman yelled back with a grim note of satisfaction. "A few weeks shut away in the workhouse, and you won't be recognisable. In fact, nobody would ever know you were raised by Sir William Cavendish." He whipped the horses to go faster. "It will do you good to work hard like the rest of us have to," he added, with a slightly deranged note in his voice.

"Please, I beg of you." Katie wrapped her shawl around her arm and jabbed her elbow against the window. A crack splintered across the top corner, and she jabbed it again, shattering enough of the glass to make a jagged hole. "Stop the carriage and let us out. Uncle Norman will never need to know you let us slip away into the night. We…we'll go somewhere new, far away."

Giddings roared with laughter. "You think I'd make an enemy of Mr Cavendish just to save four brats?"

"If you don't stop, we'll send for the constable as soon as we arrive. They'll throw you in jail for kidnap. Our grandfather is a person of influence."

"Was a person of influence…but he ain't no more. You're to give me that note your uncle wrote for you, then Mr Smethurst will shut you away and put you to work. You won't have any contact with the outside world for a while." Giddings chuckled again but suddenly broke off. "What the devil—" The carriage lurched. "Woah! Stop, you stupid animals, before we crash…can't you see there's a tree across the road."

Polly yelped as they all landed in a tangle on the floor of the carriage before scrambling to sit in their seats again. The horses whinnied and stamped with alarm at Giddings' rough handling of them, and a moment later, there was a loud thud as the coachman jumped down.

He loomed at the window, scowling with frustration. "There's a tree across the road, although goodness knows why. It's not as if we've had a storm."

"Would you like us to help you move it?" Wilbur asked politely. "It's probably too much for one person—"

"Don't take me for a fool," Giddings snarled, shaking his head. "The minute I unlock this door, you'll be off. Luckily, your uncle gave me the key." He fished it out of his waistcoat pocket and held it up with a grin. "I'd rather rouse a farmer than let you brats escape."

"But—" Wilbur began, stopping only when Katie surreptitiously tapped him on his knee. "Very well, have it your own way, Mr Giddings, but don't blame me if you can't do it."

The coachman pressed his face to the glass, peering into the carriage. Up close, Katie could see his skin was pockmarked, and his nose looked like it had been broken. A true thug, doing Uncle Norman's bidding. She sat back, trying to look serene despite her pounding heart.

"Don't try to escape while my back is turned," he growled menacingly. "Not that you'll be able to. And there's no point screaming for help. Nobody will hear you, and all it will do is annoy me even more." He pulled a hip flask from his jacket and gulped a mouthful, wiping his mouth afterwards with the back of his hand before glaring at them again and stomping off.

"This is our chance," Tim whispered. "Do we have anything in here we can use to break the door open?"

"Just smash the rest of the glass," Polly suggested. "If we're careful, we can squeeze through the window."

"No, that's too dangerous." Katie rubbed her hands over her face, forcing herself to think. "He'll hear the glass smashing, and I can't risk us getting cut."

They sat in silence for a moment, and Giddings' angry rant drifted in their direction so loud that it was clear he knew they were far enough away from any dwellings that nobody would hear. "...it's one turn of bad luck after another...never should have gone to that fortune-teller who told me to look for work elsewhere..." He grunted, and there was a faint dragging sound as though he had managed to move the tree trunk a few inches. "...the last thing I need is Norman Cavendish finding out about this delay... pray I can make it to the workhouse before daybreak..."

"He's getting so worked up about everything," Polly whispered.

Katie peeked through the window, noticing that there was a bend in the lane ahead of them and that the coachman was almost out of their view as he grappled with the tree, trying to snap smaller branches off to make it easier to manhandle.

Suddenly, a movement caught her eye, and a figure crept towards them, looming out of the shadows. "Who—?" she gasped.

He wore scruffy clothes and a battered cap. Shaking his head, he pressed a finger to his mouth, warning her to be quiet. "Miss Anderson?" he whispered. The burly man glanced towards Giddings, then pressed himself against the side of the carriage so he wouldn't be seen.

"Yes," she nodded. The others crowded forward around her.

"Who are you?" Wilbur demanded in a low voice. "We're locked in and being kidnapped."

"Hush," Katie said quickly. "Let me speak to him." The others nodded, looking by turns hopeful and terrified.

"I'm here to rescue you." The stranger pulled a knife from his pocket, and Katie sensed rather than heard Polly's sharp intake of breath to scream. "Don't worry," he said hastily. "This is to prise the door open. As soon as I've done that, we must leave…there isn't much time."

"Wait!" Katie looked him directly in the eye through the window. "How do I know I can trust you when you won't even say who you are?" Her heart thudded, and her mouth was dry. "I have to protect my sister and brothers."

"Gabriel," he muttered, not bothering to add a surname. "I'm just a friend in your time of need." The man shot her a reassuring smile and jerked his head back towards the shadows he'd just emerged from. "My carriage to help you get away is hidden in the trees just yonder. And there's an important acquaintance of Sir William's in it to explain everything."

Katie turned to the others. "This is like some sort of surreal dream, but we have to trust him. It's our only chance."

With a twist of the knife, the door clicked open. As they clambered out and scurried behind the carriage to keep out of Giddings' sight, the stranger jumped nimbly up the steps and handed down their four bags. "It's that way," he mouthed, gesturing towards a small gap at the edge of the lane that led into dense woodland.

"Are you sure this is wise?" Wilbur looked anxious. "Perhaps I should go on my own to see if he's telling the truth."

Katie hesitated, then glanced up to the inky sky. She could see that the clouds would move, revealing the moon again soon, which would make it more likely that Giddings would be able to follow them once he discovered they had escaped. "No. Remember, Beryl always said we must stick together."

"Follow me," the stranger whispered, this time with more urgency. He carefully closed the carriage door again, then grabbed hers and Polly's bags so they could go faster.

As they stumbled along the narrow path, brambles snagged at their clothes, and every footstep sounded unnaturally loud. Luckily, a breeze had picked up, and the trees rustled overhead. *Please let us get a good distance away before Giddings realises we've gone.* Katie's breath sounded loud in her ears, and she gripped Polly's hand firmly, dragging her behind their rescuer as fast as they could go, half walking, half running, with Tim and Wilbur bringing up the rear.

After they had walked for a good five minutes, Katie was beginning to have grave misgivings. The trees were getting so dense scarcely any light from the moon lit their way, and there was no sign of a carriage. She decided to risk speaking.

"Gabriel…or whoever you are. None of this makes sense. How did you know where to find us?"

"There are good people looking out for you, even though you might not think it," he muttered over his shoulder.

"Good people?" She wracked her brain. "Who? Tell me, please. All this secrecy is making me worried."

"You'll find out shortly, but it's not my place to tell you." He strode ahead, pausing every so often to hold branches aside.

"I don't like this," Wilbur muttered under his

breath. "Perhaps we should have chanced our luck escaping when Giddings arrived at the workhouse."

Katie was almost inclined to agree.

"There's the carriage," Tim whispered loudly. He pointed towards a faint glimmer of light ahead of them, and sure enough, the outline of two horses and a carriage took shape in the gloom.

"Thank goodness." She led them into the clearing, still following Gabriel. "Are we going to discover who Grandpa's mysterious acquaintance is now?"

Gabriel nodded. "Give me your bags, and I'll stow them up top. "Then get in and close the door. We'll follow the track yonder out of the woods for half a mile or so."

"There are no lanes nearby?" Katie still had no clue where they were going.

"The grassy track will muffle our hoofbeats and ensure Mr Giddings doesn't hear the horses." He grinned, his teeth white in the lamplight. "Mind you, I made sure to choose the biggest tree I could find to put across the lane. I reckon he'll be struggling with it for a while longer before he realises you've escaped."

"You felled the tree on purpose?" This was getting stranger by the moment.

"Aye, but not with a wood saw, Miss Anderson.

Nothing was left to chance. The roots are still attached so it looks like it toppled over in the wind, thanks to the farmer was very willing to hitch up his carthorses earlier to help us." He tipped his head slightly as if he'd heard something in the distance. "Get in…he'll explain everything."

She approached the carriage with some trepidation, wondering who could have known that Uncle Norman had planned such a terrible change of circumstances for them when it had all happened so fast. The door was already open, and she could see a shadowy figure inside.

"Are you sure this is safe?" Polly whispered. "We only just managed to escape from one carriage. We don't want to end up trapped in another one."

"A perfectly reasonable question," the voice from within the carriage said with a wry chuckle. "Sir William told me you might wonder. Allow me to introduce myself."

Katie held her breath as a tall man exited the carriage, holding the lantern, which he lifted up so they could get a better view of him.

"Y…you?" she croaked. His cheeks were still sunken and cadaverous, and his dark eyes bored into her, just as they had all those years ago. His coat hung loosely on his rangy frame, but now his hair was more grey than black, and his shoulders were slightly hunched.

"Indeed." He nodded politely. "Last time I saw you, you were hiding on the upstairs landing when I visited Castleford Hall to assist your grandfather with a legal matter." He turned to look at the others and then smiled at her, taking her by surprise. "I'm Ebenezer Black, Sir William's solicitor. Please get in the carriage and I will explain everything on the way to your new home."

CHAPTER 11

By the time they emerged from the woods and started clopping along a narrow lane, enough time had elapsed since their daring escape, and Katie slowly felt herself start to relax slightly. Even if the future was still uncertain, they had overcome the most pressing issue, which was to get away from Mr Giddings and Uncle Norman's wicked intentions for them.

"You don't think Giddings will follow us, do you?" Polly asked. She kept peering out of the window every few minutes as though she couldn't quite trust the situation.

"Gabriel chose this spot very intentionally," Ebenezer said, eager to reassure them all. "Even if Mr Giddings has an inkling that this is the way you came, it would take him an hour to turn his carriage around and retrace his route to get back to the crossroads to follow us. I think he'll be so worried about your uncle's reaction that he will simply claim that you ran away into the night."

"How did you know Uncle Norman would send us away tonight? Was it a coincidence that you and Gabriel rescued us before we arrived at the workhouse? We didn't even know that he and Amelia were coming to Castleford Hall today; it was a complete surprise."

He shifted in his seat and gave a slight cough as though he didn't want to reveal too much. "I have connections who are paid to keep me informed of certain comings and goings."

"I still find it strange that Grandpa never mentioned to me that you are his solicitor." Katie stifled a yawn and noticed that Wilbur and Tim were both looking drowsy. "I always believed that Uncle Norman had taken over legal matters to do with Castleford Hall and the estate to help make Grandpa's life easier. I just assumed the family solicitor would be someone in London."

Mr Black looked thoughtful and nodded. "Yes, I'm sure it was in your uncle's interests to give everyone that impression. The truth is, there might well be another solicitor based in London. My arrangement with Sir William was rather discreet—you might even say secretive—at his insistence. It's quite possible your uncle had no idea that I was taking care of some legal matters for your grandfather for many years. Sir William was shrewder than many people gave him credit for."

The gentle rocking motion of the carriage felt comforting, and Polly leaned her head on Katie's shoulder. "Just going to close my eyes for a minute," she mumbled.

"I have so much to ask you." Katie stifled another yawn.

"The journey will take a while. Why don't you all have a nap, and then I can explain everything when you wake up? There's no rush now that Gabriel is taking us to our destination."

Part of Katie wanted to know all the details immediately, but a wave of exhaustion washed over her, and her thoughts felt woolly and disjointed in a tangled web of half-truths and deceits. She let out a long sigh, and her eyelids grew heavier as sleep beckoned. "Very well…maybe just for a few minutes," she murmured to herself.

* * *

"Thank you, sir. It's always a pleasure stopping at your humble abode." Gabriel's cheerful comment filtered into a confusing dream Katie was having, where she was running blindly through the hallways and passages of Castleford Hall, desperately trying to find Sir William. Every time she thought she saw him hobbling away in the darkness and she chased after him, he always remained just out of reach and couldn't hear her cries for help.

"Looks like we're in for a fine summer's day," Gabriel continued. "And all the better for that mug of tea, Mrs Watts."

She jerked awake, and her reality came flooding back in an instant. The others were still fast asleep, and she saw that they had stopped outside a thatched cottage. A young boy had brought buckets of water from their well for the horses to drink, and Gabriel was putting away the empty nosebags after giving the horses some oats. She was surprised to see that it was just getting light. She carefully leaned forward so as not to disturb Polly and looked outside. It was the quiet moment just before dawn when the birds would start their enthusiastic chorus of song. The stars were fading, and a hint of pearly pink glimmered towards the east, heralding that sunrise was not far away.

"How are you? I expect that feels a bit better now that you've slept for a couple of hours." Ebenezer's smile was kind, and Katie realised she had judged him wrongly in the past when his dour expression and serious demeanour had frightened her on that dark night while hiding on the upstairs landing.

"A lot better, but I expect it will still be a long day." She folded her hands together in her lap, feeling much older than her nineteen years as she thought about the responsibility of trying to do the right thing for the four of them. "Are you able to explain everything to me now?" she asked quietly.

The others started to stir, and Ebenezer waited until everyone had woken up. "Of course. I didn't mean to come across as secretive, and I admire your pluckiness. You have shown the sort of fortitude tonight that Sir William told me you displayed after your parents sadly perished in that terrible accident." He paused, choosing his words carefully. "I say that because you will need courage in your new life, Katie. All of you will need to work together because things will be rather different from what you've been used to until now."

"Why did Grandpa make separate provision for us aside from what was in his will if that's what you're saying?" A torrent of questions swirled in

Katie's mind. "Perhaps if you start at the beginning, it will make more sense to us."

"Yes, you're quite right. I forget that you're not privy to the beginning of the story in quite the way I am." The solicitor pulled out his pocket watch and checked it, glancing outside as they bowled along through the lanes again now that the horses were refreshed. "I'll explain everything, and by the time I finish, we'll be there."

"Aren't you going to tell us where we're going?" Polly asked, jumping ahead.

"Soon." He held up one hand to slow them all down. "Back when you first saw me, Katie, Sir William had recently suffered from that bout of influenza if you recall."

She nodded. "It was bad. We feared he wouldn't pull through, but thankfully he did."

"It made him think about getting his affairs in order. I don't wish to cast your uncle in a bad light, but I suppose I must in order to give you the context of your grandfather's decisions."

Wilbur huffed and pulled a face. "I think our uncle has done a very fine job of revealing what sort of person he is all by himself, Mr Black. Please don't spare us any details out of politeness or thinking we might be offended by how you speak about our family. We need to know everything if we are to make a success of our future."

"Sir William feared that your uncle might not honour his word to look after the four of you after he was no longer alive and in charge of the estate. It pains me to say it, but he confided in me that Norman's jealousy towards your mama, Grace, might warp his sense of morals."

"It's sickening to know that Grandpa's suspicions were correct," Katie said quietly, still finding it hard to believe everything that had happened in the last few hours.

"I'm afraid family ties and kindness can be tested when inheritances and wealth are involved. I see it all too often, but admittedly, never something quite this shocking."

"So are you saying Grandpa thought Uncle Norman might plan something like this?" Tim asked in a small voice. "Does this mean we will never see our cousin Max again? We think of him as one of us, another brother almost."

Ebenezer's dark eyes narrowed as he considered the question. "All I can say is that your grandfather asked me to put provisions in place to secure your future if the worst ever happened. He hoped it would never be needed, but he was adamant that I should draw up an arrangement that was legally binding so that no one could challenge it. As for your cousin, I can't really say."

"We have to cut off all ties with everyone to do with Castleford Hall," Katie said hastily, looking at the others and feeling as upset as they were about it. "Dearest Max, we love him like a brother, but if he knows where we are, I'm sure it would only be a matter of time until Uncle Norman did as well. Perhaps it would be wise to keep our location a secret, don't you agree, Mr Black?" She turned back for the solicitor's confirmation.

"I think that would be a good idea, at least until you get settled. To be honest, I got the impression that your uncle is rather lazy. He likes to take the easy path in life, and now that he's cast you out of the family, he probably won't be very bothered about where you are or what you're doing. He has inherited the estate and practically everything Sir William owned, which is all he cares about."

"Max is probably away overseas now that he's in the army," Wilbur pointed out. "We can send him a letter once we feel more secure about things."

Katie let her thoughts drift, wondering what was waiting for them at the end of this journey. Was it a quaint cottage where they would be able to live quietly? And what about work? Without the privileges afforded to them she had always taken for granted, being known as the grandchildren of Sir William Cavendish, they would have to put their minds to finding employment. She wasn't afraid of hard work and tried not to look too far into the future for fear of being overwhelmed.

Another thought slid into her mind, which she knew she had to say out loud. "Uncle Norman wrote me a note, Mr Black." She retrieved it from her reticule and passed it across to him, blushing slightly. "Is it true that Grandfather didn't marry our mama's mother, Abigail? You can see that Uncle Norman is convinced that Sir William was only ever married to his first wife, Norman's mother, and that, as a consequence, our mama was born out of wedlock. As you can see, he makes no bones about saying this is why we don't belong to Castleford Hall and that we're not a legitimate part of the Cavendish family."

The solicitor frowned as he read the note and looked apologetic as he handed it back to her. "I'm sorry, my dear. That must have been a shocking thing to read."

"Just one of many shocks we've had since yesterday," she said, her voice catching with emotion.

"Mama never said anything to hint at it, but perhaps they kept it secret from her."

"The honest answer is that I don't know. Your grandfather never discussed that with me, and I've never heard any rumours to imply your mama was born out of wedlock. As you know, your grandmother, Abigail passed away when Grace was a child. I can assure you he adored your mama and your grandmother. But I always felt he went out of his way to treat Norman and Grace equally as his children, even though Norman was convinced he favoured your mama." He ran his hand over his grey beard. "I can certainly look into it for you, but I must warn you that you might not like the answer."

She glanced at her siblings, and they all nodded. "We just want to know the truth, Mr Black. It doesn't change how we feel about Mama and Grandfather, but if you can find out more, we would be very grateful."

"I'll do my best." Mr Black reached under his seat and pulled out a basket. "On a more practical note, are you hungry? It's not much, and we'll arrive soon."

Tim's eyes lit up, making Katie laugh. "The boys are always hungry."

"Don't forget about me," Polly added, leaning forward as he lifted the wicker lid to reveal apples, cheese, wedges of fruitcake, and water. "Running away from that rogue Mr Giddings is hungry work."

Silence fell for a few minutes as they all tucked into the unexpected picnic, and by the time Katie was wiping her fingers after finishing her slice of cake, a new sound reached her ears. It was the plaintive mewing of seagulls. She slid the carriage window open and looked up from between the high-sided lanes they were travelling through that were lined with cow parsley and elegant spires of pink foxgloves. The sun had risen, casting golden fingers of light through the trees, and overhead, she watched three white gulls wheeling in the sky just as she smelt the refreshing salty tang of the sea.

"You've brought us to the coast?" A surge of excitement and optimism bubbled inside her, and she grinned as Polly leaned over her and sniffed deeply.

"Wait until you see the view…any minute now," Gabriel called from his seat perched up in the front of the carriage. Even the horses seemed to sense everyone's shift to a happier mood, trotting faster along the lane.

"What made Grandpa choose for us to come here?" She brushed a couple of crumbs off her dress, giving Mr Black a quizzical look.

"He had some ties here in the past, is all he told me."

"Woah there." Gabriel reined the horses to a stop, their harness jingling. "Is there time for everyone to have a moment to stretch their legs, Mr Black? It might be a good chance for them to get a first glimpse of where we are."

"Please say we can have a look," Polly said, grabbing Ebenezer's hand and giving him her most persuasive smile.

He looked momentarily flustered and then rather touched. "Of course you can, my dear. It is rather spectacular, and the only sadness is that your grandfather never lived to know that you would see it."

With no second bidding needed, Katie flung the door open, held her skirts, and clambered down the steps, grateful to be released from the cramped carriage.

"What do you think, Miss Anderson?" Gabriel spread his arms wide to embrace the stunning view ahead of them.

"It's…it's like paradise," she murmured.

They were on top of a hill that looked like common land, given that there were sheep and cattle grazing freely without any drystone walls or fences to keep them in. Below them, the lane continued down a hill to a jumble of whitewashed cottages and red-brick houses, some with slate roofs and some thatched. It was smaller than Pembrey Minster but too large to be called a village. Several steep-sided wooded valleys fanned inland, one of which was carved by a winding river that ran into the sea. The coast stretched away in either direction, a mixture of sandy coves, pebbled inlets, and steep-sided cliffs with folded strata that formed strange stripes and patterns where it had been forced up from the earth's crust millennia ago. There was a small harbour, sheltered by the stone jetty that curved around it, and beyond it, white-tipped waves rolled towards the land, carried by a brisk breeze that tugged at her bonnet. A short distance out to sea, a small island rose from the foaming water, with forbidding dark cliffs and seabirds circling overhead.

"I never thought I could like somewhere more than Castleford Hall and the moors, but I think this might prove me wrong," Wilbur said, standing next to her, shaking his head slightly in disbelief.

"What's it called?" Polly asked as Gabriel jumped down to adjust one of the harnesses.

"Stonehaven." He grinned and pushed his cap to the back of his head, all traces of weariness from travelling through the night gone from his face. "I think your Grandpa chose wisely. You could have an enjoyable life here."

Katie walked across the common a little way, closer to where it started to slope down to the cliff edge. The springy grass was more akin to what she had seen growing on the moors rather than lush pastures. Her shawl fluttered behind her shoulders, and the wind snatched playfully at her dress.

The salty tang of the sea, combined with a stronger smell of seaweed and the noise of the gulls mewling overhead, tugged at the edge of her consciousness and then suddenly unlocked a memory deep in the recesses of her mind. "I think I came here once with Mama and Grandpa," she blurted out, whirling around to tell the others and feeling strangely emotional. "You were just a babe in arms, Polly, and Wilbur, you must have been only a year or two old. It was before you were born, Tim."

"We've been here before?" Wilbur sounded shocked.

She nodded and laughed. "Sometimes I dream about standing on a sandy beach, with the waves lapping over my toes. I always thought it was just something in my imagination, but now I think

Grandpa must have brought us here to visit. It must have been a happy day for them."

Polly came to stand next to her, and they linked arms. "I wish I had such memories."

Katie squeezed her hand. "It means we have some sort of tie to this place, which can only be a good thing. Grandpa didn't just choose a town at random to send us away to. It makes it feel like they're a little closer to us... still with us in spirit if he and Mama came here and had fond memories of the town."

The horses tossed their heads, eager to carry on, and Ebenezer cleared his throat politely from where he was standing next to the carriage. "There will be plenty more time to get to know the countryside around Stonehaven, but I think it would be prudent for us to continue on our way. I would like to ride through the cottages and past the harbour before too many people are awake to see us arriving."

"Must we keep our presence secret?" Katie's question came out slightly sharper than she had intended.

"It's not so much that." He exchanged a glance with Gabriel that was hard to read.

"It's more that Stonehaven is a small coastal town and a close-knit community," Gabriel explained hastily. "You know what it's like, Miss Anderson.

New arrivals give the gossips plenty to tattle about, eager to spread rumours about folk they don't know."

"It will be good for you to have a few days settling into your new home before you start meeting everybody," Ebenezer added rather mysteriously.

As Katie smoothed down her skirts in the carriage again a moment later, she wondered what he meant. She had thought they would quietly move into a small cottage perhaps and slowly get acquainted with their new neighbours, but Ebenezer made it sound altogether different…as though the whole town of Stonehaven would want to get to know them whether she was ready for it or not.

CHAPTER 12

"I think we really could be happy here," Katie murmured to herself as Gabriel steered their carriage through Stonehaven with little more than the occasional flick of the reins and soft command to the horses. The rhythmic hoofbeats sounded loud, echoing through the narrow cobbled streets, and a couple of plump old women smoking clay pipes paused from scrubbing their cottage steps to wave.

"The townsfolk are just beginning to stir," Ebenezer said.

"What are those men doing? And why are they dressed strangely?" Polly pointed towards four men gathered around a mound of what looked like wooden cages before Katie quickly reminded her that it was rude to point.

"Those are lobster pots." Ebenezer lifted his hat politely as one of the men turned to stare at them.

Katie was fascinated by how different the small town looked compared to what they were used to seeing in Pembrey Minster inland. Here, fishing nets were draped over cottage walls, and she noticed that many of the whitewashed cottages had a couple of lobster pots in their small front gardens. Smoke curled up from their chimneys as the women started their morning chores, and she spotted lines of herrings, gutted and butterflied, on wooden racks next to a warehouse, which she assumed was the smokery where they would be turned into kippers.

"They send them up to London now that the train line has opened this far west," Ebenezer said, following her gaze. "They've become rather in demand with the discerning wealthy folk."

"It must be good for the town to keep everyone employed."

"Yes, there are plenty of hardworking fishing families in Stonehaven. It's a good mixture of folk making a living from the sea and the land. Not grand, but people are honest salt-of-the-earth types."

She heard the underlying message that he wasn't saying. "Don't worry, we'll fit right in. We might have come from the well-known Cavendish family, but we don't put on airs and graces. Mama made sure of that."

Wilbur grinned at him, getting it, too. "We grew up tramping across the moors foraging for blackberries and fishing for trout in the rivers. Not to mention, Grandpa always encouraged us to help in any way we could on the farm."

"That's good to know." Ebenezer fidgeted on the carriage seat, looking worried. "Gabriel and I will visit often to see how you are, but I'm afraid it's going to be down to you four to settle in and adapt to your new lives now."

Katie lifted her chin, determined to show she was up to the task. "Anything is better than being thrown in Monkton Workhouse." She watched the boats bobbing in the harbour, noticing two men had already rowed out to one of the boats and were preparing to set sail. One pulled up the anchor while the other raised the sails, which snapped taut as they filled with wind, sending the boat cleanly through the waves for an early morning fishing expedition. "We will have to give some thought about how to earn money, but I'm sure we'll manage. I could do tuition. Wilbur is good at doing accounts."

Mr Black shuffled on his seat again. "Your grandfather already thought of that, Miss Anderson."

They fell silent for a moment as Gabriel urged the horses to trot faster now that they were coming out of the other side of Stonehaven. The cottages got farther apart, and he turned onto a lane that looked like it wasn't used much. There was grass growing in the centre of the dirt track, and it was lined with oak, ash and hazel trees, which arched overhead, forming a dappled green tunnel.

"When Sir William wanted to provide for your future, he said he wanted you to have a safe place to live, plus a means to make an income. That's why he purchased an abandoned coaching inn. He knew Wilbur would have the business acumen needed to do the accounts and bookkeeping for such a business. And he told me you were practical enough to run the place."

Katie's mouth gaped open. Of all the different scenarios that filled her racing thoughts on their journey, running an inn was the last thing she would have imagined. "A public house? Are...are you sure, Mr Black? It seems like such a strange choice."

"Our own coaching inn!" Polly wriggled excitedly. "We can serve hot meals and make extra money with rooms for guests to stay overnight. It will be the perfect way to get to know everyone—" She stopped abruptly as they rounded a slight bend in the lane, and it came into view.

"That's it?" Katie exclaimed. "It looks like it's practically derelict." She turned to Mr Black and was disheartened to see that he looked even more shocked than she felt.

A sign hung lopsidedly from its rusty hooks, creaking in the breeze and giving the place a slightly forlorn air. The writing had faded slightly, but its name was still visible. *The North Star Inn.* "I suppose it's named after the star sailors use to navigate. But how will we even begin to bring it back into use?"

"Well…this isn't quite how your grandfather described it all those years ago when we drew up the documents for ownership," Ebenezer said cautiously.

"It's not exactly on a busy route." Wilbur looked worried.

Gabriel leaned out from his seat to reassure them through the window. "You'll be surprised. It's only this short lane that looks quiet, but the road at the end is the main route for people arriving in Stonehaven from the west."

The horses whinnied as they came to a stop on the moss-covered cobbles, and Katie gathered up her skirts and sprang out of the carriage. "If it's all the same with you, I'd like to look round by myself first," she told the others firmly. "It's a lot to digest. We mustn't get our hopes up. If I think it's unsuitable, we'll have to find lodgings nearby."

Ebenezer inclined his head. "I understand, Miss Anderson. We'll give you a few minutes. At the end of the day, I suppose I could arrange to sell the place, but I'm not sure it would make enough for you to find anywhere else to live," he added, sounding doubtful. "Your grandfather wanted to make sure you could stay together, you see. I also think he wanted a business he knew wouldn't interest your uncle."

She eyed the building again with a rueful smile, taking in the missing roof tiles and peeling paint on the door with its rusty handle. "In that case, Grandpa certainly chose well. Uncle Norman wouldn't dream of setting foot in such a scruffy building, let alone mixing with hard-working fishermen enjoying a tankard of ale after a day at sea."

"He dines in the finest restaurants in London," Polly explained. "And Aunt Amelia prides herself on having the latest fashions."

"He'd be worried about standing next to someone who might smell of fish guts," Wilbur chuckled. "I don't think we need to fear Uncle Norman swooping in and wanting to add this to his estate."

"I'll look around quickly, then come straight back." Katie marched up to the door, hiding her apprehension. *Can we really take on a coaching inn, especially in this state? What if the locals don't take to us and refuse to drink here, or we end up with no paying guests?* She tried the handle, but the door didn't budge, so she knew she would need to examine every part of the building.

"Want me to come with you?" Gabriel called, already starting to climb down.

"No, let her do as she wishes," Ebenezer said hastily. "This is an important move for them, and Miss Anderson needs to see if it's right."

"Thank you, Gabriel. I'll shout if I need help, but at this rate, I think the only thing to fear is disturbing the mice."

Katie peeked through the window, but it was too grimy to see inside, so instead, she made her way to the back of the building. Even though the tree-lined approach had made the place feel hidden away, she noticed that it was only that part of the lane. The North Star Inn sat on a slightly raised area of land with a stream babbling nearby, tumbling down through the wooded hill from the farmland beyond.

The main building was two storeys, and nearby, there was a large cobbled yard with a stable block and an array of outbuildings. Weeds sprouted along the edge of the yard, and the breeze sent dandelion seeds drifting past her like fluffy white snowflakes. She lifted the latch to look in the stable block and paused on the threshold for the sound of scurrying mice to subside as they darted away from the unexpected intrusion.

Dappled sunlight filtered through the dusty windows, and a startled squirrel ran along the top rail of the wooden stalls and out through a hole. There were still mounds of hay up in the hayloft above the stalls, with a rickety ladder leading up there, and several wheelbarrows and pitchforks were placed tidily at the end of the building. She strolled along the barn, thinking through the business side of things. "It's a good size. Enough for six or eight pairs of horses, probably," she mused quietly to herself. There was a large set of double doors in the centre of the barn, big enough to lead a small carriage inside if needed, but she noticed there was also a long open-fronted barn, little more than pillars and an overhanging roof running at right angles to the stables. It puzzled her for a moment, but then she realised it must be for travellers to park their carriages under shelter if repairs were needed.

Stepping back outside into the sunshine, Katie blinked, waiting for her eyes to adjust from the gloomy interior of the stables. "Now for the inn," she muttered. Her stomach clenched as worry coursed through her again. She had been momentarily cheered by the stables, able to see that with a good clean, they could make them useable. But if the pub itself was too ramshackle, they might have to sell up before getting started. Mr Black had made it clear there wasn't much money to make repairs.

She crossed the yard, summoning her courage, and assumed the back door would be either locked or stubbornly wedged shut, with the wooden door frame damp and swollen from years of not being used.

"Are you going to let me inside?" she asked the building under her breath. "Or will I have to break one of the windows?" Katie grasped the door handle firmly, leaning her shoulder against the wood for good measure. Much to her surprise, the door swung open easily, and she stumbled inside, practically falling over.

Gasping with surprise, Katie tiptoed further into the room. "Is someone there?" Her voice sounded high with nerves, and she huffed with frustration at herself. *Of course there isn't. It's been empty for years.* She shook the dust from her skirts, sneezing as it stirred up more dust where it lay thickly on the flagstone floor.

A faint whispering sound made her shiver.

"Hello?" Her voice echoed, and the only reply was a rustle and the sound of scurrying mice again. But she couldn't shake the feeling that she was being watched and spun around to look over her shoulder. Other than a blackbird hopping on the cobbles outside, the yard was still completely empty.

"Come on, Katie. Stop being scared of your own shadow." This time, she spoke more firmly and decided to continue exploring before the others came trooping in to come and find her.

Taking a deep breath and putting aside the thought that she should have brought a lantern to light her way, she continued onwards, forcing herself to look at everything more carefully. The first room looked like a storeroom, and there was still one old barrel in the corner, along with a pile of hessian sacks.

Following through from there, Katie stepped into the taproom, which still smelt faintly of ale. There was a bar along one end, with room for the barrels of ale to be stored behind and shelves practically up to the ceiling. A lone empty glass bottle sat on the shelf next to a battered tankard, and a glass on its side. She slipped behind the bar and looked out, stifling a scream as she walked into a cobweb, disturbing a huge black spider that dropped from above her head and scuttled down her arm onto the floor. Clutching her hands together so as not to encounter any more creepy crawlies, she looked out at the taproom, trying to imagine it full of customers, with the sound of jovial laughter ringing out over the hum of chatter and a fire crackling in the inglenook fireplace. It had the potential to be a welcoming room, but would people visit an inn on the edge of town? She had spotted several other taverns in Stonehaven as they passed through. Perhaps Gabriel's optimism was misplaced.

"At least the furniture is still here," she murmured to herself, prowling around the room, running her finger through the thick dust. There were plenty of chairs and tables, an old upright piano in the corner, and hooks on the wall behind the door to hang coats and hats on. She caught sight of her reflection in the mirror in the corner and pulled a face. Somehow, she had managed to smudge dirt on her cheeks, and her bonnet had picked up some cobwebs along the way, too. Not only that but her dress was torn in several places from running through the woods, and her hair had long since fallen out of the neat coil at the back of her neck and hung in tangled tendrils around her face, *It's a good thing nobody can see me looking like such a fright.* Passing by the piano, she ran her fingers over some of the keys, and they let out a discordant jangle. They would have to get it tuned, she thought absentmindedly.

Katie was mindful of the minutes ticking by and hurried through the rest of the downstairs. There was a large kitchen, a smaller bar near the kitchen, which served as a snug where people could eat, plus several more storerooms. Peeking into the remaining room, which was a parlour, Katie was surprised to see that it looked much cleaner. There was an empty bookcase in an alcove, more tables and chairs, plus two wingback armchairs on either side of the hearth, with two empty glasses on an occasional table next to one of them. Her heart beat faster as she crossed the room and opened the shutters to allow some fresh air in. A shaft of sunlight revealed a half-burned log surrounded by white ash in the hearth and what looked like the corner of a document which hadn't burnt fully. It looked like the fire had been lit in the last few days. She eased the scrap of paper from the ash and turned it over on her palm. All that remained was the edge of a gold-embossed crest. The ornate curl, similar to a fleur-de-lis, looked slightly familiar, and she wracked her brain, trying to think where she had seen it before before reminding herself it was commonly used in all manner of things.

Someone has been here recently. Can I smell the remnants of cigar smoke?

The thought filled her with alarm, and she glanced over her shoulder nervously, half expecting to see a person silhouetted in the doorway behind her. Her imagination was running away with her again, and she forced herself to hurry back to the corridor and run up the stairs. A quick exploration showed her there were upstairs living quarters for a family, with the furniture shrouded in dust sheets and a separate narrow back stairway to reach those rooms that looked like it led back down to somewhere near the kitchen. Then, there were eight other bedrooms for guests and another small flight of stairs leading to several smaller rooms under the eaves, presumably for servants.

Katie opened the shutters of the window on the upstairs landing and gave the others a cheery wave so they would know she was almost finished.

Hurrying along the upstairs corridor, her footsteps sounded loud on the wooden floorboards, but her sense of unease that she wasn't alone had gone now that she had made up her mind about their future.

Smiling to herself, she clattered down the stairs again, pausing at the bottom as a wave of gratitude mingled with pangs of grief came over her. "Thank you, Grandpa," she murmured, tears suddenly misting her eyes from missing his calm, reassuring presence in their lives. "I know you would rather Uncle Norman hadn't turned his back on us, but I'll do my best to take care of the others...and it's all thanks to your kindness buying the inn for us."

She pulled a lace handkerchief from her sleeve and wiped her eyes. This was a time for looking forward and not feeling sad about the past. Taking a deep breath, Katie squared her shoulders and hurried back through the building. She had spotted that the main entrance to the taproom was bolted from the inside. She would throw open the doors and welcome the others in. If they started work cleaning up immediately, she reckoned they could open to paying customers within a week.

Humming to herself, she bustled through the door, already wondering who might be able to tune the piano and where they would source barrels of ale from.

Suddenly, two figures rushed towards her from the shadows, and her blood ran cold.

"Burglar!" a plump woman screeched, brandishing a brass warming pan in front of her. "Get away from us!" She jabbed it in Katie's direction, forcing her into the corner, looking formidable despite being in a patched dressing gown with her nightcap askew.

"The constable's on his way. You're no better than vermin…sneaking around at the crack of dawn. He'll arrest you and throw you in jail like the crook you are, but I ain't letting you get away!" The man looked as though he'd just woken up with half his shirt buttons still undone and glimpses of a hairy belly between them, but there was a determined glint in his eyes as he strode forward with a length of rope to tie her hands together until help came.

Burglar? How much more must I endure? After everything she'd been through in the last twelve hours, Katie felt like she was in a nightmare that would never end where nothing made sense. A feeling of outrage surged through her. She charged towards him, lowering her head to barge her way out, and let out a bloodcurdling shout.

CHAPTER 13

The man stumbled out of Katie's way and let out a horrified bellow of alarm as Gabriel and Wilbur burst through the front door, sending splintered rotten wood everywhere. Ebenezer hastened in after them.

"We're being burgled in our own home," the woman shrieked.

Ebenezer strode into the middle of the taproom and held his hands up to try to instil a sense of calm. "We are not burglars or marauding criminals. Sir William Cavendish owns this property, and these are his grandchildren."

"Grandchildren? But…what…why? You can't just turn up. 'Tis enough to frighten anyone, let alone two innocent folk still sleeping," the man spluttered indignantly at Katie. "I'm not a mind-reader," he added, glaring at Gabriel, who was towering over him, ready to intervene if things turned nasty again.

"What were you doing creeping around?" The woman lowered her makeshift weapon and put her hands on her broad hips, looking equally indignant. "'Tis a strange sort of time to arrive at the crack of dawn." She gave Gabriel a long look, still not ready to back down. "This madam was marching around talking to herself like she owned the place. What were we meant to think other than that she must be an intruder?"

"Perhaps we should all introduce ourselves properly," Wilbur suggested, giving the middle-aged couple a genial smile.

"I'm Wilbur Anderson, and this is my older sister Katie, my younger sister Polly, and the boy over there eating an apple is Tim, the youngest of us all and still hungry no matter what's going on, it would seem." He rolled his eyes slightly as Tim gave him a guilty grin, still munching.

"I thought you said you're Sir William Cavendish's grandchildren. How come you're called Anderson?" The woman sniffed, her eyes narrowing with suspicion. "How can we trust you are who you say? You could be vagrants looking for a roof over your heads, for all we know."

Glancing down at her torn, crumpled dress and remembering her dishevelled reflection, Katie thought she had a point. "Mr Black is our grandfather's solicitor. I'm sure he will be able to provide whatever proof you need," she said quickly. "We travelled through the night and haven't had a chance to smarten ourselves up."

Ebenezer nodded and pulled a document from the inside pocket of his coat, snapping it open with a hint of irritation. "It's not often my professional judgement is questioned, but if you must continue to doubt us, here is Sir William's signature, as you can see. He purchased the North Star Inn many years ago with the sole purpose of it being a home and business for his grandchildren, should they ever need it. These are his daughter's children, which is why they have a different surname."

The woman's cheeks turned red, and she bobbed her head apologetically, glancing at the man who Katie figured was her husband. "You check it, dear. You know reading fancy documents like that isn't something I like doing."

Ebenezer held it up for the man to read before

folding it up and putting it away again once he had nodded his acceptance.

"So that's who we are," Wilbur said. He folded his arms and strolled slowly around the couple. "Now it's your turn. Who are you, and why do you act as though this property is yours to defend?"

"We live in a small cottage in the woods back yonder," the woman said plaintively, edging closer to her husband, who threw a protective arm around her shoulder.

"Agatha and Vernon Tremaine is who we are." The man drew himself up to his full height, hastily adjusted his shirt, and smoothed his wiry mop of greying hair. "We've been caretakers of this place ever since your grandfather bought it, as it happens. Valued guardians of his property, no less, so we were only doing our job."

Katie let out a long sigh of relief and couldn't help but break into an amused chuckle as she caught Agatha's eye. "It seems we both got the wrong end of the stick...or should I say the wrong end of the warming pan."

Agatha looked embarrassed, so Katie stepped forward and patted her on her shoulder. "I suppose you were fast asleep in your cottage and then heard me clattering about outside?"

"Yes, Miss Anderson. I didn't mean to frighten you. We usually walk around the outside of the buildings most mornings after breakfast, but we've never had any trouble like this before."

"They're not making trouble, Agatha," Vernon corrected hastily. He gave her an ingratiating smile. "So many years have passed; we never imagined anyone would actually turn up. We only met Sir William Cavendish once, you see."

"A very grand gentleman he was," Agatha murmured. "Dressed in the finest suit I've ever seen, but he was kind, not stuck up like some toffs. We're not from Stonehaven originally, but further along the coast. My Vernon was looking for work after our fishing boat was wrecked in a storm. We'd travelled to Pembrey Minster, thinking there might be more chances. He saw us asking folk in the town square, then said he was looking for a caretaker for an old property."

"He told us not to breathe a word about him being the owner to anyone," Vernon said, taking up the story. "Our instructions were just to look after the place and turn nosy folk away."

"People did ask why we weren't running it as a coaching inn when we first arrived, but they soon lost interest. Sir William said that someone official would tell us if anything ever needed to change."

"And that it might be years in the future," Vernon added.

Agatha's eyes widened with sudden understanding, and she stared at Ebenezer. "He must have meant you, Mr Black...the person who would tell us more about his wishes."

"Indeed. What exactly were Sir William's instructions about caring for this place?" The fastidious solicitor winced slightly as Tim rearranged some of the chairs and brushed against a curtain, sending up a cloud of dust. "Were you meant to keep the inn clean, by any chance?"

"No...I mean...yes. Well, I suppose so." Agatha suddenly clasped one of Katie's hands and gave her a beseeching look. "You're not going to throw us out of our cottage, are you, Miss Anderson? We didn't mean to let the place get so dusty, but when we used to clean it in the past, travellers kept asking if they could stay the night or wondered why we weren't serving food."

"And my arthritis has been playing up these last few years," Vernon said, sounding slightly aggrieved that their comfortable existence was being questioned. "It's not an excuse," he blustered. "We took the view it was best just to leave the place locked up so folk would stop wondering why we weren't running it as a proper coaching inn."

"A very convenient decision," Ebenezer said dryly. He gazed around the desolate-looking taproom, festooned with cobwebs, and wrinkled his nose as a rat popped out from behind the piano and eyed them all curiously before scuttling away again. "It would seem you have been paid handsomely with a delightful cottage and a wage for doing very little, but that is about to change, Mr and Mrs Tremaine. Katie and her siblings are going to resurrect the pub into a thriving business again, and I'm sure you will be eager to help to make up for all these years of idleness. You're lucky Sir William never made an unannounced visit."

Agatha exchanged a worried glance with Vernon but then nodded eagerly. "Of course, Mr Black. You and the youngsters can rely on us. We've kept to ourselves most of the time, but we can help introduce everyone to some of the locals. And will we still be paid?"

"Yes, as long as you help. I was thinking of more practical things," Ebenezer said firmly. "Like cleaning, and mending the roof. Not to mention getting rid of the rats."

"Oh." Vernon took a sharp breath, preparing to list out all the excuses why they wouldn't be able to, so Katie hastily stepped in before it escalated into an argument. She had a feeling the Tremaines would respond better to flattery and encouragement than firm demands.

"I appreciate that you didn't feel it necessary to keep the place spotless when it was empty, but just think how marvellous it will be to bring the inn back to life again, Agatha. Won't it be wonderful to have the fire crackling in the hearth and hear tales from travellers stopping for a hearty meal and a pint of ale?"

"When you put it like that." Agatha nodded slowly, glancing around. "I always did think it was a terrible shame that the place sat empty." She lowered her voice and leaned closer. "Folk say this used to be where smugglers would drink and plan their terrible deeds."

Tim paused from moving furniture, his face bright with interest. "There are still smugglers around here?"

Gabriel harrumphed sarcastically. "Don't listen to that nonsense, Master Anderson. I'm sure all that stopped years ago. This will be a good, honest coaching inn, and I'm sure you will all make it a great success. With the right sort of help," he added, glowering at Vernon again, who gulped and nodded.

"I had a good look around the stables, Vernon," Katie continued. "I'm sure you're very good at knowing what repairs are needed, and they seem to be in good condition apart from a few areas of rotten wood. If you can oversee the outside chores, the boys will be happy to do the hard work required."

Tim bounced on his toes. "At last, proper work instead of sitting in the library learning about history and geography."

Polly nudged her brother. "Don't think you can disappear outside for hours at a time, boys. We must draw up a proper plan, clean the place from top to bottom, and then figure out where to get supplies. It's all very well having the place look tidy, but it won't be a business if we have nothing to sell."

"I've already thought of that." Ebenezer pulled a notebook from his pocket and flicked through the pages. "Gabriel and I need to leave now, but I've arranged for a few deliveries to be made over the coming days. I'll call again in a week, and hopefully, by then, you will be ready to open the doors of the pub and have your first paying customers."

Katie hurried over and shook hands with him

and then Gabriel. She suddenly felt close to tears and rather overwhelmed by the task ahead of her. "I sincerely hope so. I'll never be able to thank you both enough for rescuing us. If it weren't for you and what Grandpa put in place all those years ago, we would be locked away in Monkton Workhouse by now. We will always be in your debt, and I hope you will visit often."

Gabriel coughed with a bashful smile, and Ebenezer looked touched by her heartfelt words. "I was only doing your grandfather's bidding, Miss Anderson, but I would like to continue supporting you from afar however I can. Sir William was a fine man and believed in behaving with integrity. It has been an honour to help you, although I'm sorry it had to come to that."

"Rest assured, I'll visit whenever I can," Gabriel said cheerfully, rubbing his hands together. "A nice pint of ale by the fire and a plate of stew will be the perfect evening while I check up that everything is going well."

Katie swallowed the lump in her throat, not wanting to embarrass herself by crying. "Right," she said brightly, turning to the others. "There's no point trying to sleep now that it's daylight. I propose we start cleaning immediately. There's no time to lose if we're to become landlords of the North Star Inn, and I want the business to be a success so that Grandpa would be proud of us."

She and Polly linked arms, and they all followed Ebenezer and Gabriel back outside.

"I'm sure we'll see a great difference by the next time we visit." Ebenezer slipped a card into her hand with a twinkle in his eyes. "You're a determined young woman, Katie. Your grandfather was always very proud of you all when you were younger, and I know with grit and determination, you will do well in this new chapter of your life. My office address is on that card if you ever need to send a letter to get hold of me. Also, the bank manager in Stonehaven, Mr Mayberry, is expecting you to visit soon. There is a modest sum of money in yours and Wilbur's names which is for emergencies, and use this to get started." He dropped a pouch into her hand and she knew this time it would be proper money, not the metal scraps Uncle Norman had tricked her with.

Once Ebenezer was in the carriage, Gabriel handed down the carpetbags and climbed up onto his seat, picking up the reins and telling the horses to walk on. "Here's to new beginnings," he said cheerfully with a backward wave farewell. "Mind you do what your new mistress says, Vernon," he added with a hint of firmness beneath his jovial demeanor to underline his words. She'll be firm but fair, and remember, she might not have the Cavendish surname, but she's every bit Sir William's granddaughter."

"Of course, Gabriel. They can count on us."

"And don't entertain smugglers."

Agatha pulled a face and shivered. "That's not something to jest about. Careless words like that might bring a curse upon the place."

Gabriel chuckled and tipped his hat.

"Goodbye." Katie blinked rapidly as she waved them off, feeling a sudden sense of abandonment, which she knew was probably just from being tired. "To new beginnings," she added under her breath.

Once the carriage had disappeared from view, she turned around and gazed at their new home, full of mixed emotions: relief that they had foiled Uncle Norman's plan, excitement at the thought of having their own business, but also trepidation. They were strangers in Stonehaven and didn't have the advantage of their family name being known and respected in the area.

Can I really do this?

She squared her shoulders and marched back inside, determined to lead by example. She had to succeed for the sake of Wilbur, Polly, and Tim. But it was more than that. Their upbringing had been privileged in many ways, but they had suffered loss as well, which she knew had given her inner strength. Failure was not something they could countenance. She would work her fingers to the bone if she had to and prove to the naysayers that they could be a valuable part of their new community.

"Perhaps you should have a cup of tea and some porridge before you start, Miss Anderson?" Agatha suggested. "It won't take me but half an hour to make it back at my cottage and bring it down on a tray."

"I think that's an excellent idea." She smiled at the older woman. "Please call us by our first names, Agatha. If we're to work together and make this business a success, even though I'm the mistress of the house, we need to be friends."

"Very well, Miss…I mean, Katie." Agatha bobbed a curtsey. "Vernon will fetch all the brooms and mops and buckets. He might grumble about his arthritis, but it isn't too bad if I keep him going with plenty of cake." She watched her husband fondly as he hobbled away towards the stables, answering Tim's stream of questions."

"I think we'll have the inn sparkling in no time." Katie sighed again, but this time with less trepidation. There was a lot of hard work ahead, but for the first time, she had a sense this strange new family of hers would manage perfectly well.

"It's nice to see the place coming to life. Sorry I nearly drove you away with the warming pan."

"You looked formidable, even in your nightgown. But it takes more than that to put me off." The taproom rang with the sound of their laughter as Katie rolled up her sleeves.

CHAPTER 14

Polly jumped up as soon as they had finished their porridge, eager to make a start. "I think I'll explore our living quarters upstairs and start taking the dust sheets off the furniture."

"Good idea." Katie drummed her fingers on the edge of the table, running through all the different options in her mind. "I suppose Agatha and I should tackle the kitchen range first. Once we get that going, we will have as much hot water as we need, and we'll be able to cook for ourselves."

"I spotted some fishing rods in one of the sheds." Wilbur stifled a yawn and rubbed his eyes to banish his weariness from the long night of travel. "Vernon told us there's a good spot to fish for trout in the river, just a short walk through the woods. If we can catch enough for supper we'll be fine for food today. There's also half a sack of coal, which will keep us going until the coal merchant visits with more."

"Yes, I don't want to go to the grocer for supplies until tomorrow. Agatha has flour, so I can bake bread later, and we still have more cheese and apples that Ebenezer left behind. I think we'll make good progress today." Katie collected the dishes and put them next to the big sink. Tim was already outside helping Vernon pump water into buckets. At first glance, the pump had looked broken, but with a bit of oil to stop it from squeaking and a few firm bashes with a hammer that Katie declined to watch, the sweet clear water from the well was soon flowing again. It was good to know that was one less thing to worry about.

Once the others had hurried away to tackle their jobs, she coiled up her hair and started attacking the kitchen range with gusto. It was almost as big as the one they'd had in Castleford Hall, and once she had scooped out the old ash and scrubbed away the grease and grime, it was in surprisingly good condition. A little while later, Agatha appeared in the doorway holding a broom. Her hair was wrapped up in an old scarf, and she was still coughing and spluttering from making a start on brushing down all the cobwebs from the taproom ceiling.

"I'll black the range with lead if you want me to," she offered. She plucked a sticky cobweb off her shoulder and absentmindedly flicked a spider away that was still clinging to the bottom of her apron. "That's not the sort of job Sir William's granddaughter should be doing."

Katie was kneeling in front of the range, and she dunked the old rag in the bucket of water and swished it around, noticing how filthy the water was and that it needed tipping away and replacing. "It's good of you to suggest it, Agatha, but there's no need. The range has scrubbed up well, and I already polished the parts that show with an old tin of lead blacking I found in the cupboard. It's good enough for now, and it's more important that we get it lit."

"True enough. Once the range is going, the place will feel more like home."

Katie stood up, not bothering to shake the dirt off the bottom of her gown. It would have to be consigned to no longer being for best, she thought with a rueful smile. Her thoughts turned to all the gowns she and Polly had left behind at Castleford, hanging in their wardrobes, and she huffed with annoyance. They had left so many of their belongings behind, never dreaming their departure would be forever. They would have to scrimp and save and watch every penny, and new clothes would be a luxury they couldn't afford for a while. "I don't look like I came from a large country estate and a well-to-do background," she muttered.

Agatha patted her arm with a sympathetic expression. "I won't press you with questions about why it seems like you've run away, Katie. It's not my place to pry. All I'll say is it seems like someone's done you and your siblings wrong."

"That's about right. Someone I thought we could rely on had other ideas." She didn't want to share any more details.

"A snake in the grass." Agatha sniffed with disapproval. "A young lady like you should have more than just one carpet bag of belongings, but don't worry, there's a copper tub in the laundry room out the back. It hasn't been used for years, but with some elbow grease, we'll be able to get it going again so you can wash your clothes. I'm a dab hand at dressmaking…at least I was when I was younger. I used to take in mending and work as a seamstress when Vernon was a fisherman. I have some nice scraps of fabric and lace to dress up a plain gown with pretty collars and trims. You'll need to look smart once we have customers, and I'll make sure you and Polly look the part."

Katie chuckled as she looked down at her dress. As well as the rips from being torn by brambles earlier, it was now covered with streaks of soot. "We used to live on the edge of the moors, Agatha. Papa used to say that Polly and I were tomboys, but I suppose you're right. I did manage to bring a couple of nicer gowns with me. That will be enough to start with, and I'll see if I can persuade Ebenezer to let us use some of our money for warmer dresses once winter approaches. Other than that, the priority is to use what money we have to buy ale and ingredients to start offering food for hungry travellers."

"Are you a good cook?" Agatha asked, suddenly sounding worried.

"Beryl was in charge of that at Castleford Hall. We used to help out, but her cooking was wonderful." She let out a long sigh, suddenly realising they would never see Beryl, Jacob, and Mr Dryden again. It felt shocking to face up to the fact that they had to walk away from everyone in their old lives, at least for the time being. She wondered whether she would be able to somehow secretly send a note to let Beryl know that they were okay and decided she would ask Wilbur later. Perhaps it would be better to let Beryl and the others stay blissfully unaware of what had happened, thinking they were all having a jolly time in London. It was a dilemma.

"Will you be wanting me to cook the meals we sell?" Agatha shot a dubious look towards the range, looking slightly alarmed as if it was an unpredictable animal. "I don't mind cooking on my little potbelly stove in the cottage, but I've never done more than provide for Vernon, you see. I suppose I could learn…" Her words tailed off, leaving no doubt that it was the last thing she wanted to do.

"Polly and I will have to figure it out," Katie said, sounding more confident than she felt. Even though they had helped Beryl often in the kitchen, cooking for paying customers was a different prospect altogether. She had a feeling that the inn's reputation would rest on whether the ale was good and the food was tasty. It would only take a few dissatisfied travellers and locals spreading the word that what they offered wasn't very good, and that could be the difference between success and failure. *Surely it can't be that hard?* She couldn't show her doubts in front of Agatha. "Once we've got the place clean, Polly and I will sit down and draw up a list of hearty dishes we can make that we won't find too challenging. I'm sure we can come up with a handful between us.

Perhaps I could make a few discreet enquiries to see if a woman in Stonehaven could come daily to work in the kitchen with us." She thought about having to pay a wage and wondered if Wilbur would agree.

"Yes, a cook and perhaps a housekeeper." Agatha backed out of the kitchen, looking relieved. "That sounds like an excellent idea. Cleaning and collecting the glasses is something I'll be far better placed to help you with."

* * *

THE NEXT FEW days passed by in a frenzy of cleaning and tidying. Once the fire was lit in the range, the kettle whistled merrily, and they found large pans to use as well to boil water. Cobwebs and spiders were banished, and woodwork was polished with Agatha's supply of beeswax polish and buffed until it gleamed with a rich patina. The windows were washed and polished until they sparkled in the sun. Finally, she and Polly knelt side by side with hot water, lye soap, and scrubbing brushes to clean the floors, working their way from the corners of each room backwards to the door.

Vernon had managed to get the copper laundry tub up and running, and Tim discovered a wood store behind the stables filled with enough chopped logs to last until they had time to cut more ready for winter. Agatha was tasked with doing the laundry, which she did with good cheer, her cheeks turning pink from the heat in the laundry room and the exertion of tackling all the sheets and blankets they had found in the linen press.

Katie was eternally grateful to whoever had thought to leave so many mothballs between all the sheets. Not only did her eyes water with the cloud of camphor that greeted her when they discovered the linen press, but the sheets were mercifully free from holes apart from a few mouse nibbles.

It was perfect drying weather, and before long, the bed linen flapped in the breeze on the various washing lines that Vernon had strung up between the apple trees beyond the neglected kitchen garden. The freshly laundered sheets smelled of sunshine and the coastal breeze, and with each folded pile that Katie gathered to take upstairs again, she began to feel more optimistic about the future. She and Polly had worked out they had enough bedding for four guest rooms. That would be enough to start with for visitors who needed to stay overnight, and hopefully, once they started to make a small profit, Katie would be able to hunt around for more second-hand sheets and blankets for the remaining rooms if there was enough demand. It wasn't ideal, but with Agatha's lavender bags and rosewater spritz to keep the bedding nicely scented, it would have to do until they could afford to purchase new sheets the following year.

By the end of the week, they had started to become acquainted with a trickle of locals as well, thanks to Ebenezer's kindness.

The first visitor was Angus Bishop, the local coal merchant, who came slowly up the lane bright and early one morning, whistling tunelessly. The sturdy cob pulling the coal cart nuzzled Katie's hand when she proffered half an apple, and Mr Bishop's teeth gleamed white in his soot-blackened face when Agatha brought out a mug of steaming tea and a spiced fruit bun for him.

"I've been told to bring a delivery every couple of weeks." He pulled a chit of paper from his shapeless jacket and squinted at the writing. "Billed to Mr E. Black, care of The North Star Inn for the time being. Is that right?"

"Yes, that's wonderful." Katie was in the middle of pegging out another pile of washing.

He eyed the newly weeded cobbles in the yard and spruced-up stables with interest. "What a change to behold. I never used to like coming here 'afore, especially when there were a storm blowing in from the west, but it looks quite different now you'm taken over, Miss…?"

"Miss Anderson. Thank you. It's been a few long days of cleaning, but it's nice to know you can see a difference."

"Oh, aye. The place were like a den of thieves 'afore. Never knew whether I'd be paid for my troubles or if I was taking my life into my hands asking for what I were rightfully owed." He thumbed his cap back and scratched his head. "I expect you'll have a nicer bunch of folk staying here these days. Where did you say you hailed from 'afore this?"

"Just a small market town inland," Katie said, keeping it vague. They had all agreed it was best not to mention they were Sir William Cavendish's grandchildren for a while until they had established themselves in Stonehaven.

The following day, Gethin Cowley, the owner of the local brewery, trundled up the lane with three barrels of ale on the back of his wagon. At first, Katie was reluctant to accept all three.

"What if we don't sell enough, and it goes off?" she whispered to Wilbur. "We haven't even put the word out about opening for business yet. Who knows how many people will visit…it might only be a trickle the first few weeks."

Gethin's eyebrows shot up, and he let out a rumbling chuckle of amusement. "You think folk don't know you're here, Miss Anderson?" He chuckled again. "It's all everyone is talking about."

"Is it? I'm surprised. I haven't been into town yet to introduce myself, although I planned to visit the grocers and bakery this afternoon," she added hastily. "It's not that we're being unfriendly, just that we've been busy cleaning."

"News travels fast in Stonehaven and the local villages," he said, undoing the bolts on the back of the wagon so he could roll the barrels off. "You'll get plenty of curious visitors, and you don't want them to go thirsty, do you?"

"No, but—"

"We can always reconsider the amount once you know your regulars. Mr Black was most insistent on getting you well-stocked to start with. Then he said he'd leave it to you to agree on deliveries with me."

"I'm sure you know best," Wilbur said, beckoning for Tim to come and help roll the barrels into the taproom.

"See you again soon." Gethin's round belly jiggled as he laughed and heaved himself back onto the wagon seat. "It might be my boy, Walter sometimes. Depends whether I'm busy brewing, but I thought it would be good to make your acquaintance. I might even come and sample a nice dinner of pie and vegetables one evening." He fixed Katie with a direct look. "You will be making pies, won't you? 'Tis something of a tradition for the North Star Inn. The locals will expect it."

"Pies?" Katie winced, thinking back to her last attempt, where the pastry had been like chewing shoe leather. "Yes…of course."

"That's the way." The jovial visitor slapped the reins on his horse's back, eager to get to his next customer, and no sooner had he left than another horse and cart appeared ten minutes later. It was a mid-sized cob gelding with a dappled chestnut coat, and he whinnied as the man reined to a halt and jumped down from the cart.

"Farmer Garton." The man had weathered, wrinkled cheeks and muddy trousers that he hitched up with his braces. "Yon' horse and cart are for you."

"For us?" Katie asked faintly, wondering who else might appear with unexpected offerings.

"Yes. Mr Ebenezer said I was to give you a reliable animal that wouldn't eat you out of house and home and doesn't spook easily. So this 'ere is Robin.

Bred him myself and swore I'd never part with him, but needs must. He's a hardy cob, so he'll get by on rough grazing and a little barley now and again." He rattled a few coins in his pocket and suddenly grinned. "Mr Ebenezer named a sum of money I couldn't say no to…at least, not without Mrs Garton giving me merry hell if I did." He thrust forward a calloused hand and shook hands with Katie, suddenly looking misty-eyed. "Look after him. He's from my favourite mare who died from colic this spring."

"Are you sure?" Katie felt guilty. "Maybe we could wait a while and buy a different horse."

He looked offended. "Certainly not, Miss. You won't get better than a homebred horse from Garton Farm. I'm known for my horses around these parts."

"In that case, thank you. And I promise we'll take good care of him."

"Can't say better than that." He patted his horse's muscular neck one last time and strolled back down the lane. "Pop round when you want some chickens. We're just over the hill. I've got good layers, and you'll want your own eggs for cooking, I'm sure," he called back over his shoulder.

"We will. Perhaps in a week once we're open to guests." Katie smiled inwardly. Ebenezer had promised he would help them get settled and he had certainly done that. All that remained was to visit the grocers to purchase ingredients and to cook the modest selection of dishes she had devised with Polly, and they would be ready to welcome paying customers to the inn.

"Have you decided when our opening night will be?" Polly asked as she carried out another basket of wet washing just as Tim came hurrying across the yard to unhitch Robin from their new cart.

"Yes, Katie," Tim chimed in. "We've cleaned and repaired so much the place looks as good as new. It's time to bring some money in."

"When do you think?" She beckoned Wilbur over to join the conversation. "Our grand opening? Should it be this week?"

"How about tomorrow? If everyone's already talking about us, we may as well use their curiosity to our advantage."

Her heart beat faster, and she nodded. "Tomorrow it is, then! I'll tell a few of the shopkeepers this afternoon when I go to the grocer. Hopefully, good old gossip will do the rest for us." There would be no looking back then. She would be the landlady of a coaching inn, and their new life would well and truly have begun.

CHAPTER 15

Katie stood in the doorway, watching the last customer of the day wander away into the dusk, whistling under his breath. "That didn't go as well as I'd hoped for our grand opening," she said, turning to her siblings with a worried frown.

"I don't agree." Wilbur put the brass fireguard across the hearth in front of the dying embers of the fire to stop any sparks from flying out onto the rug they had put down to make it feel cosier. The taproom smelt of a pleasant combination of woodsmoke mingled with hoppy ale. "I think you're being hard on yourself, Katie. Perhaps it was my fault for suggesting we should open so quickly instead of waiting a few more days."

Tim yawned behind the bar and rested his chin on his hands. "I think it's better that there wasn't a mad rush. We had a steady trickle of customers. To be fair, a lot of them only came out of curiosity, but we sold plenty of ale, and everyone was friendly."

Polly was busy gathering dirty glasses on a tray and nodded in agreement. "Tim is right, Katie. Word will soon spread, and then we'll be busy night and day. It was bound to start off slowly."

"Word spreading is what I'm worried about." She walked between the tables, wiping them down with a wet cloth before lifting the chairs and resting them upside down on the tables so they would be able to clean the floor more easily the following morning. "We had one gentleman grumbling that the ale was too expensive, and those three fishermen said that our ham and vegetable pie was practically inedible. That's not the sort of remark I want people to associate with our business."

"Never mind about them, ducky," Agatha said, rolling her eyes as she bustled in to take the tray from Polly. "Those three fishermen aren't local. They're from one of the ships passing through on their way to Bristol docks and anchored up for the night, so we'll probably never see them again. And as for Ernie Waite, he's well known for complaining about the price of everything. He's a skinflint, always harping on at his wife if she buys fresh bread from the bakery instead of getting a stale loaf for half the price. Even if you'd given him a pint of ale for free, he still would have found something to grumble about."

Katie felt somewhat reassured by Agatha's remark, but she was still worried. "If we're being honest with ourselves, the comments about the pie were justified."

Polly bobbed her head looking guilty. "We'll just have to be more careful next time. I didn't know you'd already added salt to the ham and vegetables, and I didn't think to taste it before I added more."

"Also, we weren't to know that the range was running hotter than what you were used to in Castleford Hall," Wilbur pointed out.

"Yes, but a pie that tasted practically as briny as the sea, with pastry that was so rock hard it would break your teeth, is hardly what we're striving for." She sighed, feeling the weight of responsibility resting heavily on her. "I wish I'd paid more attention all those times I sat at the kitchen table at Castleford watching Beryl when she was cooking."

"We can't turn the clock back now," Polly said, patting her arm as she passed to collect more empty glasses. "We'll just have to make enquiries in Stonehaven to see if we could persuade someone to come and cook the meals until we get better ourselves."

Everyone worked busily together for the next ten minutes tidying up, until Tim yawned loudly and declared it was surely time to stop and have a cup of hot chocolate before retiring for the night.

"My head is still swirling with lists of things we need to do over the coming weeks." Katie walked to the window and looked out, noticing how bright the moon was. "I don't feel tired yet, so I think I might take a stroll down to the harbour. There's something about being by the sea that feels wonderfully relaxing. It's a nice benefit of our new home."

Wilbur's eyebrows twitched up, and he looked concerned. "Do you want me to come with you? I'm not sure it's safe for you to be out alone."

"I'll be perfectly fine. You've worked so hard these last few days you deserve to put your feet up and have an hour off before bed. Leave everything else in the taproom until the morning. I won't be gone for long, and it's not even fully dark yet, with it being midsummer." She reached for her shawl and wrapped it around her shoulders.

"Very well, but if you're not back within an hour, I'll come and look for you," Wilbur chuckled. "I suppose it's not very different from when you used to walk on the moors on a midsummer evening."

"Exactly. I'm just going to sit on the harbour wall for a bit, that's all."

As Katie walked briskly down the lane, bats flitted overhead in the gloaming, squeaking as they passed her, and she caught a waft of sweet scent from wild roses in the hedgerow. Most of the birds had started to roost, but there were still a few blackbirds hopping ahead of her, and two magpies chak-chacked with alarm in the oak tree as she walked past it. She wondered whether she would hear the soft hooting of barn owls and see them gliding silently on white wings, hunting for mice. She hoped so because it would remind her of being back at Castleford Hall.

When they had first arrived early that fateful morning, the North Star Inn had felt quite far out of Stonehaven, but she quickly realised she had got the wrong impression. It was only a ten-minute walk from the inn to the heart of town and a few minutes extra to walk through the cobbled streets down to the harbour. In spite of Wilbur's warning and the late hour, she felt perfectly safe. She thought it might have something to do with the way the town was nestled between the protective curve of the coastal cliffs on either side and how friendly the townsfolk had been on her first visit to various shops to introduce herself and tell them about the opening.

I'm beginning to like it here. She hurried down a cobbled lane that opened up onto the seafront, and the gentle lapping of the waves felt soothing, just as she had hoped.

Katie took a deep breath, savouring the smells that were quite different from living inland, and strolled along the stone jetty that sheltered the boats in the harbour. Now that she was not near any trees, the moonlight was brighter, leaving a silver pathway across the sea that she found delightful. Every so often, the beam of light from the lighthouse around the headland swept in an arc across the water, steady and reassuring to keep sailors away from treacherous rocks.

As she neared the end of the harbour wall, her thoughts turned to how much had changed in such a short time. She was still fearful for their future, knowing that everything was riding on whether they could make a success of the coaching inn. She thought about how considerate Ebenezer had been and suspected that even though Grandpa had paid him handsomely for his services, he was going above and beyond what he had agreed with Sir William. It felt good to know that Ebenezer and Gabriel would do their best to help them succeed and that she could always send a message to them if she needed help.

Katie listened to the rhythmic slap of the seawater against the jetty and noticed the first few stars appearing in the mauve sky. *It would be nice to share this moment with someone special.* The unexpected thought left her gripped with a sudden pang of loneliness, which caught her off guard. It was as though all the recent events had suddenly caught up with her, not to mention everything from the past... losing their parents when they were still so young, Grandpa dying, and then Uncle Norman throwing them out in such a devious way.

"I just wish I had a friend and confidant here in Stonehaven," she murmured to herself. She could only say so much to Wilbur and the others because she didn't want them to worry. Katie wanted to stay strong for them, but she longed to have someone who might have a special place in her heart one day...a person she could confide her hopes and fears in, who might perhaps fall in love with her...and who she could fall in love with.

She gazed out to sea, feeling slightly melancholy. Even more so when she heard a burst of song from one of the taverns on the far side of town that sounded like a young man serenading his sweetheart. It was a beautiful evening, but her mind raced with thoughts of keeping a roof over their heads and holding the family together.

Katie put her hand in her pocket, and her fingers closed around the farthing Uncle Norman had put in the pouch of scrap metal pieces as his cruel joke. She held it up in the moonlight, tempted for a moment to hurl it into the sea so it would sink and vanish forever, but then she changed her mind.

"You think I'm as worthless as this coin, but I'll show everyone I'm not, Uncle Norman," she muttered in a low voice, needing to say it aloud. "You might not believe we're part of the Cavendish family, but you've underestimated me. Mama and Papa raised us well, and Grandpapa instilled discipline and showed us that hard work pays off. We'll make a success of our new life…I'll make sure I can keep Polly and the boys and me out of the workhouse." That sense of fighting spirit made her lift her chin in defiance, and she tucked the farthing back into her pocket. She would keep it and look at it every day to remind herself that they were Sir William's grandchildren, despite Norman's attempts to obliterate them from their own family history.

The sound of soft footsteps behind her pulled Katie from her musings, and she spun around, alarmed that she had been so engrossed in her thoughts a stranger been able to creep up behind her without her noticing.

"Sorry," the man said, holding his hands up in an apologetic gesture. "I thought you'd seen me walking along the harbour wall. I didn't mean to frighten you. I just wanted to check that you were safe."

Katie's heart thumped in her chest, but it wasn't so much from fear as from surprise at his kindness. Just at that moment, a cloud drifted over the moon, and she realised it was darker than she had thought. She couldn't see his features clearly but had the impression he was a couple of years older than her. He was tall, and his voice was warm, as though he laughed often. Something about him seemed familiar, and she wondered if she had passed him in town earlier but been too distracted to notice.

"It's unusual to see a young woman alone on the harbour wall at night," he added.

"It's kind of you to ask. It's such a lovely evening, I thought I would walk down here to stand and watch the sea for a while to see if it would help me sleep better tonight." She tightened her shawl and smiled, not feeling self-conscious in his presence.

"I've got a lot on my mind at the moment. You know how it is."

He gave a nod of understanding and shook hands with her. "I certainly do. I'm George Morgan, by the way. Nice to make your acquaintance."

His hand felt warm with a firm grasp, making the breath catch in her throat. "N…nice to meet you."

They started strolling side by side back along the harbour wall, and he tilted his head. "So, did it help?"

"What?" she asked, feeling slightly flustered as she caught a faint scent of wood smoke and seaweed from the fisherman's smock he was wearing.

"Watching the sea. Did it help soothe your mind?"

"Oh, I see." She tried to concentrate, but it was hard as she tried to figure out where she had seen him before, especially as it was still so dark and she hadn't had a clear look at his face yet. "Yes, but I expect I still have some difficult days ahead. I should probably explain: I'm Katie Anderson, the new landlady at the North Star Inn."

"Yes." He didn't sound surprised. "I hope your opening night went well and you had a good turnout."

Of course he knows who I am. Katie smiled inwardly. She should have remembered that everyone seemed to know about them, even though they hadn't been here long.

She considered his question. If anyone else had asked, she would have found a way to change the subject, but with George, for some reason, she felt her defences crumble. Walking together on the harbour wall under the moonlight made it feel like they were the only people outside, which lent a certain air of intimacy, making her want to confide in him. "My sister and brothers think it went well, but I'm not so sure. A few people only came to have a look around and didn't buy anything. My ham pie was a disaster, which I shall need to remedy as soon as possible. But what's worrying me most is this niggling doubt that we've made a terrible mistake even opening the pub again. People probably think I'm too young to be a landlady, and if we don't get regular visitors, who knows what will happen?"

George didn't rush to offer meaningless reassurances, which she liked. Instead, he walked in silence for a few more moments, thinking about what she had just told him.

"It's bound to take a few weeks for word to get around beyond the townsfolk of Stonehaven. And I'm sure the incident with the pie was probably just opening-night nerves," he added kindly. He sounded as though he was close to laughter, and Katie suddenly found herself laughing as well.

"I added salt, and then Polly did as well. The pastry could have doubled as roof tiles, it was so hard. Those poor fishermen probably wondered if we were trying to poison them."

He grinned and shook his head. "I expect they were just chancing their luck to see if they could get away with having the meal without paying. At least next time, you and your sister will know to check before adding any more seasoning."

As they got closer to the sandy beach, where a few rowing boats were moored in the shallow water, Katie still couldn't shake the feeling that she knew George from somewhere. She stopped walking and gave him a quizzical look. "Have we met before? You seem so familiar, but I can't put my finger on it…"

He wandered away from her to where he'd left a lantern nearby and picked it up, holding it higher so the light shone on his face, revealing bright blue eyes and the ruggedly handsome features of a man who worked outside. "We certainly have. I was wondering when you might remember."

Katie gasped as the memories of the violent mob in Pembrey Minster four years earlier came flooding back. "It's you! You rescued me and Polly when those protesters chased us into the alleyway, and I feared for our lives."

George shrugged modestly. "I just did what anyone would have done. Those men were thugs looking for trouble, and you happened to be in the wrong place at the wrong time."

"I've thought about you often since then," she blurted out unthinkingly.

"That's good to know," he said with another grin, his blue eyes twinkling with amusement. "I thought about you as well. I made a few discreet enquiries to make sure you got home and wondered if I might bump into you again. And here we are…all these years later."

"Yes, it's a strange coincidence…fate perhaps." Katie was glad they had started walking again so he wouldn't see the blush colouring her cheeks. *All those nights I dreamed about him, wondering if we would ever meet again.* "Do you live here, or are you visiting and about to vanish again?" The words flew out of her mouth before she could stop them, and she glanced away, hoping she hadn't sounded too forward.

"Yes, Stonehaven is my home, so I shall come and visit you at the inn and tell everyone how good it is."

She pulled a face. "You might want to wait a few days until Polly and I have improved our cooking."

This time, it was his laughter that rang out into the night. "I've eaten some terrible meals on fishing trips; you don't need to worry about that."

"Bring your parents as well, if you like. We wanted to make it the sort of coaching inn where everyone feels welcome."

A shadow crossed his face momentarily. "It's just me and Ma these days."

"Oh, I'm sorry."

"You weren't to know," he said easily, briefly resting his hand on her waist to steer her away from a man staggering along the cobbled street who had clearly had too much to drink and was in danger of barging into her. "It's been a few years now since Pa passed away. Things were hard for a while, but you know what that's like."

She looked at him in surprise. "You're right; we did lose our parents and were orphaned quite young. How did you know?"

"It's like I said when I helped you and your sister in Pembrey. I overheard a few folk talking about your family. You're Sir William Cavendish's granddaughter."

She took a sharp breath, instantly feeling worried that if he knew, perhaps everyone else did as well.

He gave her a kind smile. "Don't worry, Katie. I'm

not the sort of person to gossip about others. I just wanted you to know that I understand. Everyone in Stonehaven has been wondering why you turned up out of nowhere to reopen the North Star, but they will soon get bored and start gossiping about something else. If you want to tell me, I'll always be happy to listen, but if you don't, that's fine as well. We all have things in our past that are best left there."

"I...I will tell you, but perhaps I should check with Wilbur and the others first." She felt comforted by his solid presence next to her. "Sir William... Grandpa died recently. That's why we ended up coming here. Running away from our uncle. It's complicated."

George made a disapproving noise. "If he ever makes trouble for you, I'll make sure he regrets it."

"He doesn't know we're here, and I'm hoping it will stay that way for a while."

They reached the end of the lane, and George held the lantern aloft to light their way. "It can get a little spooky walking through those trees at this time of night. I live in a little fishing cottage the other side of the harbour, but Ma would have my guts for garters if I don't escort you back home."

Katie was about to explain that she didn't need to be mollycoddled but bit her comment back. It felt nice knowing he cared for her, and she enjoyed his company. She wanted to know more about him and what it was like being a fisherman in Stonehaven.

Perhaps I finally have someone to call a friend...or maybe more? If she was being honest with herself, his tousled brown hair and tanned cheeks set her heart aflutter. She had dreamt of meeting him again so many times since he rescued her in Pembrey that it felt like fate that he lived in Stonehaven and their paths had crossed again.

"That's very kind of you, George. As long as your Ma won't mind you getting home late."

"She's used to me being out at all hours."

"You mean you go fishing at night?"

"Something like that. Keeping an eye on the boat, watching the tides, that sort of thing," he said, sounding rather vague.

Tramping along the track, with the trees rustling overhead, and blocking out the moonlight, Katie sensed they were being followed and looked nervously over her shoulder. *There's nothing there; I'm imagining it.* She put it down to feeling jittery because she was tired and overwrought and reminded herself it had been foolish to go out without a lantern.

By the time the pub came into view, Katie was

grateful for the extra time in George's company. He was easy to talk to and interested in her without being nosy. He entertained her with tales of Stonehaven's past and a few colourful characters she would likely meet in the coming weeks.

Polly had left an oil lamp burning brightly in the window, but Katie could see that the curtains were closed upstairs in their bedrooms. She wasn't surprised everyone had gone to bed already, as she finally felt weariness creep over her as well.

"I really appreciate you walking me home, George." She suddenly felt shy and cleared her throat to cover it. "Come and see what we've done with the place one day soon. I'd like to introduce you to Wilbur and Tim as well, and you'll probably be surprised to see how grown-up Polly looks now."

George shifted the lantern from one hand to the other and nodded eagerly. "I'd like that. I really do hope you stay here, Katie. I meant it when I said I thought about you in the four years since we last met." He shuffled his feet and grinned at her. "You look grown-up too, but I would have recognised you anywhere. I admire your courage in starting over far away from your home. I'll do whatever I can to help you and your family settle in."

Before Katie had a chance to thank him, there

was a louder rustle in the undergrowth, and she let out a startled cry as she caught sight of two eyes glowing like hot coals in the darkness. "What is it? A wild animal, George, look."

He lifted his lantern higher, and she grabbed his arm as the beast stepped forward. "It's just a dog."

Katie gasped with relief and hastily let go of George's arm. "It's a wolfhound." The dog had a fine head and intelligent eyes. "The poor thing must be lost." A thought occurred to her. "Or does he belong to you, George? I did hear a few sounds behind us as we were walking up the lane, as though something was following us, but I didn't want to say anything in case you thought I was being jumpy about nothing."

"No, he's not mine. Ma has a little terrier who spends most of her life snoozing in front of the fire or on Ma's lap."

Katie took a couple of cautious steps closer to the tall, shaggy dog, and held her hand out. "Hello, boy. Who do you belong to?"

The dog whined and wagged its tail at the same time. "Get along home; otherwise your owners will be worried about you." She took her shawl off and flapped it slightly, trying to shoo the animal away, but it had the opposite effect, making him whine more.

"He doesn't have a collar, George. Do you have any idea who he might belong to? I don't want to take him in for the night, knowing that her owners will probably be worried sick. I certainly would be if I had a dog that went missing."

"I don't think he's a stray." George had a strange expression on his face.

She glanced at him, wondering why he was looking at her with newfound respect. "So you think I should just leave him out here to make his own way home?" The dog walked up to her and nudged her hand with his head, his brown eyes never wavering in their devotion.

"You might not want to hear this, but I feel obliged to tell you." George hesitated for a moment. "The thing is, local legend has it that a hound will appear when he's most needed."

Katie started to laugh at his absurd suggestion but realised he was being deadly serious. "Surely that's the stuff of myths and too much ale?"

"The legend says there was a wolfhound that belonged to a huntsman, and when he was killed the devoted hound sat by his master and refused to leave, even after his master was buried. A few drunkards have claimed to see the dog over the years, but never in daylight. The story goes that one day the hound would appear again and stay, to protect his new master or mistress from those who wished them harm."

Someone wants to harm me? Katie shivered and couldn't help but glance at the dense shadows under the trees, which felt claustrophobic now, pressing in on her. The dog nudged her hand again, and she felt comforted.

"It does feel like he has chosen me, whether the rumour is true or if he's a stray." The dog wagged its tail again and then sat beside her, leaning against her legs, making her chuckle. "Either way, I think I have another family member at the inn now. I just have to think of a name. Any ideas?"

"Galahad," he said without hesitation. "That's what I always thought I would call him. And for what it's worth, I feel happier knowing that he's here guarding you, especially when I'm not around."

"Galahad it is," Katie said. "Pure and noble. One of the knights of King Arthur's round table." She stroked the dog's head. *And known for his bravery.* She shivered and glanced at the shadows again. At least if anyone followed her again, Galahad would bark and alert her.

"I'd better get off before Ma starts worrying and sends one of the neighbours out to look for me."

George shot her another grin and hurried away. "I'll pop in tomorrow evening and risk a plate of your infamous pie," he added, teasing her.

Katie watched him as he strode away into the night, feeling unexpectedly happy. The only thing she knew about her new life was that there seemed to be daily surprises. But now that she had George as a friend and Galahad looking after her, she realised everything somehow felt more manageable.

CHAPTER 16

"What's that burning smell?" Tim asked as he carried a basket of logs into the taproom to place next to the hearth.

"Oh no." Katie threw her hands up in dismay. "I forgot all about that cake I left cooking in the range. I got distracted by Wilbur showing me the storage bin he's built to stop the birds from getting into the sacks of barley over in the stables." She dropped her duster and darted away to the kitchen, even though the acrid smell that greeted her told her she was too late. Grabbing a tea towel, she hastily pulled the blackened remains of the apple cake from the oven and marched back through the taproom to throw it away in the bushes, where at least the birds might be able to peck over it and find a few crumbs of goodness.

"I still haven't had any luck finding someone in the village who might be able to cook for us," Agatha called. She was pegging out washing, and Katie could tell she was trying to be helpful, even though the remark didn't make her feel any better.

"I should be able to manage." She felt cross with herself. "I used to be able to cook perfectly well when it was just for us. You'd think I'd be getting better at it now we've been open for two weeks."

Agatha clucked sympathetically. "It's because you want your customers to think well of you. When you're just cooking for family, it doesn't matter as much, but 'tis the pressure of wanting the business to succeed. I feel bad that I can't be more help, but Vernon will be the first to tell you that my cooking is plain at best."

Katie felt deflated as she looked at the empty cake tin in her hands. It wasn't just the frustration of having to make the cake from scratch again, but that they needed to watch every penny. She had wasted good ingredients because there was so much on her mind that she had forgotten to check the cake.

"Are we expecting visitors?" Polly was carrying a

bucket of corn across the cobbled yard to their new chicken coop, and she pointed down the lane as the chickens pecked at her bootlaces, eager to be fed. She scattered a handful of corn, and the birds flapped and squawked, squabbling loudly around her.

Katie brightened in an instant. "It's Gabriel. Ebenezer must have decided to pay us a visit." She waved and wished she had put on a tidier gown. Normally, she wore her old clothes in the morning and then changed at opening time.

Oh well, at least Ebenezer will see how hard we've worked. She reminded herself she had more important things to worry about than how she looked.

"Woah there." The horses' ears flickered at his command as Gabriel halted the carriage and gave her a delighted smile. "You've worked wonders, Miss Anderson. I hardly recognise the place compared to a few weeks ago." He jumped down from his seat in the front with a mischievous look in his eyes. "Is that burnt food I smell?"

Katie held up the cake tin, knowing there was no point in denying it. "It was apple cake until I got distracted, but don't worry, I have some buttermilk left over, and I'm sure I can make some fruit scones quickly, so you have something to go with a cup of coffee." She pulled a face. "Cooking for a living is harder than I thought, but we're doing our best."

"I have a surprise for you." Gabriel opened the carriage door with a flourish, and her mouth dropped open as Beryl emerged from the interior, patting her grey curls into place.

"I don't believe it...Beryl? It's so lovely to see you." She ran to their old cook and threw her arms around her.

"Now then, Katie, don't start hugging me, or you'll only make me cry. I've missed you all so much; you have no idea." Beryl looked flustered and fanned herself with the corner of her shawl to hide her emotion.

"Polly," Katie called, "tell the others our dreams have been answered...Gabriel has brought Beryl here." Her heart swelled with happiness at seeing them both. "You will stay for something to eat, won't you, Gabriel? Please say you don't have to rush off."

"I can't stay long, but a scone and coffee wouldn't go amiss." Gabriel loosened the harness on the horses and let them wander towards the water trough for a drink. "Ebenezer asked me to have a look around and see if there's anything else you need him to send your way."

Wilbur and Tim came hurrying across from the

stable block. "I think you'll be surprised to see how good it looks now," Wilbur said with a hint of pride in his voice. "At least, I hope you will, and we really appreciate everything that he's done for us so far. Please tell him how grateful we are."

"Are you staying, Beryl?" Katie linked arms with her and showed her into the taproom. "How did you know we were here? I thought it best to keep it secret from you and Jacob and Mr Dryden, but now you're here, I suppose I should tell you what Uncle Norman did."

"Well, there lies a story, cariad," Beryl said, placing her reticule on the nearest table and shrugging off her shawl. "Master Norman and Amelia told us you'd gone to London to have better opportunities, and of course, we believed them. Why wouldn't we?"

"Yes, we believed them as well."

Beryl tutted and pursed her lips. "You know I've always had to bite my tongue when it comes to your uncle, but he's ten times worse now that Sir William has gone...God rest his soul. As soon as Norman knew he was the owner of Castleford Hall, he started throwing his weight around. He put the rent up for all the tenants in estate cottages in a matter of days. Then he was trying to tell Jacob how to run the farm, even though Norman hasn't got a clue."

"Oh dear, I expect everyone was feeling rather disgruntled."

"That's not the worst of it, Katie," Beryl said darkly. "There were strange men visiting in the dead of night, talking about all manner of shady things, I'm sure." She sniffed disapprovingly. "You know I don't eavesdrop, but I did happen to walk past the study once or twice, more to see why they had to visit your uncle in the middle of the night. I only caught a few snatches of conversation, and it seems that money was being mentioned a lot. I can't believe how much the household has changed in a few short weeks; it's shocking."

"I'm sorry you had to go through that." Katie patted her arm. It was horrible to think that Norman was being so disrespectful towards the people Grandpa had cared so much about.

Beryl absentmindedly picked up a cloth and started polishing the clean glasses on top of the bar. "I always told myself I would retire once Sir William was gone and you little 'uns didn't need me anymore, but it felt too soon. Mistress Amelia is impossible. She found fault with every meal I cooked for her, and I couldn't bear the thought of spending the rest of my days being chastised for doing what I'd always done, which was perfectly acceptable to Sir William. Jacob kindly took me to Pembrey a couple of days ago because I needed to visit the grocer. I happened to see Ebenezer Black, your grandfather's solicitor, as you now know."

Katie nodded. "Yes, it seems Grandpa kept a few secrets from me and the others, but Ebenezer has been very good to us."

"I'm not ashamed to say that I begged him to tell me if he knew how you were getting on in the big city so far away. You can imagine my shock when he admitted that you weren't in London. I told him I couldn't rest until I knew where you were and if you were safe. That's when he explained that you were in Stonehaven, of all places, running a coaching inn. You could have knocked me down with a feather, Katie."

"We really wanted to tell you, but Ebenezer thought it was best that we should get settled first. Uncle Norman planned to dump us in Monkton Workhouse."

"Yes, Gabriel told me about your daring escape with his help." Beryl frowned with indignation at the thought of what her precious moppets had been through. "I had a good mind to go straight to the

THE FARTHING GIRL

constable and tell him exactly what your uncle did, but Ebenezer said it would only stir up trouble. So, instead, I told him I was leaving Castleford Hall. I asked if Gabriel would kindly bring me to visit you while I decide what to do next."

Before Katie could reply, Polly came rushing into the taproom, swinging the empty corn bucket. "Our guardian angel must have sent you," she chuckled, rushing over to smack a kiss on the older woman's wrinkled cheek. "Katie and I have tried our best with that wretched range in the kitchen, but I don't think the customers are very impressed with our cooking."

Beryl's eyebrows twitched upward, and her face lit up with anticipation. "Are you telling me you offer tasty meals to weary travellers as part of the business, not just ale or cakes with coffee?"

"I think tasty is a rather generous description," Wilbur said with a rueful smile as he joined them. "I don't like to criticise the girls, but their cooking isn't a patch on yours, Beryl."

Polly swatted him with a cloth before conceding he had a point.

Wilbur suddenly looked more serious. "I've been doing the accounts, and unless people buy our food, it's going to be hard to make ends meet. I don't suppose we could say anything to persuade you to stay and become the finest cook that the North Star Inn has ever had?"

Beryl turned pink at the compliment and started rolling up her sleeves. "I was hoping you would say that. You know I don't have any family of my own, apart from you four, and I'm not ready to spend the rest of my days sitting in a rocking chair knitting. What sort of meals are you thinking of?" She glanced around at the well-worn furniture in the taproom and the slightly threadbare rug in front of the hearth. "Hearty fare with ingredients that aren't too expensive?"

"The inn had a reputation for delicious pies before it was left empty for many years." Katie shot Polly an embarrassed look. "I think it's fair to say our pastry leaves a lot to be desired, and I was just throwing away a burnt cake when you arrived. There's just so much to think of, and I'll never be as good a cook as you are. The thing is, I don't think we can afford to pay you much—"

"A wage? Don't be silly, cariad; I won't hear of it." Beryl drew herself up to her full height, looking momentarily offended, before giving them all a beaming smile. "I'll have a roof over my head and be reunited with the people I love the most. I know I'm not your ma, but I think of you as my own children.

You don't need to worry about paying me a penny until times get better. I'm just grateful to be free of Amelia's endless criticism, and you know I like a challenge."

"I hope so." Wilbur sounded relieved.

"If the inn had a reputation for good pies in the past, folk will soon be flocking here again; you can be sure of that. How about you show me the kitchen so I can get started? No time like the present, especially if customers will be arriving soon."

Katie sent up a silent prayer of thanks as Polly led the way to the kitchen. It wasn't just that she knew Beryl would soon get the customers talking about her tasty food for all the right reasons, but she was relieved that their kind-hearted cook would no longer be subjected to Uncle Norman's horrible ways. Leaving Beryl, Jacob, and Mr Dryden without saying where they had gone to had been gnawing away at her good conscience. Beryl was part of their family and deserved to be treated well in her older years.

As they arrived in the kitchen, Katie was startled to see Agatha there. She had lifted the lid off the pan of stew and was peering in.

"Beryl, this is Agatha Tremaine," Katie said, wondering how the two strong-willed women would get on. "She and her husband Vernon have been caretakers here for many years, at Grandpa's instruction."

"Lordy, I didn't hear you behind me." Agatha spun around in surprise and dropped the lid on the floor, wincing as it clattered on the flagstones. She hastily retrieved it, gave it a half-hearted wipe on her apron and was just about to put it back on the pan when Beryl rushed forward to grab it off her.

"I'll take care of that. We don't want anything from the floor getting into today's stew for the customers."

Agatha gave her a haughty glare. "A peck of dirt never harmed anyone. I hope you're not implying I haven't been keeping the kitchen clean?"

Katie exchanged a worried glance with Polly, knowing she had to step in quickly before things got out of hand.

"Beryl, I should have explained that Agatha is doing a wonderful job of helping us in all sorts of ways. She prefers being in the taproom, clearing glasses, and she's been marvellous upstairs dusting the bedrooms for the guests and laying fires, not to mention doing all the laundry. Thanks to her hard work, we've been able to take paying guests staying overnight sooner than expected."

The two older women eyed each other warily for a moment, and then Beryl gave a curt nod. "I'm glad to hear it. It's hard work managing a place like this, and Gabriel told me the place looks transformed." She hung up her bonnet, then took down the apron on the back of the door and tied it around her broad waist.

Agatha broke into a broad smile. "I can't tell you how glad we all are to have you here, Beryl. I've always been better at cleaning than cooking. I know the girls have tried hard, bless them, but with our reputation resting on serving good food, it's a mercy you've arrived. They spoke very fondly of you."

"I'll cook. You clean. We should rub along just fine." Beryl's ample chest quivered as she laughed. "Gabriel told me you met Katie brandishing a warming pan. Folk underestimate us middle-aged ladies."

"I can see you two will be as thick as thieves," Polly chuckled. "Katie and I won't stand a chance."

Beryl began stirring the stew and dipped a spoon into the rich, meaty sauce so she could taste it. She added a twist of pepper, then started rummaging through the nearest cupboard, pulling out a bag of flour to make pastry. "Agatha is quite right. We need our own roles, or we'll all be tripping over each other. Sir William would have been very proud to see what you've all achieved so far, and I'm sure if we all pull together, things will get even better."

Katie started gathering ingredients to make scones, marvelling at how it felt like old times chatting with Beryl in the kitchen.

"I don't suppose your Vernon has any nice herbs growing outside, Agatha?" Berly asked. "I think I spotted the makings of a kitchen garden beyond the stables."

"Oh, I'm sure. He loves pottering in the garden." Agatha was keen to prove that they hadn't been completely idle all these years. "Just say what you need, and I'll ask him to cut it for you. Perhaps you'd like some bundles to dry, as well. Tarragon would go nicely with that, don't you agree? And I'm making lavender bags to make the guestrooms smell nice."

Polly giggled and nudged Katie. "Perhaps we should ask Vernon to pick some roses as well, seeing as love is in the air."

Agatha and Beryl turned simultaneously to stare open-mouthed at Katie. "What do you mean, love is in the air?" Beryl asked sharply. "Are you courting? I hope it's someone I'll approve of." She put her hands on her hips. "How can it have happened so soon? You only left Castleford a few weeks ago."

Katie rolled her eyes, deciding she would have to have stern words with Polly afterwards. "It's nothing," she muttered.

"So why has George Morgan taken to calling in for a cup of tea every night?" Polly said, persisting in her teasing.

Katie could feel the heat rising up her cheeks, and it was too late to pretend otherwise. "We're not courting, Beryl," she said quickly before Beryl got the wrong end of the stick.

"Oh. Does he think he's too good for you?" Now, the older woman looked offended.

This was not the response she had expected. She couldn't win either way. "George is my friend, and it just so happens he was the kind-hearted young man who saved me and Polly. Do you remember that day a few years ago when we got caught up in the unrest at Pembrey Minster? The angry mob started turning on us once they realised we were part of the Cavendish family, and George hid us in an alleyway until the danger had passed."

"Terrifying," Beryl muttered. "It's a good thing the constable restored order."

"I didn't know who he was at the time, so it was purely a coincidence that I bumped into him in my first week here when I walked down to the harbour wall in the moonlight." She sighed wistfully at the memory of his hand on her waist for that delicious moment and the connection she felt growing between them. It was true that he visited almost every day with a few fish he'd caught or to help Wilbur and Tim with the endless list of things that needed fixing. "We were both as surprised as each other—"

"I know it's none of my business," Agatha said, butting in, "but I'm not sure you should be out walking at night, Katie."

"Exactly," Beryl agreed, looking worried. "It seems I arrived just in the nick of time. I know you're a young woman now, but you mustn't forget that you're still Sir William Cavendish's granddaughters, girls. Just because you're the landlady of a coaching inn now doesn't change that."

"George was very gentlemanly and escorted me home. He even protected me when Galahad suddenly appeared out of the bushes and gave me a fright."

At the sound of his name, the wolfhound came trotting into the kitchen, and Beryl squawked with shock. "What's that?"

"My new dog. Rumour has it that a ghostly hound roamed these woods for centuries and would reappear one day to protect his new master... or, should I say, mistress. He's very sweet."

Beryl blanched and backed away in alarm. "He's enormous…more like a scruffy donkey. Must he live inside?"

"Yes." Katie ruffled his ears, and Galahad wagged enthusiastically.

"Lawks, things have certainly changed, but I suppose that was inevitable." Galahad's tongue lolled out of his mouth in an amiable grin, before he flopped down under the table with a long sigh, with only his paws poking out. Beryl stepped over them cautiously, darting nervous glances in his direction as she weighed out some flour.

Katie glanced at Polly again, and they both started laughing. "Things certainly have changed, Beryl, but we're just glad you're here. You'll soon get used to it, and I hope you'll like George." She looked around the kitchen, realising it was true. The place felt like home now, especially with their old cook joining them. She took it as yet another sign that they were on the right path.

CHAPTER 17

Katie's eyes snapped open, and she lay in the darkness, her heart thumping, wondering where she was. Instead of the familiar sight of the tree outside her bedroom window at Castleford Hall, she had a clear view of the starlit sky, and it was only as she heard the faint sighing of the sea in the distance that she remembered she was at the inn.

She sat up in bed, wondering what had startled her awake, and tucked her hair behind her ears.

Just as she was about to snuggle under her patchwork quilt again, she heard a soft whine outside the bedroom door, and Galahad nudged it open. He padded across the floorboards and pawed the side of the bed. The hairs on her arms prickled with a sense of foreboding, and she quickly swung her legs out and grabbed her shawl to wrap around her shoulders.

"Go on then, show me what's bothering you." Tiptoeing down the stairs, she decided against waking any of the others. As long as she had Galahad next to her, she was protected, and it was probably nothing, she told herself. A few weeks had passed since Beryl's arrival, and it had been the busiest evening yet for customers. She had taken longer than usual to fall asleep when they all went to bed, her mind whirling with snippets of conversation and things she had to remember for the following day. She figured that perhaps Galahad was still getting used to living in a busy coaching inn as well. They were learning together, and disturbed nights were to be expected.

Katie collected the candle in its holder from the alcove at the bottom of the stairs and lit it, shivering as tall shadows immediately loomed on the walls around her. Her long white nightgown looked ghostly in the light of the flickering flame. Something about the building felt different, and her skin prickled as Galahad cocked his head, and a low growl rumbled in his chest.

"It's nothing to worry about, boy," she whispered, resting her hand on his shoulders for a moment.

The flame flickered again, almost blowing out, and she felt a draught around her ankles. *That's what isn't right...why can I feel a breeze?* Katie hurried into the taproom. "What's going on?" She was surprised to see that the front door was wide open, and she could hear the trees rustling outside, so she quickly shielded the candle flame with her hand.

Have we been burgled? She looked around, but everything was exactly how she had left it. Clean glasses behind the bar, bottles of spirits lined up neatly on the shelves. The fireguard was across the hearth in the inglenook, and chairs were lifted up ready for mopping the flagstones in the morning. The breeze picked up outside, making the door creak on its hinges. "We must have forgotten to lock it." She was puzzled by the oversight and hurried across the room to close it. Before she had a chance, Galahad bounded ahead of her into the dark night, letting off a volley of deep barks, which did little to reassure her. She followed him out, picking her way cautiously to the damp grass and thinking she should have put her boots on. Despite straining to look in all directions, it was impossible to see if anyone was hiding in the dense shadows. Ragged clouds raced across the sky, blocking out what little light there was from the moon, and the guttering candle flame barely pierced the darkness around her, let alone further into the woods. Her only comfort was that if anyone was skulking nearby, Galahad would be sure to sniff them out. She gave a low whistle, and the hound loped towards her, wagging, which reassured her.

After double-checking that the door was properly locked again behind them, Katie was wide awake. She hurried along the corridor and poked her head into the kitchen. It was silent, with not even the scurry of a mouse behind the cupboards now that Tim had put mouse traps there.

"I suppose I should go back to bed now." She yawned as tiredness washed over her again and ruffled Galahad's ears. "Want to come with me, boy?" Katie decided she would let him sleep at the foot of her bed, even though Agatha had looked horrified at the idea of a dog being allowed upstairs.

He gave a low woof in reply, making her smile.

"I thought so."

Walking past the parlour, her breath caught in her throat as she saw out of the corner of her eye that the window was open. "Not again," she groaned.

This time, she knew something was amiss because she clearly remembered closing it herself just a few hours earlier. A merchant and his wife were visiting from London, and they had enjoyed a meal in there, followed by coffee and port, before retiring to the biggest guestroom upstairs. They'd hinted that they would be coming to Stonehaven regularly, needing somewhere to stay each time, so she wanted to make sure that everything was perfect for them. Tim had kept the fire crackling merrily in the parlour, and Katie had shut the curtains to make the room even cosier when she saw the woman only had a thin silk shawl over her ruffled gown.

But now the window was ajar, and the curtains were flapping in the damp breeze, which was most definitely not how she had left it.

Katie hesitated on the threshold, wondering whether it would be wiser to go upstairs and fetch Wilbur. Galahad loped ahead of her, then looked back over his shoulder as if to encourage her to follow. She put the candle on the nearest table and leaned out of the window, this time giving her eyes a moment to adjust to the darkness beyond without being affected by the candlelight. At first, she saw nothing, but then her breath hitched as she suddenly spotted a glimmer of lamplight in the

THE FARTHING GIRL

distance. *How strange.* She felt the prickle of foreboding on her skin again because she knew there was no footpath in that direction. Tim had been exploring a few days ago and came back scratched by the brambles. Then, when Vernon found out where he'd been, he'd issued a stark warning that it was dangerous to wander off because the clifftops were that way, and it would be easy to tumble over the crumbling edge and fall onto the jagged rocks below.

"Who goes there?" she yelled. The bobbing lantern light stilled and then vanished, leaving nothing but inky darkness again. "Who are you?" she asked, sounding more uncertain this time. She wondered whether she had imagined it.

"I don't know what's wrong with me, Galahad," she mumbled. "This is the second time I've heard noises and now seen strange goings-on in the middle of the night." She laughed shakily, trying to convince herself it was simply that one of them hadn't closed up properly at the end of the evening. She shut the window firmly and tugged the curtains across again, making sure there wasn't even a chink of a gap between them for someone to peek in.

Turning back into the room, Galahad was standing in front of the fire, staring intently at the grey ash in the hearth. His hackles rose, and the growl rumbled in his chest again.

"What is it?" She patted him, then knelt down for a closer look, remembering the two glasses in the parlour on the day she had arrived. She had never asked Agatha about that, assuming that it must have been her and Vernon using the room for themselves, even while the rest of the inn was filthy and shuttered. But now, as she saw another scrap of paper in the hearth, a chill ran down her back. She picked it up and angled it towards the candlelight. It had the same charred fragment of a fleur-de-lis crest on it, which seemed like a strange coincidence. It was only at that moment that she caught sight of the mirror and shrieked with fright.

The words 'Go Now' had been scrawled on the glass in black soot.

Trembling, Katie tiptoed closer to the mirror. Her face looked pale and gaunt in the candlelight, and with the writing angled across her reflection in the mirror, it felt as though the stark message was meant directly for her alone.

Go now? What does it mean?

A sudden spurt of anger replaced her fear. She was trying so hard to make their new business successful, and the heartless words made her huff with irritation. She whipped off her shawl and rubbed the cruel message away. "No," she exclaimed. "We're not going anywhere. We're here to stay. This is our business, and I'm going to make it work." She stomped away, with Galahad close at her heels. Clearly, one of the locals was upset with them reopening the inn, but she wasn't going to be bullied into leaving. She would have a quiet word with George to see if he might know who held a grudge against them and try to win them around.

CHAPTER 18

"Is something wrong, Katie?" Beryl stared at her, pausing from chopping up potatoes and carrots to add to the evening's rabbit pie. "You've been quiet all morning, and you seem a bit jumpy."

Sunshine streamed through the open kitchen doorway, and she gave the cook a bright smile, resisting the urge to look outside when she heard an unexpected clatter from the direction of the stables. "I'm just a bit tired, that's all. Galahad was scratching to get out, and it took me a while to fall asleep again." She felt bad for not being entirely truthful but didn't want to worry anyone until she'd had a chance to speak to George about the alarming discovery in the middle of the night. Part of what she said was true, though. Katie had tossed and turned after going back to bed and only fallen fast asleep about half an hour before it was time to get up again, being jerked awake by the cockerel crowing.

"I hope you're not sickening for something." Beryl clucked sympathetically as she bustled between the table and the sink. "I brought a few bottles of my rosehip syrup with me. I'll make you a hot drink in a minute."

"I don't want to make any extra work for you." Wilbur and Tim had skinned and gutted several rabbits for her, and she diced the meat, hoping there would be enough. She would fry it off in a little flour and pepper before adding it to the vast saucepan. She didn't mind that sort of cooking at all, but it was a relief to hand over the more delicate dishes to Beryl, such as the buttery, flaky pastry she would shortly be making and the fish terrine she planned to offer guests, with the trout Tim had caught early that morning.

"Nonsense, it's no trouble, cariad." Her eyes twinkled. "I like that young gentleman of yours. Polly was right; he seems to visit most nights."

"He's not my young gentleman," Katie said hastily. Between Polly and Beryl and now Agatha too, it seemed everyone was convinced she and George were in some sort of courtship. Even though she secretly hoped it might come to that, she didn't want the others interfering. "He's been a good friend, and it's nice knowing that we have someone on our side."

"A good friend?" Beryl bit back a smile. "If you say so, my dear." She frowned as she considered the second part of what Katie had just said. "Have there been some locals not on your side? Do I need to have a word with any of them? Because I won't stand for anyone thinking they can be mean to Sir William's grandchildren."

She shook her head. "No, that's not what I meant. Also, we haven't told anyone that we are part of the Cavendish family. George knows because of our encounter during the riots at Pembrey Minster. And Agatha and Vernon Tremaine know who we are, of course, because of being caretakers here for Grandpa all those years. But as far as all the other locals are concerned, for the time being, we are just the Anderson family from a town inland."

"Very wise. Not that folk should judge you for who you are." Beryl let out a gusty sigh and shook her head, setting her grey curls bobbing. "I'm so worried about what your Uncle Norman is going to do with Castleford Hall and the estate. Honestly, Katie, I'm terrified he's going to besmirch your grandfather's good reputation and damage the Cavendish name, the way he's carrying on."

Katie could see that Beryl was starting to upset herself with how things had changed. "All we can do is put the past behind us," she said soothingly. "I hope we'll be able to see Max again in the future, but we can't be held responsible for anything that Uncle Norman and Aunt Amelia do from now on. We just have to do our best with this new life."

Beryl's eyes suddenly misted with tears, and she bustled around the table to give Katie a hug. "You poor little moppets, you've been through so much. Your ma and pa would have been so proud of you, Katie. You can't see it, but you remind me of Grace so much. She was strong-willed with a kind heart, just like you. Don't ever forget where you come from, my girl."

As much as Katie tried to put the previous night's events out of her mind, she found it almost impossible. Rushing through her jobs and keeping busy helped, but she was grateful when it was opening time. With each day that passed, they had a few more customers, and she even considered some of them regulars now, which was very gratifying.

They were far from the only tavern and drinking establishment in Stonehaven, but now that Beryl had taken over the cooking and their prices were sensible for the drinks, it was nice to know that they were starting to feel accepted in the community. At least, that was what she had thought.

"Is that a fresh barrel of ale?" Ernie Waite frowned suspiciously at the amber liquid frothing in his favourite tankard as he watched her pour his drink.

"Delivered first thing this morning by Mr Cowley himself." She put it on the bar and smiled politely. Most of their regulars were friendly. Bert Garten always liked to chat about what was happening on his farm, and Amos, Melvin, and Owen, the three fishermen who liked the table near the window and enjoyed a game of cards as they supped their beer, liked to tease Agatha and Beryl, but always with a twinkle in their eyes.

Ernie Waite, however, always seemed to see the worst in every situation. He would grumble that the beer was off, but only after he'd drained the last drop and wiped his mouth on the back of his hand before saying he should get his money back. And he generally managed to find fault with the food, even when everyone else said it was delicious. Beryl muttered darkly about barring him from the premises if he complained again, but Katie didn't want to go down that route. In spite of his mean-spirited ways, Ernie knew everyone in town. His cobbler's shop was on the main street, where he could see all the comings and goings from his workbench in the window, and nothing escaped his beady-eyed gaze, judging by how much he liked to discuss everyone's personal matters. She had a feeling that if she didn't keep on his good side, he would soon start dripping out poisonous comments about their business, and they couldn't afford to have any negative talk. They needed every customer that walked through the door.

Ernie wandered away, clutching his drink and sat down heavily in the chair he always chose. It gave him a clear view of everyone else in the taproom and along the corridor to the kitchen so he could see what everyone was doing.

"You're far more patient than I am," Polly whispered as she squeezed past Katie. "He's a miserable old so-and-so."

"We just have to put up with it as long as he's paying most of the time."

Agatha bustled past, collecting dirty glasses, and Katie poured strong coffee with a dash of cream for her to take to Mrs Kemp. The old woman used to own the fish smokery until her arthritis got too bad, and her son took it over. Since being widowed, she was lonely and would hobble up the lane to the inn for some company. Katie found that she was a treasure trove of wisdom, reminding her of the old lady on the moors who made herbal potions. Mrs Kemp would nurse a large mug of coffee, making it last as long as she could, and Beryl would slip her a slice of cake, free of charge. When Wilbur had questioned giving food away, Katie pointed out that she had no doubt the old lady would return the favour in other ways, perhaps by telling them the best places they could forage berries and wild plants to use in the kitchen or supplying them with a herbal tonic during the winter to keep them all healthy.

"We've got a good turnout today," Wilbur said as he popped inside for a few minutes. "Two well-to-do merchants from Bristol have just arrived. Is there room for them to stay the night? They've heard about the quality of the cockles from the estuary and want to see about getting them sent up on the train to sell at the markets and for the new hotels."

"Of course. Agatha cleaned all the rooms just in case after yesterday's guests left. The fires are already laid; they just need to be lit."

"Tim is stabling the horses, brushing them down and making an oat mash for their feed. I wonder how they heard about us? I should ask."

"And more importantly," Katie added, "if they are happy with their stay, I must ask them before they leave if they would very kindly tell their business acquaintances in Bristol. A recommendation from people who have enjoyed our hospitality is sure to help."

Agatha put the tray of glasses on the bar. "Did I see some new folk arriving?"

Polly joined her. "Two gentlemen needing rooms for the night. I'll come upstairs with you to make sure everything is just right, and I'd better tell Beryl to bake fresh bread for breakfast tomorrow."

KATIE ENJOYED the busyness of customers coming and going, but when she spotted George walking briskly up the lane, her pulse quickened. It wasn't that he was the most handsome man she had ever known, but there was something about the way he always gave her his full attention and wanted to know her opinion on all sorts of matters that made her glow with happiness every time she saw him. Where some locals had been quick to point out how inexperienced she was, George did the opposite. He encouraged her at every turn, sympathising with her mistakes and reminding her that everyone had to start somewhere. It had quickly reached the point where she looked forward to his company and couldn't imagine a day without seeing him now. It was hard to believe they had only known each other for a few weeks, and she smiled to herself as she remembered the whispered conversation she overheard between Beryl and Agatha earlier that day, discussing what a well-suited married couple they would make.

I only hope George might feel the same one day.

She patted her dark hair into place and smiled as he came through the door. "Good evening." Yet again, she marvelled at how fate had conspired to bring them together again.

"I have a few spare mackerel from today's fishing trip if you think Beryl could make good use of them." George unfolded the parcel tucked under his arm and held them out towards her.

"You're far too generous, and they look delicious. We've never been spoiled with so much fish as we have since moving here." She admired the iridescent silvery pattern on the skin just as Beryl appeared. "George brought these for us."

Beryl's face lit up with a beaming smile, and she gathered them up. "I'll fry these for our supper with caper sauce. Why don't you stay and eat with us once things get quieter, George? It's the least we can do for all these treats you keep bringing us."

"Thank you." He nodded, much to Katie's delight, even though she suspected Beryl was trying to play matchmaker.

Katie poured a jug of ale and took it across to the three fishermen, then returned to the bar to talk to George.

"I'm glad to see you today. There have been a few unusual goings-on the last few nights, which I haven't told the others about yet." She lowered her voice. "I've heard strange noises. And last night, when I went to investigate with Galahad, the parlour window was wide open, and I saw the light from a lantern in the woods, in the distance, as though someone was running away."

"That doesn't sound very good." George frowned with worry. "Do you think someone broke in, or was it just the breeze that caught the window?"

Katie leaned closer to him, glad he was taking her seriously. "There's more. The taproom door was wide open as well. I think someone had been in the parlour, and Galahad was behaving most peculiarly. Someone wrote 'Go Now' on the mirror—"

A shadow suddenly loomed over Katie, making her jump, but then she realised it was just Ernie wanting another pint of ale. For a large man, he could be surprisingly quiet on his feet, she thought.

Ernie sucked on his teeth, not hiding the fact that he had been listening to their conversation. "I've heard rumours that the smugglers are operating in this area again, Miss Anderson. 'Tis well known they used to meet at the North Star Inn because it's out of the way of prying eyes."

"I thought the Customs officers put an end to all that years ago," she said sharply. "Along with the Free Trade laws. Besides, this building was abandoned. It's obvious nobody had used it for a very long time." A memory of the two glasses and the scrap of paper in the parlour hearth slipped through her mind. She had a sickening feeling that someone had been using the building…she just didn't know who or why.

"Don't go putting frightening ideas into her mind, Mr Waite." George's expression was pleasant, but his tone was firm. "You know very well there haven't been any smuggling gangs working along this coast for a long time."

Ernie's dark eyes narrowed, and he gave them

both a long stare. "Times are hard for many families, and those new laws might have changed things in London, but many of us rural folk still have to look to the ways of the past to keep a roof over our heads. Who's to say the people who made easy money in the past from smuggling haven't started again?" He paused for a beat. "Or perhaps they never stopped."

"Nonsense." George was starting to look annoyed. "That's why they built the new lighthouse up on Rhoswell Head, to make sure there wouldn't be any more ships lured onto the rocks or shipwrecks to plunder."

Katie wondered why Ernie was so involved in their conversation. He had a habit of worming his way into everybody's business that didn't sit right with her, and she decided she didn't want to listen to any more of his gloomy ramblings.

"I'm sure it was just the breeze that opened the windows, and the light was probably just from someone out catching rabbits or something like that." She didn't quite believe her own words, but she wasn't about to show her fear in front of Ernie and then have him gossiping about it with everyone in Stonehaven. "I remember my pa telling me a long time ago that those criminal types who took to smuggling and terrifying the locals had all been thrown in jail."

Ernie sipped his ale and wrinkled his nose as though it didn't meet his high expectations. "Some folk who were raised inland don't know what they're talking about when it comes to smugglers," he said. He tapped the side of his nose as though he had a secret. "You should remember Stonehaven is a coastal community, and we live differently from the toffs. It's not your fault that you don't understand. It seems to me you come from a well-to-do background, so you wouldn't know the sort of struggles that poor folk have to suffer." His gaze flickered towards George. "You should ask your young man; he'll tell you how bad things were. His father was killed by smugglers, after all."

Katie gasped at Ernie's thoughtless words, and her heart went out to George as she saw a shadow of loss darken his blue eyes.

"Anyway," Ernie continued blithely. "I'll drink this up and be on my way. I don't have any more money on me tonight, but I'll make sure I pay you next time." With that, he returned to his table with a smug expression.

"I'm so sorry, George. He really is a very tiresome customer, and I'm starting to think Beryl might be right about telling him not to come here anymore. He never has a good word to say about anyone."

George shrugged, but she could tell he wasn't happy about the way the conversation had turned. "It's something I've been meaning to talk to you about, but you've been so busy getting the inn up and running I thought it could wait." He glanced towards Ernie with an expression that was hard to read. "I should have known better. People like Ernie love nothing more than spreading gossip."

"You don't have to tell me if it upsets you."

"No. I want to be honest with you about everything. Now that Ernie has brought it up, I may as well tell you what happened."

Polly had just returned from getting the bedrooms ready for their guests, and Katie beckoned her to take over at the bar for a little while. "George and I are just going outside for a few minutes. For some fresh air," she added when Polly fluttered her eyelashes, teasing her.

"There's no need to hurry back," Polly said, shooing her away. "We've taken the food order for the two gentlemen from Bristol, and they're settled in the parlour. It doesn't look like anyone else will arrive this evening, so take your time."

Katie wrapped her shawl around her shoulders,

not bothering with a bonnet, and they left through the back entrance before any other drinkers stopped her to chat. "Shall we walk along the stream a little way? It's so beautiful—I go there often."

"It's one of my favourite spots as well," George said, falling into step next to her. "My parents used to come up here before it was abandoned. We used to go blackberry picking so Ma could make jam, and afterwards, we would sit by the stream with a picnic, but it wasn't often because Pa was always so busy working. It brings back nice memories."

Katie led the way along the short, winding footpath, enjoying the dappled evening sunlight on her face. The ground was slightly damp underfoot, smelling rich and loamy. Ferns and yellow iris were growing in the boggy parts, and strands of moss hung from the trees closest to the water. There was a large flat boulder in a natural glade next to the stream, and she perched on one end of it, looking up at the blue sky with a sigh of contentment.

"I remember when people used to talk about the accident that took Mama and Papa from us. They meant well, but the speculation about what happened was hurtful."

George nodded and settled himself on the other end of the rock, maintaining a polite distance between them. He picked up a pebble and rubbed it between his hands to clean it. "Pa died at sea when he was out fishing. There was a big swell that night, and I wasn't with him because Ma was unwell, so he said I should stay at home with her. We'd had two bad winters, one after the other, and storms kept the fish away. But our fortunes changed, and he was luckier than most with the catches he landed that summer."

"It sounds like a precarious way to make a living."

"It can be, but Pa was good at what he did. He caught the best fish and got the best prices. Some of the other fishermen were jealous and started spreading rumours that he was doing well because he was working with the smugglers, but I know Pa. He never would have done that. It went against everything he believed in."

"That's the trouble with rumours; once they start spreading, they take on a life of their own."

"They found his body washed up on the beach." George sounded matter-of-fact, apart from a slight hitch in his voice. "The people who spread the rumours said it was a falling out between rival smugglers. They said Pa got greedy, and the other smugglers wouldn't stand for it."

"It must have been a terrible loss for you and

your mother." She reached across and squeezed his hand briefly, and he gave her a grateful smile.

Katie felt a ripple of shock at the very idea that George's family had been linked to smuggling. *But not George, surely?* It seemed absurd, and every instinct told her he was a good man. She had truly believed that illegal activities along this rugged coast had ended years ago, but now she was beginning to wonder if she was mistaken. Perhaps there was some truth in what Ernie had said, and the smugglers were still continuing with their lawless ways, hidden away from the Customs officers in the local coves and wooded valleys. She shivered despite the warmth of the evening, and she couldn't shake the thought that the North Star Inn would be the perfect place for them to meet.

"We had to carry on, and I took over the boat. I knew what they were saying was nonsense. It's true that Pa did some work for John Flanders, who was the smuggler everyone feared the most. But it was never anything illegal. Flanders had several fishing boats, and occasionally, he asked Pa to mend his nets and check his lobster pots because he was so good at it, but that's all. I think that night, Pa just got caught in the swell and thrown out of his boat. Fishing is a dangerous profession, and the sea can be a cruel mistress."

Katie nodded slowly. "I'm starting to understand that now we've been here a while." She looked at him shyly, then glanced away again. "You will be careful, won't you, George? I...we are all very fond of you, and I don't want to worry that something bad could happen when you're fishing, especially as you manage the boat alone."

His blue eyes glinted with amusement. "Don't worry. I never take unnecessary risks because I have to take care of Ma. Besides, I have a new set of friends to consider now as well, so I'll be extra careful."

She felt her cheeks getting warm as he held her gaze for a moment, making her feel slightly flustered. "I wouldn't have managed any of this without you," she blurted out, gesturing towards the tavern and stables.

He shrugged. "That's what friends are for, isn't it? Just don't let Ernie take advantage of your kindness." He jumped up again and handed her the pebble, which is when she saw it sparkle in the evening sun.

"It's fool's gold," he explained. "When the stream floods, it sometimes gets washed down from the mountains. Perhaps one day I'll be able to give you real gold if I have a good year fishing," he added, looking slightly bashful.

"I'd rather have this. You don't need to impress me with fancy trinkets." As they walked back along the path, Katie tucked the pebble away in her pocket, treasuring the gesture.

George suddenly turned to her. "Before we go back inside…you do believe me when I say that my pa wasn't involved in smuggling, don't you?"

She nodded without hesitation. "Of course I do. There's probably a lot of history in Stonehaven that I don't understand yet because I wasn't raised here, but I know you wouldn't lie to me, George. You have a kind and true heart."

He looked relieved. "It means a lot to know that."

"You're our friend," she said simply.

"Also, if anyone ever makes you feel unwelcome here, they'll have me to answer to. I'm going to ask a few of the old fishermen in town if what Ernie said is true. I'm too young to know if the smugglers did use your inn, but if I find anything out, it's best that we know what we're dealing with."

"Maybe we should tell the constable?"

He frowned. "Constable Parry? Let's keep it between ourselves a little while longer. I've heard a few rumours that his father, who was the constable before him, turned a blind eye to the smugglers in return for a handsome cut of money. It was never proven but…" His words trailed off.

"It's hard to know who to trust, but if you think that's for the best, I agree."

A new sense of intimacy hung between them for a moment until a burst of laughter and the sound of tinkling piano music caught her attention. "Let's go inside before Beryl sends Wilbur to look for us." She hurried into the taproom feeling a lot better about the threats now that she had confided in George.

CHAPTER 19

Katie took the washing basket from Agatha's hands and saw relief flash across her face. "I've noticed you've not been yourself these last few days. I'm not busy, so let me get the sheets off the line."

"Oh, it's no trouble." Agatha looked doubtful. "I don't want you to think I'm being idle."

Beryl appeared on the kitchen steps carrying a bowl of vegetable peelings for the chickens, and the mouthwatering smell of beef stew wafted out. "There's no point keeping on if you're not feeling well."

"It's just a headache that won't shift." She pressed the back of her hand to her forehead, looking glum. "Vernon always says it's the changing of the season that causes it, but my mother used to suffer the same. He doesn't like seeing me in pain, but the poor man doesn't know what to do to make it better." She glanced across the yard towards Vernon, who was busy digging manure into one of the empty vegetable beds in the kitchen garden.

"Feverfew tea is what you need," Beryl said with a sympathetic smile. "I'll bring you one in the snug. Then, if you have a snooze afterwards, I'll wager you'll be as right as rain again before we start serving."

"Are you sure? Maybe just for half an hour."

Katie nodded firmly. "You and Vernon work hard. What sort of person would I be if I didn't look after the people who care for all our customers so well? And we seem to be busy every day now, so I don't want any of us getting sick now that autumn is almost here."

Standing by the washing line a moment later, a chilly wind tugged at the bottom of Katie's gown, and the dry sheets flapped, making it hard for her to unpeg them and fold them up. The long, hot summer had come to an end, and it wouldn't be long until the woods would be transformed into a glorious wash of orange and red as the leaves changed colour and started falling from the trees. As if to prove her point, she spotted a few leaves spinning down from the sweet chestnut trees at the top of the lane. It would soon be time to harvest the prickly fruits and have roast chestnuts by the fire.

Our first winter in Stonehaven. She sighed wistfully, trying not to think about the tall Christmas tree decorated with glass baubles and candles they always had in the parlour at Castleford Hall. Instead, she hoped they would start new traditions. Perhaps there would be carol singing along the cobbled lanes in the town, followed by mulled cider. George had mentioned it was tradition to throw flowers into the sea on Christmas Eve in memory of the sailors and fishermen who had lost their lives at sea, and that he hoped she would join him. "We'll have to invite George and his ma to join us for Christmas dinner," she murmured, folding another sheet and laying it in the basket. She hadn't seen him much over the last week because he had been at sea every day, making the most of the fine weather for fishing before the autumn storms arrived.

Her thoughts drifted back over the last few months. Part of her felt proud of what they had achieved in such a short time, although she was mindful that it was because everyone had pitched in to work hard, and Ebenezer was still helping out by paying for a few deliveries of coal now and again. But she was also conscious that she often felt on edge. Even now, standing a little way away from the buildings, she couldn't help but look over her shoulder towards the woods, trying to see into the shadows.

As far as she knew, she didn't think anyone had broken in again during the night, but that was little comfort.

Katie found that she often jerked awake, straining to listen for strange noises, before tiptoeing downstairs with Galahad to double-check that all the windows and doors were shut properly. She had seen bobbing lights in the woods again on numerous occasions. At George's suggestion, she had told the others what had happened on that fateful night. Beryl had blanched when she described the message written on the mirror, then pursed her lips, angrily declaring she would give the culprit a sharp talking-to when they found out who it was. Wilbur had hacked a pathway through the brambles in the woods to try and investigate where the lights might be coming from, but his searches were futile. Even George hadn't been able to find out anything more despite making discreet enquiries with friends and acquaintances who were born and raised in Stonehaven.

Who wants us gone? The troubling question filled her thoughts, but she couldn't answer it.

The one thing Katie did know was that where she had originally only spotted the lights occasionally when she first started checking, she had seen them three times in the last week. It felt as though danger was brewing and things were escalating. She glanced over her shoulder again, not knowing whether the chill that trickled down her back was from the wind or some sort of sixth sense that something bad was going to happen. She remembered how her mother sometimes foretold things and that the old lady who lived on the moor had once told Katie that she should always pay attention to what her gut feeling was telling her. Ironically, Katie hadn't thought about those two things again for years. But as the autumn breeze rattled the leaves in the trees and the wheeling seagulls mewled in the sky above the harbour, she had a feeling that change was coming and a sense that it might not necessarily be for the better.

* * *

"Must you always lie in my way, you mangy dog?" Ernie Waite grumbled to himself as he stepped over Galahad and approached the bar. Now that the evenings were drawing in, the large hound liked nothing more than stretching out in front of the fire crackling in the hearth. Everyone else patted him or fed him a titbit of food, but not Ernie, of course, Katie thought to herself as she started pouring his usual measure of ale.

"Have you seen any more lights in the woods lately?" he asked gruffly, begrudgingly handing her a couple of coins for the drink.

Katie was startled by his question. It was almost like he'd read her mind. "Once or twice," she said casually. She wasn't about to start discussing it at length with him.

He supped a mouthful of ale and perched on one of the stools at the bar instead of heading for his regular seat, much to her disappointment. That meant he wanted to chat, but she never enjoyed his barbed comments about the townsfolk she was starting to count as her friends.

"It must be ghosts then." He glanced around, and his face screwed up with disapproval at how full the taproom was with regulars and visitors alike. "That must be the only explanation if you don't know who's out there in the middle of the night." He raised his voice slightly, intent on stirring up trouble and wanting the others to join in. "They say the spirits of the past don't settle when they don't approve of what's happening in the present. I expect there are plenty of folk who would have preferred the North Star Inn to stay closed. These walls are full of secrets, Katie, dark deeds and terrible plans hatched by the smugglers that resulted in death and destruction. Theft and plundering of what didn't belong to them. No wonder you've seen spirits wandering abroad in the woods nearby. Some things are best left in the past, and who knows what might happen now that you've brought this place back to life again." He rubbed his hands with relish as a couple of visitors pulled their chairs closer together, looking alarmed.

Beryl shuddered as she served big bowls of hearty stew to Amos, Melvin, and Owen, the three fishermen in the corner, and then walked behind Ernie with a tray of baked apples stuffed with spiced raisins and a dollop of cream for two soldiers who were sitting in the corner. Katie saw her darting worried glances in Ernie's direction. This wasn't the first time Ernie had mentioned restless spirits haunting the place, and every time he did, Beryl superstitiously made the sign of the cross on her ample bosom.

Betty Kemp hobbled up to the bar with her empty coffee mug. "If it's so bad here, Mr Waite, why do you bother visiting so often?"

Ernie's mouth pinched into a thin line. He liked holding court, weaving yarns about the chequered past of this coast, and didn't take kindly to being challenged, especially by Betty, who had known him since he was a young boy with scraped knees, learning from his father how to mend shoes.

"A few ghosts don't scare me," he muttered, taking another swig of ale.

"I'd rather you didn't keep talking about this," Katie said quietly. "I told you, it was probably just a few poachers looking for rabbits."

"You tell him, Katie," Betty said, nodding approvingly.

"Poachers? Rubbish. There are far better places to catch rabbits than out yonder," he said stubbornly. "Those woods between here and the cliffs aren't known for poaching."

Betty wasn't deterred. "It's not nice of you to stir up bad feelings. We know that the dead don't always rest easy, but all the bad things that used to happen along this coast are in the past now." She gave him a firm stare. "You've been a troublemaker ever since you were a little boy, always finding fault with kind folk like this delightful family. Perhaps you should pay more attention in church instead of dozing through the sermons," she added crisply.

Ernie shifted on his stool under the old woman's direct gaze, with a hint of embarrassment at being told off so publicly. Katie hoped it wouldn't make him even more belligerent. He wasn't the sort of man to accept he'd done wrong and apologise, she was coming to realise.

"Perhaps you should mind your own business—" Ernie countered, but the retort died on his lips as the taproom door swung open and a tall man stepped over the threshold.

When Wilbur asked her about it later, Katie told him the atmosphere changed in an instant. The hum of conversation faltered as people fell silent, and Amos, Melvin, and Owen all stopped chewing their stew and glanced at each other before resuming eating furtively.

The newcomer, who hadn't visited before, strolled slowly across the taproom floor, seemingly unperturbed by people's reactions. He was well over six feet tall, with broad shoulders and greasy dark grey hair that curled on his collar. He wore a long greatcoat that only added to his bulk, and his boots were stained white with salt as though he had recently walked through shallow seawater.

"Good evening." His voice was low and hoarse, and he looked at Katie curiously with dark eyes that held no warmth. "A tot of rum, please. In fact, you can put the bottle on the bar, and I'll help myself." He removed his hat, placing it tidily on the bar.

"I prefer to do one serving at a time," Katie said casually, wanting to make him understand she was the landlady in charge. "I find it saves some of my customers from having a sore head the following morning," she added, trying to lighten the mood.

"Fair enough." His lip curled in a half-smile. "There are plenty of men around here that need protecting from their bad habits, that's for sure." He pulled a coin from his coat pocket and slid it across the bar. As Katie turned with the bottle and glass, she saw a jagged, silvery scar on the back of his hand. He followed her gaze and held his hand up to the light, turning it this way and that, drawing attention to the fact that she had stared at it.

"Caught my hand on some rigging many years ago," he explained. "I was lucky not to lose a couple of fingers, wasn't I, Doctor Hawkesworth," he added loudly, giving the bespectacled man in the corner an amused glance.

"Yes…yes indeed…I remember that night well," the doctor stammered.

The man chuckled as he turned back to Katie. "One of my men had to rouse poor Doctor Hawkesworth from his slumbers in the middle of the night. He said he was delighted to be woken up… imagine sewing a man's hand back together while still wearing your dressing gown and night cap."

The doctor laughed uneasily and lifted his newspaper a bit higher so he could disappear behind it.

Just at that moment, Tim came striding in from the back corridor, carrying a sack full of logs for the fire. "That makes you sound like a pirate," he said cheerfully. "Or perhaps a smuggler," he added with a chuckle.

Katie heard Amos' spoon clatter as he dropped it, and Ernie coughed as his ale went down the wrong way.

"How is business going, Miss Anderson?" The man carried on speaking in a perfectly normal tone, ignoring the others.

"We've been very fortunate. The locals have supported our endeavours, and we appreciate all our customers. Word seems to be spreading afar to travellers as well, as we've had quite a few people staying overnight to break up their journey."

"What about some food for you?" Beryl asked as she brought another bowl of stew from the kitchen, this time for the doctor. "I didn't catch your name…"

"Another time, perhaps." He sniffed appreciatively and peered into the bowl as she walked past. "It looks nice. Good food and friendly company keep a tavern like this thriving." He nodded for Katie to pour another tot of rum for him. "Mind you, it would be a shame for something to spoil your success."

Beryl turned after she had put the doctor's food down on the table and looked at him suspiciously. "What are you implying?" she asked sharply.

"Yes, what do you think would spoil our success?" Katie added, thinking it was a strange and rather unsettling comment.

The thickset stranger leaned over the bar and lowered his voice. "I've been keeping an eye on you since you arrived. There are dangerous men in these parts who don't want you to succeed, Miss Anderson. It would be a terrible shame if something bad were to befall you and you had to close the inn so soon, don't you think? Or what about if your young man George had an accident at sea?"

Before Katie could reply, Betty Kemp hobbled up to the bar and plonked her coffee cup down firmly, making the nearby glasses rattle. She glared at him. "If anyone's dangerous around here, it's you."

He ran a hand through his grey hair and laughed loudly. "Don't tell me you believe those silly rumours from all those years ago, Widow Kemp? You know very well I was just a humble fisherman like so many others around these parts." He leaned sideways and nudged Ernie, who was looking rather pale. "You can vouch for me, can't you."

"Err...yes...yes, of course." Ernie nodded and gulped another mouthful of ale. He was gripping his tankard so tightly, his knuckles had turned white. His gaze flickered towards Katie and she saw something she had never seen in his eyes before. Sympathy. And fear.

"Fishing is a young man's game, though, Miss Anderson. I gave it up years ago, and now I'm a rent collector for Lord Bevan. He's one of the wealthiest landowners in the area." He reached for the rum bottle, which she hadn't put away yet, and poured himself some more, throwing it back in one mouthful.

"Well, that's very interesting, but I have other

customers to serve. Would you like to pay for those extra couple of drinks before I go?"

His eyes narrowed, and he pushed himself away from the bar, reaching for his hat. He put it on and pulled it low over his eyes. "I don't think you understand. As I said, I'm a rent collector. A bit like you, I always make sure folk pay what they owe."

"We aren't tenants, so we don't owe anything." She wondered whether he had been drinking already and had got them confused with someone else. "My family and I own the North Star Inn."

"I wasn't talking about paying rent," he said quietly, glancing at Ernie, who hastily looked away again. "I'm talking about paying for my protection, Miss Anderson. I already told you there are dangerous men in these parts. Those who don't pay up…well, it's surprising how unexpected bad things happen to them and their premises."

Beryl's mouth gaped open with shock, and she put her hands on her hips, looking outraged. "Now, listen here…do you know who you're talking to—"

He held up his hand, stopping her in her tracks, and grinned menacingly. "Don't treat me like a fool, old woman." He gave Katie a challenging stare. "I know exactly who you are, and a quiet word with

Norman Cavendish might set off an interesting chain of events."

She snatched the bottle of rum back from him, too shocked to feel afraid. "I'd like you to leave—"

"Maybe Norman Cavendish would like this place for himself," he drawled, drumming his fingers impatiently on the wooden counter. "I suggest you give my offer the thought it deserves. If you don't start paying for my protection, you might regret it."

This time, it was Katie's turn to put her hands on her hips. "I won't stand here and be bullied on my own property, least of all by you."

Out of the corner of her eye, she saw Amos shaking his head and Melvin gesturing for her to be quiet, and the blood draining from Ernie's face, but she couldn't stop herself.

"Are you sure about that?" he asked coldly.

Agatha and Vernon wandered through from the back room, hearing the commotion. "Oh no, Katie… you don't understand—" Agatha began.

It was too late. Katie didn't often get angry, but she wasn't going to be extorted into paying money they didn't have. They were barely making enough to get by, and she had a nasty suspicion that if she agreed, the monthly amount he demanded would soon increase.

"Perhaps Lord Bevan should be told that you're threatening people and causing all sorts of unwanted heartache for local businesses," she snapped. She marched briskly around to the front of the bar, grabbed his arm, and propelled him through the door. "Don't cross this threshold again; you're not welcome," she said, brushing her hands together after she shoved him outside into the dark night. "If anyone is going to have regrets from this conversation, it will be you for trying to take advantage of people who are just trying to make an honest living."

"Katie, stop...you mustn't say that...not to him," Agatha whispered urgently, rushing to her side.

The man snatched up the reins on his horse and jumped onto the saddle, looking furious as he galloped away down the lane.

"I'm fed up with being threatened and told there are ghosts and smugglers and all sorts of nonsense," Katie said, still simmering with annoyance. "Who is he anyway? He didn't even have the courtesy to introduce himself."

Agatha wrung her hands and groaned. "That's John Flanders. He used to strike fear into the hearts of many folk round here in years gone by."

John Flanders? The name sounded familiar, and with a shock, she remembered George saying that's who his father used to do occasional work for before the accident that took his life. *The man some people said was a vicious smuggler.* "That's no reason for us to fear him," she said, trying to reassure Agatha, Beryl, and Tim, who had also come to join her.

"Lawks, this is going to cause trouble."

"I'm afraid you've made an enemy out of a powerful man, Katie." Vernon put his arm around his wife's shoulder, looking worried. "I expect several people who pay that scoundrel money to protect their business are sitting in this pub here tonight. Nobody says no to John Flanders. He has a way of getting what he wants."

"Well, not this time." Katie tossed her head, even though a cold worm of fear squirmed in her belly. "If we give in to his demands, it will just get worse. That's how people like him work. Somebody has to stand up to him, so it might as well be me."

CHAPTER 20

Polly stood in the doorway looking down the lane, watching Galahad loping between his favourite spots to sniff out any creatures that had been on his territory. He had already done it once at the crack of dawn, but even though it was midmorning now, he was hopeful there might be new smells to track down.

"Any sign of Ned from the grocer's yet?" Katie joined Polly, hoping to spot Alwyn Jones's eldest son with his piebald pony and cart making deliveries. The lane was empty, and she chuckled as she saw Galahad pounce on a clump of grass, his long tail waving much like when Agatha shook her feather duster. The clock on the mantlepiece behind them chimed, signalling that the day was getting on. "He's never late."

"No. It's unusually quiet today. I haven't seen anyone walking by or heard any wagons on the road. Shouldn't we have had a delivery of ale from Gethin by now as well?"

Katie sighed and turned back into the taproom to finish mopping the floor. Once that was done, she had to polish all the furniture with Agatha's new lavender beeswax polish. Many taverns spread sawdust on the flagstones to soak up spilt beer, but she preferred not to, thinking it made the place look rough, which was not the impression she wanted to give. It meant mopping more often, but she figured it was a small price to pay.

Agatha bustled in, closely followed by Beryl. "Let me do that," Agatha said, getting to the mop before Katie.

"I told you that feverfew tea would work wonders." Beryl peered outside, looking disappointed. "Has that lazy boy delivered our groceries yet? I need dried fruit, girls. You know I like to make the plum puddings and cakes for Christmas nice and early with a good splash of brandy so they have time to mature. I'm making extra this year as gifts for a few folk who are struggling to make ends meet."

Katie came to a quick decision. "I'll walk down and get everything. I've been meaning to visit the haberdashery as well, and my boots need to be re-soled."

Polly snorted. "Ernie Waite doesn't deserve our business, spreading all those silly rumours about ghouls and ghosts."

"I know, but he's the only cobbler in Stonehaven. It's not desperate, but I thought he could measure up, and then I'll go in another time to get the rest of the job done. It will give me another chance to remind him not to alarm our customers with his tall tales."

Polly grabbed her bonnet and grinned. "If you're walking into town, I'm coming with you. We never get a chance to have fun anymore."

"Buy yourself a twist of humbugs or some fudge." Beryl beamed as she slipped a few pennies into Polly's pocket. "Don't roll your eyes," she added, pinching Polly's cheeks like she used to when she was younger. "You'll always be two little girls to me, and I like to treat you now and again."

"I ALWAYS FEEL a bit nostalgic to see the swallows leaving. It means summer is well and truly over."

Katie pointed to where the last few birds were gathering in a line on one of the new-fangled telegraph wires, noisy with their whistling song at the start of their autumnal migration. They reminded her of ladies chattering at a church social, she always thought, and she marvelled at the thousands of miles the tiny birds would travel to overwinter in warmer climes. "They will be heading to Africa following all the others that have already gone."

"Don't worry, we'll have them back again next April." Polly walked briskly beside her, more interested in the shopping expedition than Katie's observations about the plentiful wildlife around them. "Do you think Ebenezer might let us have a new gown each for Christmas?"

"We can only ask." She thought back to the green velvet dress she'd had last Christmas with a pang of regret. They'd had no idea at the time how privileged their life was, but it wasn't necessarily a bad thing for them to learn to be more frugal.

As they reached the end of the lane, she had a sudden urge to take a slight detour. "Let's go up the path to the cliff top. We're not in any hurry." Without waiting for Polly to agree, Katie hurried up the narrow track. The grass on the headland was springy, but the sea pinks had long since stopped flowering. Drawing closer to the edge of the cliff, the wind snatched at her dress and buffeted her. She could feel the elemental force of the sea as she looked out at the white-crested waves and took deep breaths of the damp, salt-laden air. The colour of the water reminded her of grey-green pewter. It was far from the sparkling blue she had enjoyed in the summer, and she was beginning to understand how the changing seasons were so important for the fishermen. She had missed George these last few days and sent up a silent prayer that he was safe. She found herself wondering what it would be like to be married to a fisherman, anxiously keeping watch at the window at every sign of bad weather that might catch an unwary fisherman out. The gulls wheeled above her, and she saw a few inquisitive grey seals popping up out of the waves, their smooth heads looking like buoys, before they dived again, looking for fish.

"Come on, we can't stand here looking at the view all day." Polly fidgeted impatiently. "By the time we've run our errands the first customers might be arriving at the bar, wanting food and ale."

They walked briskly back down the hill, reminiscing about times gone by when their lives had been simpler and then discussing plans for their first Christmas at the North Star Inn. Tim had already earmarked the perfect-sized pine tree to cut down and decorate with baubles and tinsel in the corner of the taproom for the festive season, and Wilbur had grinned mischievously when he told Katie he'd found some mistletoe growing in the woods on the poplar trees. He'd said it just loud enough for George to hear as well, which made her blush.

Katie was surprised that Latimer Lane was deserted. Usually, the fishermen's wives were busy scrubbing their front steps, cleaning fish, or mending nets for their husbands. Today the place seemed eerily deserted, and she was gripped by another sense of foreboding.

"Why is it so quiet?" Polly asked, echoing her thoughts. "Something doesn't feel right."

A gust of wind hit them as they emerged from the shelter of the row of whitewashed cottages, and the harbour came into view. She frowned as she realised where everyone was. "Look, something must have happened. They're all on the beach."

They hurried across the road, stopping at the low stone wall to watch. There was a gaggle of fishermen wearing their distinctive smocks, with their wives, They were all standing around something on the sand, but they kept moving, making it impossible to see exactly what the indistinct shape was. Snatches of conversation drifted towards them.

"I'm telling you, 'tis a bad omen after all these years."

"...trouble for the town...had it coming..."

"...thought those worrying times were over..."

"Do you know what's happened?" she asked two scruffy boys running towards them. They were carrying empty buckets, wearing ragged trousers made from old, patched fabric, rolled up to reveal scrawny ankles and bare feet. She presumed they were children of the fishing families, who picked mussels off the rocks at low tide for a few extra pennies' income each day.

The boys stopped running, and one of them sneezed noisily, then dragged his sleeve across his face to wipe his nose. "Ain't you heard, miss?"

"Heard what? Has something washed up on the beach from the sea?"

The boys exchanged a glance and their eyes rounded in a mixture of fear and alarm. "You could say that, miss."

"Well, what is it? A seal? Some old timber from a

shipwreck?" Polly was getting impatient again, and the sky was darkening with the threat of rain.

"'Tis a dead body...a man." The older of the two brothers stood taller, wanting to be the one to impart such shocking gossip. "They don't know whether he died at sea or was attacked by someone else. Pa said it could cause all sorts of trouble...bring the Customs officers sniffing around again—" He stopped abruptly as his brother gave him a sharp jab with his elbow.

"Shut up, Ioan," he hissed. "Don't tell strangers."

Before Katie could ask any more questions, the two boys ran off, darting down the slipway onto the sand. A death in the town was no excuse to get out of work, and their ma would tan their backsides if they came home with an empty bucket.

"Goodness, what a horrible thing to happen," Katie murmured, clutching her shawl.

The circle of people parted for a moment, and she saw it was true. The body had been wrapped in a sheet, and two fishermen were lifting it onto a stretcher at Doctor Hawkesworth's bidding. The doctor glanced in their direction with a grim expression, then gestured towards the slipway, saying something to the young man next to him who had recently come to Stonehaven to complete his physician training under the doctor's tutelage.

"Who do you think it is?" Polly looked momentarily guilty for having wanted to rush away. "I wonder if it's someone local or just some poor soul washed ashore from their boat."

Katie fought the urge to rush down the beach and check that it wasn't her dearest George. Doctor Hawkesworth would surely have come to tell her if it was George; he had seen them talking at the inn often enough to know they were close.

Four of the fishermen picked the stretcher up, grunting slightly with its weight. It was a horrible sight, and her heart went out to whoever was going to get the bad news that their loved one had died. But she also felt relieved that the battered hat Doctor Hawkesworth picked up off the sand and laid respectfully on the shrouded corpse was nothing like the cap George wore when he was sailing.

"We should carry on with our errands, Polly. I'm sure we'll hear who it is soon enough if it's someone we know. It doesn't feel polite to stand and watch."

"You're right." They paused momentarily to show their respects, then hurried towards Long Street.

"We'll go to the haberdashery first, then I'll pop

into the cobbler's, and you can go ahead to Alwyn's for the dried fruit and sugar and flour that Beryl needs. We'd better check that Ned hasn't gone out delivering anyway, or we'll end up with double of everything."

"It's probably because of the body on the beach that nobody has done any deliveries today." Polly looked shaken. "Perhaps there's some truth in what that boy said. If the person died because of a fight, the constable might be questioning people."

"Well, we mustn't gossip," Katie warned. "Remember, we're relative newcomers to Stonehaven, and something like this makes people close ranks. With the wind getting up like it is, I expect George will be back from his latest fishing trip today. He'll keep us informed."

* * *

"It's closed." Polly tried the door handle of Mrs Gaskin's haberdashery shop again, but it wasn't budging.

Katie peeked through the window and thought she saw a shadowy figure slip out of sight into the back room. "Never mind. I expect people are on edge. We can come back another day. That's what I'll buy." She pointed towards some of the pretty lace in the window that she was hoping Agatha would be able to use to make a new collar on one of her older dresses to smarten it up. There were some lovely velvet ribbons as well that caught her eye, and she tucked the information away, knowing they would be perfect as part of Polly's Christmas present.

"I hope the grocer isn't shut as well." They continued along Long Street, noticing that the quaint bookshop was also closed.

"I'm sure it won't be. People still have to make a living, and the baker can't throw away all his fresh bread. The townsfolk need to eat."

"What about your boots? Are you going to bother calling at the cobbler's?"

"I may as well now that we're here." They turned onto Hawthorn Lane and walked briskly towards Ernie Waite's shop. He had a sign hanging above the bow-fronted windows portraying a fancy boot and swirly writing, announcing it as 'Lloyd Cobblers, Shoemaker and Repairs', named after his father, who had started the business.

"Well, at least he hasn't shut up shop," Polly muttered. "Looks like he's having a good old gossip with Constable Parry, mind you. No doubt Ernie will be eager to tell us the worst possible version of what might have happened." The two men were standing further along from the cobbler's shop, deep in conversation, and something about Ernie's demeanour set alarm bells ringing in Katie's mind. He seemed agitated and kept looking over his shoulder.

As Katie walked ahead of Polly in single file to let a horse and carriage go past, she was just about to greet them when Ernie suddenly nudged the constable, pointed at her, and then scurried away. His shop door slammed shut behind him, loud enough to echo between the other buildings, and Katie was startled to see him hastily close the shutters, making it crystal clear he was not open for business.

"How peculiar," she whispered as Polly caught up. "I've never seen him move so fast."

"Why was he pointing at you?" Polly blanched as Constable Parry started running towards them, with his truncheon raised and a determined expression on his face.

"Stop! Stop right there, Miss Anderson."

Katie stepped in front of Polly, shielding her, and folded her arms. "I don't know why you're shouting like a banshee, Constable," she said mildly. "We're not going anywhere, and if you need to talk to us, you only have to say."

The lawman's face was red with exertion under

his hat, and he sounded slightly breathless as he put his truncheon back in the leather belt around his portly waist. He glowered at her and clamped his hand on her shoulder. "Don't get any bright ideas about running away."

"What on earth are you doing?" Polly asked indignantly. "Take your hand off my sister."

On the other side of the lane, a cottage door creaked open, and Katie felt the heat of embarrassment flood her cheeks as a woman with two toddlers clinging to her skirts peeped out, agog with curiosity. An old gentleman pushing a handcart stared as the constable tightened his grip, then shook his head with a pitying look, as though it had already been decided she had committed some terrible crime.

Katie took a deep breath, determined not to be rattled by the constable's strange behaviour. She gave him a polite smile. "I think there must be some sort of mix-up, Constable Parry. If you could kindly explain why you need to speak to me, I'm sure I can sort it all out immediately."

"Have you heard about the death?" Sidney Parry's pale blue eyes narrowed, and he jerked his head in the direction of the beach. "A body...on the sand, discovered not two hours ago."

"We saw there was a gathering, and Doctor Hawkesworth was overseeing matters. I'm still not sure what this has to do with me."

The constable's expression hardened, and she saw a flicker of disbelief in his eyes. "The dead man is John Flanders. I have it on good account that he visited your coaching tavern last night, and you threatened him—"

"What a ridiculous claim," Polly interrupted, looking outraged.

Katie patted her arm. "It's okay, Polly." She turned back to Constable Parry. "It's true, Mr Flanders visited us yesterday for the first time since we took over the place. He had a few tots of rum, then tried to extort money out of me. If anyone was behaving threateningly, it was him."

"I have a witness who will swear under oath that you threw him out of the pub and said he would pay for his actions."

"Well...it wasn't quite like that—" Katie's stomach lurched as she realised why Ernie Waite had just pointed her out and then scurried away to hide in his workshop. She had a sickening realisation that despite all his bluff and bluster, Ernie was probably paying protection money to John Flanders, and was terrified of the finger of blame pointing at him.

"All I know is that Flanders died by foul play." The constable gripped her arm and his bushy moustache quivered as he became even more officious. "You will have to accompany me to the police station for questioning. I'll have to send a message to my superiors, but I expect they will need to be satisfied that you had nothing to do with it." He started propelling her in the direction they had just come from, towards the town's small police station.

"Wait, this is silly. This was nothing to do with me." Katie was still hopeful that common sense might prevail and they could sort it out quickly. "Yes...I told him to leave. Perhaps I spoke a little more firmly than usual, but I was upset that he thought he could bully business owners into paying him their hard-earned money to guard against spurious threats and vague hints of dangerous men in the area. After Flanders rode away on his horse, I carried on serving the other customers. Then my family and I cleaned up, just like we do every night. I locked up, and went to bed."

"That's as maybe, but it seems like too much of a coincidence that you threatened him, and then he was found lifeless on the beach just a few hours later." The constable's tone was firm and uncompromising.

"Run and get Wilbur and the Tremaines, Polly," she called over her shoulder. "Tell everyone not to worry...I know I'm innocent, and Constable Parry will know the same, too, before the day is out."

As she watched her younger sister run back the way they had just come, Katie shook the constable's hand off her arm and lifted her chin defiantly. "There's no need to manhandle me like a common criminal. My grandfather was Sir William Cavendish from near Pembrey Minster, and he raised me to know right from wrong. I will happily come to your office until you get the proof you need. You'll see that this had nothing to do with me, and I think you should remember that the law states someone is innocent until proven guilty."

Constable Parry harrumphed and let her walk next to him with grudging acceptance. "You're related to Sir William Cavendish?" he muttered, sounding less sure of himself. "I believe he was a keen patron of the constabulary in these parts. Probably knew quite a few judges."

"Yes, and he was involved with getting many laws passed in parliament to help improve the lives of working-class people before he retired." Katie marched briskly towards the police station, her stomach churning with terror. It was the first time she had used her family connection that way in her whole life, but desperate times called for desperate measures. She was determined not to be accused of a crime she hadn't committed. Especially something so heinous as murder.

CHAPTER 21

"Is it really necessary to have her locked up behind bars?" George was struggling to stay polite towards Constable Parry but knew that anger would get him nowhere. "Surely you can let her sit quietly in your office while you wait to hear from your superiors?"

The constable threw him an irritated glance as he reached for another pile of paperwork and pulled his oil lamp closer now that it was getting dark. "I wouldn't be doing my job properly if I didn't keep criminals locked up," he replied, sharper than necessary.

"Suspected criminal," George corrected. "Based on a garbled accusation from someone who was

THE FARTHING GIRL

scared of John Flanders." He hoped Ernie Waite was feeling guilty.

"Count yourself lucky I'm allowing you to sit here meanwhile. I could barely hear myself think with the rest of her family in the room. I've never known such a rabble."

George walked to the window, gazing out unseeing, and reflected on the peculiar day.

It was fortunate that he had just rowed ashore from his fishing boat and taken his catch of mackerel and herrings to Kemp's Smokery when he heard the news. He had run all the way to the police station, arriving just at the same time as all of Katie's family, as well as Agatha and Vernon Tremaine. Beryl had dumped her reticule on Sidney Parry's desk and demanded Katie's immediate release. Wilbur was gasping for breath because he had already run ahead to the post office to send an urgent telegram to Ebenezer Black, which he told Sergeant Parry, implying that the solicitor would be heading to Stonehaven the moment he heard about Katie's plight. Polly had burst into noisy tears, overwhelmed by the whole situation, while Tim pleaded to be allowed to see his sister.

It was fair to say that mayhem had broken out in

the usually sleepy police station, but the only effect it had was to make Sidney Parry dig his heels in even more, like a stubborn mule.

After listening to everyone talking over each other, he had finally thumped his fist on his desk, sending a teetering pile of dusty books and ledgers crashing onto the floor, making him even more bad-tempered.

"Let me remind you all that I uphold the law in Stonehaven. Miss Anderson admits her encounter with John Flanders ended on a sour note. People drinking at your coaching inn clearly heard her say he would regret their altercation. I understand the situation is complicated by the fact that Mr Flanders had also behaved in a threatening manner, but only one of them ended up dead. She deserves to be behind bars."

Beryl stumbled backwards as though the constable had slapped her. "I've known my Katie since she was a baby, and if you think a grand-daughter of Sir William Cavendish would stoop so low as to commit such a dreadful crime, I might be left wondering whether you've been on the whiskey. The idea that Katie took Mr Flanders' life is absurd." The poor woman looked close to tears, and

Constable Parry had the grace to turn away to look out of the window, clearly uncomfortable with so much emotion and the clamour of everyone questioning his decision.

"You don't know the Andersons like we do," Vernon said, trying to plead Katie's case from a different angle. "Agatha and I have lived here for many years. We've worked alongside Katie since the day she arrived, and she's as honest as the day is long. Kind-hearted, too. You know John Flanders is a scoundrel. It was probably his past misdemeanours catching up with him."

After nearly an hour of much back-and-forth, Constable Parry had had enough. He marched to the door and yanked it open, gesturing for them to leave. George could see that behind the family's insistence that Katie was innocent, they were afraid that the blame might be pinned on her anyway, simply because they were outsiders.

"I'll stay here with her," he said, patting Beryl's arm to reassure her. "The thing with Constable Parry," he added, lowering his voice, "is that the locals have long memories. When his father was the town's constable, there were rumours that he should have done more about the smugglers. Parry isn't always very confident that he's doing the right thing, which is why he's waiting to hear from his superiors."

Wilbur had reluctantly agreed it was time to leave. "I suppose Katie did tell us that we should go back to the inn and open up as normal. We still have guests to serve food for, and even if the locals don't come, we might get travellers turning up."

The family had trooped off again, and George had been there ever since, apart from ten minutes to run home to tell his ma what had happened. *That's something else to worry about*, he mused. *Ma hasn't been herself lately. Something is bothering her.*

"Do you want a cup?" The sound of Constable Parry pouring himself another cup of bitter coffee from the pot warming on the potbelly stove snapped George back to the present. Parry's housekeeper had left a plate of ham rolls, too, and the constable munched on one, dropping crumbs on his waistcoat. He held out a battered tin mug. It was the first hint that he might be relenting. "I'll make one for Miss Anderson as well. I was hoping she wouldn't have to stay here all day. You can take it through to her."

George's heart went out to Katie as he carried the steaming mug of coffee into the back room a moment later. The cell she had been locked in was austere, but Beryl had insisted on leaving her cloak behind so Katie could fold it up and use it as a cushion or wrap herself up in it to stay warm.

"I don't think he can keep you here for much longer," George whispered as he handed her the cup of coffee through the bars. "He's got no evidence other than hearsay, and I'm sure there are plenty of people in Stonehaven who Flanders counted as an enemy."

"I know you're doing your best. Sorry it's taking so long. I hate thinking how worried the others must be." She gave him a warm smile, wrapping her hands around the mug for comfort, and his heart flipped in his chest. She had that effect on him. It wasn't just her sparkling green eyes and lustrous dark hair but the fact that he felt he wanted to protect her from life's harsh knocks. He felt drawn to her in a way he couldn't explain, and it was her heart-shaped face that filled his dreams and made him work harder than ever in the hope that one day he could offer her a future where they could be together. But first, he had to keep her spirits up until Constable Parry let go of this ridiculous notion that she was some sort of hardened criminal.

"I promise I'll do everything I can to get you out

of here." He didn't want to leave her alone, but she shooed him away.

"You'd better go back and sit with Parry. We need to know if anyone else speaks to him about this, or perhaps he'll drop a hint about who else he thinks could have done it."

George reluctantly walked away, but his heart jumped with renewed hope as two people suddenly burst into the police station, clearly in a hurry.

"I've just heard about John Flanders being found dead on the beach." The first man was a fisherman George recognised, who lived further around the coast but occasionally brought his catch to Stonehaven to sell to a costermonger, who took fish to the local market. "I came as soon as I could." He sounded panicked.

"Aye. What of it?" Parry grunted suspiciously.

"I was moored in Stonehaven Harbour last night. It was a bright moon, and I was late heading out to sea because I had a problem with my sail. I heard two men arguing on the beach."

The constable's chair scraped as he abruptly stood up and leaned over his desk. "Are you absolutely sure about that?"

The fisherman nodded firmly. "Yes, sir. You could tell they were trying to be quiet about it, but the more heated it got, the louder they started shouting at each other. There was nobody else around, and then they started fighting. I was tempted to row back to shore to break the fight up, it was that vicious."

"But you didn't."

"The tide was running, Constable, and I couldn't afford to stay inshore any longer. Money's tight with another little 'un on the way and four more mouths at home to feed."

"And why are you only telling me this now?" Parry's neck turned red, and he ran a finger around his collar, glancing nervously in George's direction.

"It's like I said, I've been out with my nets all day." The fisherman shrugged. "I shouldn't have bothered staying out for so long, not once the wind got up, but I kept hoping I would catch a few more fish. You know how it is. I heard everyone talking about it at the tavern as soon as I got back." His eyebrows twitched upwards in disbelief. "Folk are saying you're blaming that nice young lady who owns the North Star Inn? I think you're making a terrible mistake—"

Constable Parry strode round from behind his desk, barging past George, and bundled the fisherman back outside again. "Thank you, Mr Carson.

I'll bear what you said in mind, and please don't go gossiping about this to all and sundry."

"Aye, well, the man Flanders was fighting with was a similar build. A nasty piece of work with no conscience if you ask me, so you'd better catch him quickly. We don't want someone like that roaming the town."

Constable Parry hurried back inside again, jingling the keys on his belt.

"What do you want?" he barked at the other fellow, who had been watching everything with interest.

"I'm just a messenger," the young man explained quickly, worried that the constable was in danger of losing his temper. "Chief Inspector Pritchard told me to deliver this message to you."

Parry snatched the letter from the man's hand and turned away slightly.

"I must say, the Chief Inspector didn't seem in a very good mood when he gave it to me," the young man added, rather unhelpfully, George thought. "Sounded like he couldn't believe what you did."

George edged a little bit closer, and Constable Parry finally cracked, throwing up his hands and handing him the note. "You may as well read it while

I go and let her out. But if you ever speak one word of this to anyone else, I shall—"

"Don't worry, my lips are sealed as long as you do the right thing for Katie," he said hastily, doing his best to keep the relief out of his voice.

"I take it there's no reply?" The young man in his smart uniform smirked as he waited.

"Just tell the Chief Inspector I've done as he wished, and this unfortunate incident won't be logged in any of my notes." He coughed awkwardly. "It's just an unfortunate misunderstanding…"

Constable Parry strode out to the back to unlock the cell. George heard him apologising profusely and took the opportunity to read the note, which had been written on thick vellum paper with the senior policeman's flourishing signature at the bottom.

It was clear Chief Inspector Pritchard was exceedingly cross that Constable Parry had arrested Sir William Cavendish's granddaughter…the same Sir William who had, in the past, played a significant role in the great institution of British governance and attended Parliament in London, not to mention being a generous benefactor to the local constabulary for many years. He tucked the letter under the edge of one of the books on Parry's desk, almost feeling sorry for him.

"At last!" He grinned as Katie ran towards him a moment later, her face radiant with relief. "I'll walk you home." He offered her his arm, and she tucked her hand into the crook of his elbow.

"Please accept my heartfelt apology again, Miss Anderson." The constable rushed past them to open the door and escort them out. "I'm sure Ernie Waite meant no harm by suggesting you had something to do with this dreadful crime."

"He's probably scared stiff of Mr Flanders." Katie gave him a polite smile. "We all make mistakes, so let's forgive and forget, and I hope you catch the awful person who actually took John Flanders' life."

"I shall certainly be following up every line of enquiry."

George held back what he wanted to say, following Katie's lead of kindness. "If you want our help with anything, just ask."

"I'm not sure that will be needed."

"If John Flanders was up to no good again, it might not be over, even though he's dead now. Stonehaven doesn't deserve to be dragged back into those terrible days when people were afraid to walk the lanes at night."

"I quite agree, Mr Morgan." Parry stepped outside and looked up and down the dark, empty lane with a new glint of determination in his eyes. "I know what people say about my father, but whether it was true or not, I don't condone smuggling or any other criminal behaviour. Good evening, Miss Anderson."

"Do come and visit us at the inn. Beryl makes delicious pies, and now this misunderstanding has been sorted out, I'm sure we can all behave in a neighbourly fashion."

George was filled with even more admiration for her as they left the police station behind. Most people would have had harsh words to say to the constable for his bumbling error, but Katie wasn't like that. It only made him love her even more.

They walked in silence for a while as they passed the beach where the terrible death had been discovered; then he told her how Beryl had practically snatched the keys off the constable's belt in her quest to get her released, trying to lighten the moment.

"I swear, Constable Parry looked like he'd met his match when Beryl and Agatha both started on at him. They're a formidable pair."

Katie laughed, and he thought it was the sweetest sound he had heard all day. "You're telling me. When Beryl first arrived, I thought we'd have fireworks; they're both so strong-minded. But once they realised they had different skills, and I needed them both if we were to make a success of the inn, things settled down. They're firm friends now."

"That sounds a lot like my Ma." He sighed as they turned off the road, and the lights from the inn's windows twinkled up ahead in the darkness.

"Is something wrong?

"Oh, sorry, it's nothing." He shook his head.

"You can tell me, George. I don't want us to have any secrets."

"Ma hasn't been herself lately. A few times, I thought she was going to tell me what's on her mind, but she didn't."

"I'd like to meet her," Katie said quietly. She checked herself. "I…I mean, not in a formal way that implies we're more than friends," she added hastily.

He stopped walking and turned to face her. "After today, I've been thinking," he began. His heart thumped as the glow of lamplight from the inn cast a soft glow over them. "I know we haven't known each other long, but I feel as though we're meant to be…"

"Together?" she whispered, hope flaring in her eyes.

He reached out and rested his hands gently on her shoulders. "Katie, do you think we—"

The front door suddenly flew open, and Beryl came hobbling towards them as fast as she could, with tears in her eyes, closely followed by Agatha. "Lawks! Is it really you, Katie? God bless us all...we thought we'd have to tell Ebenezer to hire the finest barrister to defend you in court."

George hastily stepped backwards and thought he glimpsed a hint of regret in Katie's eyes before she threw her arms around Beryl's shoulders. "It was all a big mistake, there's no need to worry anymore. I promised Constable Parry he's very welcome to come here for a meal."

Beryl sniffed and dabbed her tears away. "I suppose so. As long as he pays."

Katie chuckled. "Now then, Beryl. What have you always told me about forgiveness?"

"Did we interrupt you young ones talking about something important," Agatha asked, nudging Beryl with a mischievous smile. "An embrace perhaps?" she murmured under her breath.

"No, it can keep." George wondered how the two middle-aged women could make him go red quite so easily.

"Well, don't forget to carry on the conversation you were both having. We don't want to stand in the way of true love." Beryl smiled innocently as Agatha nudged her again.

They walked into the warm fug of the taproom,

where a cheer went up from the locals, and Katie turned to make sure he felt included. "I think we've earned a celebratory plate of apple crumble, George," she said, holding his gaze. "To mark a better future for us, hopefully," she added, and he nodded happily.

CHAPTER 22

Half an hour later, Katie and George were sitting down at the table in the corner, tucked away from the other guests so they could have a bit of peace while they ate their supper. Wilbur ambled over, pulled up a chair, and leaned his elbows on the table. "I don't mind saying you gave us a fright today, Katie. Poor Beryl has been at sixes and sevens all afternoon."

She reached across the table and squeezed her brother's hand. "I had to trust that justice would prevail. Thankfully, a fisherman came in and said he saw someone fighting with John Flanders on the beach. Between that and a scathing letter from the Chief Inspector, Constable Parry was full of apologies by the time I left."

"I don't think any of you should wander the lanes alone until they've caught whoever did this." George frowned as he finished his last mouthful of roast mutton and eyed the extra-large portion of apple crumble Beryl had insisted on giving him. "He's a dangerous man and still at large."

Katie smiled at him and nodded. "I agree. I won't rest easy until we know all of this is over. I wonder who it was? It sounds like John's been extorting money from business owners for some time."

"Exactly. It's a wonder Lord Bevan never found out what Flanders was doing. Being a rent collector gave him the perfect opportunity to extort money, I suppose. Perhaps it was one of his poor victims who finally snapped. It's hard enough making a living without someone like him threatening your business."

"How have our regular customers been today?" Katie asked Wilbur, wanting to change the subject. "I was afraid nobody would show up once word got out that Parry had me locked up at the police station."

Wilbur leaned back in his chair and crossed his arms, glancing around the taproom. He nodded amiably to a couple of farmers who raised their glasses, still celebrating Katie's return. "Surprisingly supportive. If anything, the locals said that Constable Parry is rather lacking in common sense. He's fine at dealing with a bit of pickpocketing or poaching, but they all said he would be out of his depth with this. Besides, our new friends know you wouldn't do something that terrible. I heard a few whispers about Flanders' murky past. Most of them swear he was involved in smuggling back in the day, even though he denied it."

"And did we have any travellers from afar staying the night? I haven't popped across to the stables to speak to Tim yet."

Wilbur sat up straighter, suddenly huffing with frustration at himself. "I completely forgot to tell you, what with everything that's been going on—"

"What is it? Has there been a problem?" Her heart sank.

"No…yes. We have two charming old ladies staying for the night. They are cousins, and they were very complimentary about their bedrooms. They said a merchant they know in Bristol recommended staying here because it's suitable for single ladies, with no rough behaviour to contend with."

"That's nice to know. I hope they didn't get wind of me being at the police station. That's the last thing we want visitors from away to find out."

"No, it's nothing that bad." Wilbur gulped down his mug of tea as he spoke to her. "It was rather strange, actually. They dined in the parlour just like our guests always do, and even though I had the fire lit and added plenty of wood, they said they couldn't get warm."

Katie was about to eat a mouthful of crumble and she put her spoon down. "That is very strange. The watchmaker who was travelling to London to stay with his son said the same thing last week. What is it about the parlour that's making the room so cold?"

"It's an old building," George remarked. "When the wind changes direction and the autumn storms blow in, it can get chilly here on the coast."

"They were sitting by the bookcase," Wilbur continued, still looking puzzled. "I went in three times to add extra wood to the fire, but they said there was a terrible draught around their ankles."

Katie ate on in silence for a moment, thinking about what he said. "I'm going to have to investigate. I pride myself on our customers having a warm, comfortable stay with us, and feeling cold this early in the autumn isn't good. If there are gaps around the window where the wind is getting in, we'll have to block them up." She stood up and smoothed her skirt. "I'll be back in a moment."

"Let me come with you." George scraped the last spoonful of his meal and drained his mug of tea. "It might just be the wind blowing down the chimney, and you don't want to get your gown dirty with soot."

Wilbur also stood up and followed them. "I'll show you where they were sitting. The two ladies are upstairs, so there's nobody in the parlour now. They decided to retire early, and Agatha put warming pans in their beds. They weren't upset; they just wanted us to know."

Katie bustled into the parlour ahead of them. Even though it was getting late, she was still fizzing with energy and knew that if she went to bed, she wouldn't fall asleep for hours.

"This is where they were sitting?" She pointed to the corner furthest from the window.

Wilbur nodded. "Yes, the table between the fire and the alcove, and they said how nice it was to see all the books on the bookshelf."

Katie took hold of one side of the table, and George grabbed the other side, and they pulled it away from the bookshelf. Then she stood there with her hands on her hips, looking at the bookcase in the alcove. It was lined with leather-bound books which she had discovered in a tea chest upstairs and decided to put out for guests in case they wanted to read. "It's true. I can feel a cold draught around my ankles. Look, the flame on the candle is flickering as well. It seems to be coming from the direction of the alcove, not the fireplace or the window."

"That doesn't make any sense." Wilbur scratched his head. "But I agree. I can feel a cold wind seeping into the room."

A thought snagged at Katie's memory, and she rushed forward, rifling through the books. "Mama once told me there was a secret passage at Castleford Hall, Wilbur. It led from the study down to the cellar, but Grandpa blocked it off in case we ever found it and got trapped. Perhaps we have something similar here."

George's blue eyes sparkled with intrigue. "A secret passage? That would be an exciting find."

She stood back again slightly and eyed the bookcase, then kicked away the rug she had put on the floor in front of it. "Look, I'm right!" She pointed at the scuff marks on the floor in the shape of an arc. "I didn't think anything of those marks before. The bookcase must be a door, and you can see where it's been opened in the past." She stepped forward again and slid some of the books sideways, delicately feeling the wooden panelling for something unusual.

Suddenly, she felt the wood give under her fingers in the corner of one of the shelves. It felt like some sort of sprung panel. "I think I've found something," she muttered, closing her eyes to concentrate on what she could feel. "It's moving." She pressed harder, and the entire bookcase clicked and shifted a couple of inches towards her, exactly like a door swinging open. Her heart thudded with excitement.

"Crikey, you were right." George looked shocked.

"Our very own secret passage," Wilbur exclaimed.

"Run and fetch some lanterns, Wilbur, and make sure you shut the parlour door behind us. Just tell Beryl and the others that we're having a business meeting in the parlour for a little while."

"What about taking Galahad with us?"

"No, we don't know what we might encounter. He might run ahead and get stuck."

George grinned at her. "I never knew you were this adventurous."

"Well, you'd better get used to it," she chuckled. "Perhaps we have a cellar full of bottles of wine that I'll be able to sell."

"Or maybe it just leads to the stables," George countered. "It wasn't unusual to have passageways in these old taverns. Let's not get our hopes up too much."

A thought suddenly occurred to her. "Maybe that's how the person got in to write the message on the mirror and they left the window open to cover their tracks."

Wilbur returned with three lanterns, and George carefully swung the secret panel open and wedged a chair against it so it couldn't close behind them. A cold chill wafted from the opening, which explained why their guests had felt it, too. Katie expected the hinges to squeak from years of not being used, but it opened as easily as any of the doors in the building.

"I'll go first," George said, looking at her for approval.

"That's a good idea. And I'll be right behind you," she gave him a rueful smile. "It's probably only about twenty yards long, and we're going to look very silly, thinking it's something more exciting. Never mind, it will be an adventure to tell the others about. I just hope there aren't too many cobwebs."

"What can you see?" Wilbur asked from the back.

"A short passageway then steps leading down." George peered into the gloom, then reached for Katie's hand. "Are you sure you want to come?"

"Just try and stop me." She looked up into his blue eyes, enjoying the sensation of his comforting grip on her hand. "We work things out together now, don't we?" she added lightly.

As they cautiously descended the steep steps in the dark passageway, the lanterns cast flickering shadows on the damp stone walls around them, making them look like evil caricatures of themselves. The tunnel was narrow, pressing in on either side as if the earth itself was closing around them, and the steps beneath Katie's boots were worn smooth, making her wonder just how many people had made the journey before them and why.

"Is everyone fine?" George's question sounded unexpectedly loud, echoing around them before being swallowed by the heavy silence again.

"Yes, thank you," she replied quickly.

"We seem to be descending quite deep into the ground," Wilbur called from the back.

As they moved onwards, the musty air grew even colder, and the dank moisture caught in her throat, making her cough. "Do you think this leads to the sea?" Katie ducked her head as the passageway grew even more cramped for a few yards. There was a distinct smell of briny water and seaweed.

"I shouldn't be surprised." George paused for a moment and checked over his shoulder to see if she was okay.

At the bottom of the steps, the walls of the passageway changed from the wooden struts and neat bricks that reminded her of a mine shaft to be replaced by jagged rocks that scraped her arms if she didn't take care. She gripped her lantern tighter and was relieved as the passage gradually widened so they could walk side-by-side. Water dripped from unseen cracks above, and she tried not to think of the deep loam soil and woodland above her head or the fact that if the tunnel collapsed, they would be crushed and lost forever.

"We should have worn hats," Wilbur joked. He ran his hand through his hair and chuckled as another drip landed on his forehead.

"At least the air is fresher down here." George lifted his lantern up and tilted his head slightly. "Can you hear that noise?"

They fell silent, each listening to the distant thump and swoosh. "It must be the waves…that's what we can hear. We'd better hurry; we don't want to be gone for too long from the inn." Katie brushed a wet strand of something she didn't want to look too closely at off her shoulder and strode ahead. The floor had flattened out, but it was slippery, so they had to walk carefully. Every so often, there were dark puddles of water that they had no choice but to splash through, and the cold bite of it seeping through her boots up to her ankles made her gasp.

"How much further do you think it goes on for?" Wilbur asked, bumping into her as she paused to hitch her sodden skirt up higher.

"We must nearly be at the end now." George reached for her hand again. "Just around this corner..."

Without warning, the tunnel suddenly opened into a cave. The walls curved away into shadows, the rocks striped with strange markings formed millennia ago, and the ceiling arched above them. They stood there in awe for a moment before Katie suddenly realised they were not the only people to have set foot in the place.

"Look!" She pointed to the darkest corner. "What are all those tea chests and banded trunks? This is being used as some sort of store."

"Also, have you noticed how dry it is?" George bent over and picked up a handful of the sand at his feet, letting it run through his fingers. "I thought the water in the tunnel was seawater, but it must be groundwater seeping through from above. This is the perfect place to store things away from prying eyes."

"What's in the boxes?" Wilbur hurried across to

the ledge at one side of the cave, formed where the rock had been gouged out by the sea at some point. He lifted one of the lids and let out a delighted laugh. "Bottles of rum…dozens of them." The glass chinked as he moved them. "Fine French brandy as well. This will be worth a pretty penny."

Katie and George joined him. Surprisingly, only a few of the tea chests were nailed shut, so it was easy enough for them to peek inside and see what the contents were.

"This one is full of paintings." George rested his lantern on a rock and gently lifted one of the gilt-framed pictures. "I'm no expert, but that looks like the sort of oil painting a well-to-do person would have hanging in their drawing room."

"And this one is full of exquisite bone china." Katie carefully examined the teacup lying at the top. She moved the straw packed between the items and let out a low whistle as something gold gleamed softly beneath her fingers. "There are priceless figurines as well. I can't even imagine how much they're worth. Even Grandpa didn't have things this grand at Castleford Hall."

A gust of wind made their lamps flicker, and Katie looked nervously over her shoulder at the dense shadows surrounding them. "We must leave everything exactly as we found it," she said urgently, carefully replacing the teacup and closing the lid again. "Everything in here has surely been stolen. What other reason could there be to have it hidden somewhere like this?"

Walking back to the centre of the cave, the worry was palpable in the air between them.

George let out a long sigh and shook his head. "Ernie Waite was right. The smugglers are back, or perhaps they never even stopped."

"You don't seem that surprised." Katie looked at him, but his expression was hard to read. "I suppose it's because everyone here grew up knowing about the smugglers."

Before he could reply, Wilbur ran to the front of the cave, peering out to the sandy cove and the sea beyond. It was low tide, and he beckoned for them to join him. "Look up there." He pulled Katie further out, away from the cave, and pointed at the sheer cliffs rising into the night sky behind them. In the pale moonlight, she could see the jagged rocks, with loose scree and a few stubby plants clinging between the crevices. "There's no path from this cove to get to the top of the cliffs."

A dawning realisation hit Katie, and her stomach lurched. "That must be what the lights in the woods have been these last few months. The smugglers must have been using the secret passage to our inn to get their stolen goods onto dry land and away to whoever is buying them."

George nodded, his expression grim. "Of course. And since you arrived, they can't do that anymore. They've been looking for an alternative route through the woods and down to the cave."

"The smugglers have probably been using our coaching inn for years." Anger flared in her chest. "Grandpa paid Agatha and Vernon Tremaine to be caretakers, but you should have seen the state of the place when we arrived, George. It was clear they just left it locked up. I bet they had no idea the smugglers were using it as a bolt hole and part of their getaway plan for landing stolen goods."

"You don't think the Tremaines turned a blind eye on purpose, do you?" Wilbur blurted out, looking upset. "I really like them, but perhaps they've been part of the criminal activity all along?"

"No," Katie shook her head. "These smugglers are cunning. They knew Vernon and Agatha lived separately in their little cottage in the woods. All they needed was a lookout to ensure they weren't noticed. The parlour can't be seen from their cottage. No wonder the smugglers have been trying to scare us away. We've scuppered all their plans, and I expect they must be getting desperate."

"Why wouldn't they just load the stolen goods onto another boat and take them further up the coast?" Wilbur was still puzzled.

"The Customs officers patrol the coastal areas, although not as much as they used to. I expect the smugglers might think about that as a last resort, but it would be risky. They only have to encounter a fisherman out at sea asking them what they're doing."

Katie paced on the beach for a moment, her thoughts whirling. "We'd better get back in the cave. Anyone could be watching from the edge of the cliff above. The light from our lantern will reveal our whereabouts." They hurried back into the gloomy cavern, all looking shocked.

"What should we do next?" Wilbur was dragging an old branch with dried leaves on it, which had been washed up on the tide and started sweeping it across the sand to conceal their footprints.

"We have to speak to someone who might be able to help us make sense of it all," George said firmly.

"Constable Parry?" Katie shivered. Having just got away from his bungling ineptitude, she didn't hold out much hope of him being able to shed any light on what they had discovered.

"Goodness me, certainly not Constable Parry." He shot her a wry smile. "He's the last person we should tell about this."

"Who then?" Wilbur asked before Katie had a chance.

George hesitated for a moment. "My Ma, that's who. She will know what this is all about."

She couldn't keep the surprise from her face. "Is that wise, George? I thought you said your ma hasn't been in very good health recently."

He rasped his hand over his jaw. "She hasn't really been well since Pa died. But that's exactly why we need to speak to her. I have a feeling this all goes back to the past."

She reached out in the darkness and squeezed his hand. "If you think that's the right thing to do, then I agree. Do you want to do it alone, or—?"

"I want you to come with me," he said without missing a beat. "Ma's been asking to meet you anyway, and now I think it's time."

Her heart lifted with happiness. Despite their troubling discovery, she was warmed by the fact that George wanted her to get to know his ma.

"Wilbur, you'd better stay behind at the inn to

look after the others. Tell them everything that we've found and what our suspicions are, but make it clear they're not to discuss this with anyone. We don't know who we can trust at the moment. I'll go with George to find out what his ma knows, and then we can decide what we need to do next."

As they retraced their route, the shadows loomed over them like scuttling ghouls on the cave walls. She could still hear the distant thump of the waves, but as the noise gradually receded and they started the long climb up the slippery steps again, she knew they had to do something. Her livelihood and the safety of her family were at stake. Doing nothing wasn't an option; she was certain of that.

CHAPTER 23

As they walked briskly through the cobbled lanes of Stonehaven, Katie wondered whether they had left it too late at night to speak to George's mother. She was relieved to see a candle burning brightly in the window of their white-washed cottage, and there was smoke curling from the chimney.

"She said she would stay up until she knew you were safe from Constable Parry's clutches." He grinned as he held the small wooden gate open for her.

The front door opened just as they walked up the short garden path. The path was edged with late-flowering roses that released their sweet, musky scent as Katie's gown brushed against them, and there were fishing nets draped over the wall.

"What a relief, Katie." Catrin Morgan greeted her with open arms, exuding warmth and kindness. She was short and plump, and her grey dress had colourful patches around the hem. "I've been worried all day, cariad. I'm so glad George has finally brought you here for a visit. He talks about you all the time, and I know we're going to be great friends."

"It's very nice to meet you, Mrs Morgan. George talks a lot about you as well, and I can see where he gets so many of his wonderful traits from now."

"Call me Catrin, my dear." She bustled ahead of them into the cosy kitchen. There was already a teapot with three cups and side plates laid out on the table, and the kettle started whistling before Katie had even had a chance to take off her shawl.

"Ma always says she has a sixth sense about when I'm coming home," George said cheerfully, smacking a hearty kiss on his mother's wrinkled cheek.

"'Tis a mother's instinct," she chuckled.

Now they were inside, in the glow of soft lamplight, Katie could see that there was a great likeness between them. Catrin and George both had the same brown hair and blue eyes, although hers were a little faded with age now. Laughter lines fanned out from her eyes, and her skin was tanned from hours spent outside mending George's nets. The cottage smelled of dried lavender and beeswax, and there were shells dotted on the dresser and windowsills. Catrin leaned on a walking stick as she bustled between the dresser and the table. "You'll have something to eat?" She lifted the muslin cloth that was draped over half a fruitcake and cut two generous slices for them, plus a smaller one for herself.

"Thank you, and please tell me if there's anything I can do to help."

Catrin glanced at her stick and pulled a face. "Don't worry, dear, I'm not as frail as I look. I just use the stick because Doctor Hawkesworth said I might have dizzy spells sometimes. It's a legacy of that silly cough I've had ever since George's pa, Emyr, died. I spent hours on the beach that night, got soaked to the skin, and ended up in bed with influenza for months. My lungs have never been the same since, but we get by, don't we, George."

George patted his mother's shoulder and pulled out a chair for her to sit down before doing the same for Katie. She could see there was genuine affection between them by the thoughtful way he lit a couple of extra candles and lifted the heavy kettle off the stove to fill the teapot for her.

THE FARTHING GIRL

Once they were all sitting down, Catrin gave them both a shrewd look. "Are you going to tell me what's been going on then? I already found out from Betty Kemp that that bumbling fool Constable Parry let you go a little while ago. Lord knows he wasn't blessed with much common sense when he came to this earth, but he does his best."

Katie took a mouthful of the rich fruitcake to hide her smile. With her forthright demeanour, Catrin reminded her a lot of Beryl, but she liked it.

For the next few minutes, George explained about the secret passageway and all the stolen items they had found hidden in the cave. Catrin's expression grew more serious, and Katie noticed she had stopped eating. She was just crumbling the cake on the plate in front of her as if her appetite had disappeared.

"It seems a strange coincidence that John Flanders was found dead on the beach this morning," George finished. "Something doesn't feel right, Ma."

His mother took a sip of tea and then let out a long sigh before reaching across to pat George's arm. Katie had a horrible feeling bad news was coming. "There's something I have to tell you about John Flanders."

George shrugged. "It's fine, Ma. I know what the

rumours were about Pa working for him, but he only ever did legitimate jobs. Isn't that right?"

Catrin glanced away, looking at the candle in the window for a moment. "The thing is, George, John came to our home the morning your father died."

"I don't remember that." George frowned.

"I saw him loitering outside, so I sent you to buy butter and flour from Alwyn. I didn't like him being around you."

"What did he want?"

Catrin sighed again. "It was what I always feared. Your father did do a few legitimate jobs for John, but I always suspected the day would come when John would want more. Sure enough, he tried to force Emyr to carry stolen goods. He told him unless he joined their ranks and got involved with the smuggling, he would make sure all sorts of trouble would befall us."

George's expression darkened. "I always knew he was a scoundrel, but I never knew he threatened you and Pa."

Katie's heart went out to him, and without thinking, she reached across and brushed her fingers over his hand. The gesture didn't go unnoticed by his mother, who gave her a small smile of appreciation.

"Emyr told John he wanted nothing to do with it."

Her expression softened for a moment. "He was a man of principles, your father, which was one of many things I loved about him. Anyway, there was a big argument. John didn't like someone disobeying him, and he stormed off, swearing we would regret it."

"And later that night, when Pa went fishing..." George's voice hitched slightly. He didn't need to finish the sentence.

Catrin nodded, her eyes misting with tears. "I always suspected the Flanders brothers had something to do with my dear Emyr's passing, but it's water under the bridge now. Except...I think that might not be the end of it." Her face pinched with worry, and her hands trembled slightly as she poured them all another cup of tea from the pot.

A sudden noise outside startled them, and George jumped up and flung open the door, looking out into the dark night. "It's just a cat looking for scraps of fish." He shut the door firmly again and came back to the table. Katie could tell that something was troubling him. He took a deep breath and gave Catrin a straight look. "I think there's something you're not telling us, Ma. I know you're doing it because you think it will protect us, but we need to know. Finding these smuggled goods in the cave earlier…and John Flanders' murder…plus the lights in the woods by the North Star Inn that I told you about…I can't shake the feeling that they're all connected, but I don't know how."

"I think you're right, son." Catrin's blue eyes darkened with the memories flooding back, and she twisted the edge of her lace handkerchief. "John Flanders had a younger brother, Carwyn. He was a jealous, cruel man and always wanted to be in charge, but John wouldn't allow it."

"I never knew that."

"He fled to France when the Customs officers started sniffing around. Everyone in Stonehaven breathed a sigh of relief. We thought he'd gone for good, and I can assure you nobody here missed him. John Flanders might have been a bully, but Carwyn was far worse. He thought nothing of ruining the reputation of young ladies or brawling viciously for whatever he wanted. It was only his cowardly fear of being sent to jail that made him run away to France."

A gust of wind blew down the chimney, sending a couple of sparks from the fire onto the rug, so Katie jumped up and stamped them out, then put the fire guard in place.

"Thank you, dear." Catrin gave her a weary smile.

"Usually, I make sure to do that myself, but I've had such a lot on my mind the last few days."

"Please tell us what's troubling you, Ma." George squeezed her hand again. "I'm not a young boy anymore; I want to look after you."

"I visited Betty Kemp a couple of nights ago. We've known each other since we were girls," Catrin added for Katie's benefit. "We like to put the world to rights over a mug of hot chocolate."

"Friendships like that are something to treasure."

"Exactly." Catrin grinned, looking like a young woman again for a split second. "I knew Katie would be right for you, George. I could just tell by the way you described her."

He coughed awkwardly, which Katie found rather endearing. "We can talk about that another time, Ma. What about the night you visited Betty?"

"Ah yes…now let me see, where was I?" Catrin sipped her tea, then carried on. "It was dark by the time I walked home. When I got near The Rose and Crown Tavern, I saw a man in the alleyway out the back talking to two fishermen. There was something familiar about him, and it sounded like they were making plans they didn't want anyone to overhear, so I crossed the lane to get closer—"

"Ma." George's voice was sharp with worry. "What if they were dangerous?"

"Nobody pays any attention to an old lady hobbling past." She rolled her eyes. "How else was I going to find out what they were talking about?"

Katie chuckled. "You probably know more about the ne'er-do-wells in Stonehaven than Constable Parry."

"That wouldn't be hard." A glint of amusement flickered in her eyes, but then she grew serious again. "When I got closer, I heard them talking about the Rhoswell Lighthouse, then something about the full moon and hoping for a storm. It didn't make much sense to me."

"Maybe he was warning the fishermen not to go out in bad weather?" Katie knew that wasn't likely as soon as she said it. "They would know that already, though."

"I thought nothing more of it, but as I walked away, I saw the man giving them money. They went back into the tavern, and the man left." She paused, twisting her handkerchief absentmindedly again. "He took his hat off for a moment, and that's when I got a good look at him."

"Who was it?" George leaned closer.

"I swear on my life, it was Carwyn Flanders. I'd

recognise him anywhere. He's back in Stonehaven, George, and his brother ends up dead two days later. It can't be a coincidence."

There was a beat of silence as everyone digested this shocking revelation, then George stood up abruptly and shot the bolt across the door. He turned slowly, not quite meeting her eye, and Katie's stomach lurched again. *More bad news?* She gripped her hands tightly together under the table and reminded herself that George was a good man...and that she loved him. They would get through whatever was happening.

"I have a confession," he began, walking to and fro next to the table. "I've been in the pay of the Customs Officers for the last year."

Catrin gasped. "Doing what?"

"Don't think badly of me, Ma. I hated keeping it secret from you...and you, Katie, but it was too dangerous to tell anyone. They asked me to listen out for rumours of smugglers working along this coast. I did it to honour Pa's memory because he always told me that smugglers are cowards who prey on the weak and cause heartache for the people they stole from."

"You don't have to apologise to me," Katie said firmly. "I agree with you. Grandpa used to say the same about poachers, and that was why he always paid his workers a better wage than most."

"Do they think the smuggling is starting up again?" Catrin asked. "That might explain why Carwyn Flanders is back."

George's expression was grim. "It probably never stopped, Ma. They just got cleverer about it."

"Have you heard any rumours?" Katie looked up at him. "Or maybe you can't tell us."

"No, but when I saw Mr Oakley last week, the Customs Officer I meet up with secretly every now and again, he told me there's a boat carrying priceless artworks from Lisbon to Cardiff passing by here any day. It's for a grand exhibition. Even Queen Victoria and other European royals might visit it, he said."

Katie stood up as well. "If that's true, we have no time to lose. The full moon is tomorrow night."

"And you've seen how the weather is changing, George," Catrin chimed in, grabbing her walking stick and standing up as well. "The first full moon of autumn is often when we have a big storm."

"We should tell Mr Oakley about what we found in the cave. And ask if anyone local knows what Carwyn Flanders is planning."

"There's no time for that." George raked a hand

through his hair. "Oakley and his colleagues are busy in Bristol docks at the moment because they are short-handed. We won't be able to get a message to him in time for them to travel here before the storm."

"Do you think Carwyn is hoping the ship might run aground so he can steal some of the pictures?" Katie shivered at the idea of it.

"I'm not sure. Maybe he's hoping to move the stolen goods from the cave? It would be risky, but Carwyn would know folk wouldn't be out during an autumn storm."

Catrin hobbled past them and slid the bolt back on the door. "You must stay with Katie and her family at the inn tonight, George."

"Are you sure?" He looked torn. "I don't like leaving you alone."

She gestured for them to leave, patting Katie on her shoulder. "I'll be fine. Katie needs someone she can trust and who better than you? If I hear anything else, I'll get word to you."

"And we must try and work out what Flanders is planning," Katie added, linking arms with George. "Thank you for making me feel so welcome, Catrin. Once all this is over, you must come and meet Beryl. I have a feeling you'll get on like a house on fire."

Catrin waved them off, and Katie glanced up at the moon. The wind had definitely picked up in the time they'd been inside, and she could hear the thump of the waves on the beach. "Can we really go up against someone like Carwyn Flanders?" She grabbed her bonnet as the wind tried to snatch it off her head.

"We don't have any choice. It's time the Flanders brothers' reign of terror was brought to an end."

"For your pa and our friends and neighbours," Katie added.

CHAPTER 24

*K*atie yawned as she pinned her hair up the following morning, then pinched her cheeks to bring some colour to them. It had been a late night by the time she and George had sat down with all her family and Beryl, Agatha, and Vernon to tell them everything.

Beryl had been all for saddling the horse and sending Wilbur off to visit Ebenezer until he reminded her he and Gabriel would probably come in the morning anyway, thanks to the telegram he'd sent when Katie was still locked up in the police station.

Then Agatha sensibly told them they would be useless if they didn't get to bed. Vernon and Tim volunteered to take turns sitting up to make sure nobody broke in, and even though Katie's head was spinning with all the discoveries of the day, she had fallen asleep as soon as her head hit the pillow.

"Don't rush to get up," she whispered to Polly, opening the door between their two rooms a crack. "It's still early."

Her sister sat up and rubbed the sleep from her eyes. "I'll help Beryl make breakfast shortly. I had terrible dreams. Five more minutes, then I'll get dressed."

Suddenly, the sound of loud hammering on the front door echoed up the stairs. Galahad let out a volley of barks and bounded down the stairs as Katie ran after him.

The hammering started again just as she and George reached the door at the same time. He had slept in one of the empty guest rooms for the night, but Katie noticed he was already dressed, and judging by the strands of straw clinging to his trousers, he had been working in the stables.

Katie wrenched the door open and was surprised to see Ernie Waite standing there. His hair was dishevelled, his eyes were bloodshot, and he was just about to start hammering again, his fist still raised in the air. He dropped his arm immediately and gave her a sheepish look.

"Good morning, Mr Waite," she said coolly. "To what do I owe the pleasure of this early visit? I'm not serving ale yet."

He whipped his cap off and turned it in his hands. "I've come to apologise," he blurted out, looking shamefaced. "I've been up most of the night talking about everything with my wife, and she told me I should come here at daybreak. I should never have said anything to Constable Parry, and I'm sorry he locked you up. I only thought he would have a quiet word with you, that's all."

Katie could sense George glowering next to her, and she turned and gave him a gentle smile before standing back to invite Ernie inside. "I accept your apology, and let's just draw a line under it, shall we?"

The cobbler turned red as Beryl marched past carrying a bucket full of muddy potatoes and glared at him. "You've got a nerve showing up here," she snapped.

"I came to apologise, Beryl. To all of you. You've shown me kindness when I've been drinking here, and I'm aware I haven't always behaved very well. But my wife reminded me that God forgives all sins, so I'm turning over a new leaf."

Beryl paused, and Katie could tell she was wrestling with her conscience. "Very well," Beryl muttered. "Folk deserve a second chance, so sit yourself down, and I'll bring you a cup of tea. You should try being nicer to that poor wife of yours as well and stop being such a skinflint with her housekeeping money."

Ernie nodded eagerly. "I intend to, Beryl." He shuffled his feet nervously, still not ready to sit down. "You probably know why I was so scared of John Flanders, Miss Anderson?" He gave her a beseeching look that clearly showed he was hoping for her understanding.

"I guess he was probably extorting money from you as well."

"Indeed." His shoulders sagged, and he looked older than his years. "It started when my father had the cobbler's shop, and John and Carwyn's father realised he could make money from hard-working people like us. Those brothers had a terrible upbringing, not to excuse how they turned out, mind you. Anyway, when Pa died, and I took over the business, John was standing on my doorstep within a week, demanding that the little arrangement continue. It's given me many sleepless nights, I can tell you."

"I don't like to speak ill of the dead, but I'm sure there will be a few townsfolk breathing a sigh of relief now that John is gone." George's gaze flickered towards Katie, and she knew he wasn't quite ready to reveal what they knew about Carwyn.

Ernie's next comment caught them both by surprise. "I think John's brother is back from France. I've heard a couple of rumours, and I wouldn't be surprised if it was their rivalry that was the end of John."

"I've heard something similar," George said carefully.

"Apart from apologising, there's another reason why I had to see you early today." Ernie pulled a piece of paper from his pocket and handed it to Katie. "John came to my house the night before he died on his monthly visit to collect money from me. It was dark, and he accidentally dropped this note on the floor when he left. I thought you should both see it because it mentions the North Star Inn."

Katie unfolded the piece of paper, and she and George looked at it together as she read it out. At first, it looked like a random list of disjointed phrases.

"The North Star Inn…the full moon, and today's date…Steps from the parlour bookcase…The Albion…" She frowned at that last one.

"That's the name of the ship coming from Ostend," George whispered.

Ernie stepped closer, poking a calloused finger at the paper. "Look, do you see that drawing? I think it's a map. If you turn the paper around, it makes more sense. That squiggly line is the coast, and that cross there signifies the lighthouse, and the square is your inn."

Katie looked at George in shock. "It's some sort of plan about everything we were talking about, isn't it?"

"What's that, then?" Ernie sounded puzzled.

George raised his eyebrows, and she nodded, knowing without words what he was asking her. He gestured to the table where Beryl had just put a pot of tea and three plates of bacon and eggs. "I might have misjudged you in the past, Ernie. Thank you for bringing this to us, and there's a lot we have to tell you." He called Beryl back. "Can you gather everyone, please? Thanks to Ernie, we have some new information, and we'll have to try and figure out what it means."

For the next half hour, everyone tried to come up with different theories, but nothing quite seemed to fit.

"It's the drawing of the lighthouse that's

confusing me," Beryl said, looking at the scrawled map again. "What's that got to do with all the stolen goods in the cave?"

"It reminds me of that story I heard about one of the lighthouses in West Wales." Vernon nudged Agatha. "Do you remember, dear? That tramp was walking along the lane, and we gave him shelter for the night."

"Of course." Agatha's grey curls bobbed as she nodded. "He told us a lighthouse in West Wales was vandalised by smugglers deliberately so the ships would run aground."

"That's it." George groaned and glanced outside where the wind was gusting through the trees with increasing ferocity. "Pa used to tell me in the olden days, lantern men in the Fens in East Anglia would lure unsuspecting travellers into the marshes. They would rob them, and often, the poor souls would drown. This is something similar. If the ships don't see the light from the lighthouse, there's more risk of them running aground, especially in a storm. The smugglers can row out and plunder their cargo or wait for it to wash up and then steal it."

Beryl fanned herself with the edge of her apron. "Lawks, I've never heard anything so dreadful in all my life. What about the poor sailors on the ship? Don't the smugglers care if they drown?"

Ernie patted her hand. "Unfortunately not. Those of us who've grown up here have all heard those sorts of tales since we were children. It hasn't happened for a while, but I wouldn't put it past Carwyn Flanders. He always wanted to take over from his brother."

"That's what my ma said." George shook his head in disbelief. "I'll wager that John had no stomach for causing a shipwreck. Not at his age. He had a proper job working for Lord Bevan and earning a bit on the side with his extortion. I doubt he wanted to risk all of that for something that could see him spending the rest of his days in jail. I expect Carwyn tried to persuade him that they should do it together, and when John refused...well...that must have been what the fight was about."

"What can we do about it?" Katie looked at everyone sitting around the table. "If that's what Carwyn is planning tonight, which is what this note seems to imply, how can we stop it? Should we try and protect the lighthouse?"

"For all we know, he could have a dozen or more men working with him." George drummed his fingers on the table. "Other than us in this room, we can't trust anyone."

"If you can't stop them from vandalising the lighthouse, we need to think of another way to show the ship where the rocks are." Vernon scratched his head, thinking about the conundrum.

Katie clapped her hands together as an idea popped into her mind. "We have to make a beacon. They used to light them across the moors in the olden days. If you build a big enough bonfire, the flames can be seen for miles."

"Of course!" George jumped to his feet, giving her a proud smile. "Well done, Katie. That's the answer. We'll let Carwyn do whatever he and his men are planning to the lighthouse, but not far from there, I know of a flat rocky outcrop that juts over the sea. If we can build a bonfire and keep it burning through the night, that will be enough to keep the ship safe from running aground on the rocks."

Wilbur dragged his boots on and hurriedly tied the laces. "I'll start collecting as much firewood as I can with Tim. And perhaps you can help as well, George? We should have enough within a couple of hours."

"What about you, Katie?" George lowered his voice and briefly rested his hand on her shoulder.

His blue eyes were full of concern, but also something else that made her heart flutter. "Do you think you should stay here with Polly, Beryl, and Agatha? It might be dangerous."

"Certainly not. If we prepare everything now, I'll tell our guests that we are closing the inn early because of the storm later. We can't build the bonfire down by the sea until after dark anyway, in case Carwyn and his men are around, so that will work perfectly."

As they all hurried off to take care of their separate chores, Polly tidied away the plates and teacups. "You do know he loves you, don't you?" she said with a mischievous smile.

Katie just shrugged with an inward glow of happiness. "There's no time to think about romance today, Polly. We have a shipwreck to prevent. We just have to pray that luck will be on our side."

CHAPTER 25

"**G**ood horse." Katie patted Robin's neck as she looped the reins over a branch. The day felt as though it had crawled past, but as soon as darkness fell, they had all assembled to complete their plan. She clambered onto the cart seat with George. Wilbur, Tim, and Polly were in the back, with Ernie, who had insisted on joining them. Beryl, Agatha, and Vernon had stayed behind at the inn, just in case the Customs Officers arrived and needed directions.

"Are you sure it will be safe for Robin to wait here in the storm?" She eyed the thrashing branches overhead, but the placid horse just nuzzled her hand, looking for food.

"He'll be fine." Wilbur gave him a nosebag of oats.

There was already a huge mound of logs and branches nearby that they had stealthily brought down earlier in the day, plus what they had on the back of the cart.

Even though it was dark, there was just enough moonlight to see their way. "There's a track the sheep have worn in the grass where they go out onto the rocks." George pointed it out to them. "If we all carry as much wood as we can and walk single file, we can start assembling the bonfire." He hefted a log onto his shoulder, and they all followed his example. "Whatever you do, stay well back from the edge. The sea can be very unpredictable in a storm, and you're not used to it."

"Are the waves likely to come over the top?" Tim sounded worried.

"I can't say. It depends on the swell and how fierce the storm gets. I've never seen the sea come as high as the spot I've chosen for the bonfire, but…" George's words trailed off. "If I think it's too dangerous, I'll tell you to get back into the cart."

"Aye," Ernie looked serious in the weak light of the one lantern they had allowed themselves. "Listen to George, everyone. He's a man of the sea, and we all want to get home safely to our loved ones after this is over."

Galahad lifted his nose and sniffed the air. Katie had wanted to leave him at home, but the loyal dog pawed her dress until she relented. Now they were here, she was glad to have him loping along by her side. He was a comforting presence and would alert them to strangers approaching.

As she stepped out from the shelter of the woods onto the low cliff George had chosen, the ferocity of the incoming storm took her breath away. Ernie walked ahead of George, holding a blanket over one side of the lantern so it couldn't be seen from the direction of the lighthouse, and they cautiously followed.

The air was thick with the briny scent of the sea, mingling with the earthy musk of wet leaves and salt-crusted soil. She inhaled deeply, and the biting wind made her eyes water. It carried the promise of rain, though none had fallen yet despite the rumbling thunder. The sky above was a patchwork of black and silver. The thickening clouds scudded across the heavens in ragged, restless shapes, only allowing the full moon to cast its glow now and again.

They worked determinedly, in silence. Back and forth, they trudged from the shelter of the woods to the exposed rocky outcrop until their muscles burned from the exertion. Slowly, the pile of wood for their bonfire took shape. They had built it behind a low pile of rocks to keep their activities hidden from the taller clifftop along the coast for as long as possible. Every few minutes, the shaft of light from the towering lighthouse in the distance pierced the darkness, sweeping past them and out to sea, and Katie's nerves stretched tighter. There were four flashes in quick succession, then a pause before the next set of four, as regular as a heartbeat. She imagined the lighthouse keeper, high up in the circular building, checking his oil lamps, cleaning the lenses that reflected and amplified the light, polishing the glass windows, and manning the clockwork mechanism to keep it all moving during the long, dark nights.

"When should we light the bonfire?" The words were snatched from her mouth in the wind, and she leaned closer to George.

"Let me see if The Albion is out there." He waited for the next shaft of light from the lighthouse, then raised his spyglass to look out over the heaving dark water. His mouth tightened, and he lowered the spyglass again. "I think I caught a glimpse of it. Carwyn and his men will be watching, too. If I'm right, they will probably strike now and stop the lighthouse from working."

They waited with bated breath, and Katie counted the seconds passing in her head. "We should see the light again just about…now…"

Thick darkness surrounded them as the storm gathered strength. Seconds stretched into several minutes.

"That's it," George said urgently. "They've disabled the lighthouse. We have to light the bonfire now."

Ernie handed out all the torches they had made earlier, which were doused in camphine, then he carefully removed the lantern cover so they could light them from the flame.

There was a soft whoomph as the flames took hold, and she ran to the stack of wood, holding the torch to the dry kindling they had stuffed into all the gaps. The flame guttered as the wind slammed against them, and for one horrifying moment, she thought their plan would fail if the wind extinguished the flames before they could get going.

"Come to the leeward side," George cried. She circled closer to him and suddenly felt the heat of the fire on her face as the flames licked greedily up the wood.

"We did it!"

"Yes…and now we have to hope the ship will see the bonfire and that Carwyn and his men will run away thinking we have the help of the Customs Officers."

She watched the flames, mesmerised for a moment by the leaping reds and oranges and the sparks swirling upwards in the wind.

George cupped his hands around his mouth. "Stay here with Polly and keep adding more dry wood while the boys and I carry more down from by the cart."

"We will." She stumbled slightly as the wind grew stronger. "The storm's getting up. Be careful."

As George hurried away, Katie couldn't help but be in awe of the power of the elements. Beyond the rocky outcrop they were on, the sea churned in the moonlight with a wildness and raw power she had never experienced in her life. Each wave slammed against the cliffs with a mighty thud that she could feel through the soles of her boots, sending spumes of water high into the air. The swell surged and fell in menacing peaks, and the water was a mix of inky shadows and flashes of pale light as the moon briefly pierced the racing clouds. She could feel the menacing energy of the storm building, and a heavy tension hung in the air between thunderclaps, as if the sea and sky were holding their breath, waiting for the full fury of the weather to be unleashed.

"How will we know if it's working?" Katie asked after the bonfire had been burning for about half an hour.

George stood beside her, trying to shelter her from the roaring wind. He glanced skyward. "We need a break in the clouds and some moonlight."

As if on command, the ragged clouds parted, and they both ran towards the edge of the rocks, desperately scanning the heaving waves.

"There…is that them?"

"Yes," George nodded. They watched the ship being tossed about in the silvery moonlight, and Katie sent up a silent prayer as she saw the men frantically trimming the sails. The captain stood on the deck and waved at them before turning to help another crew member, who was wrestling with the ship's wheel.

"I think they've done it, Katie," George said, with a hitch of emotion in his voice. "They've managed to turn the ship just in time. Can you see the angle of the sails?"

A cloud scudded across the moon again, but as soon as the sky brightened slightly, Katie realised he was right. Even though it looked terrifyingly close to the perilous rocks that she knew were just beneath the surface of the sea, inch by inch, the ship was turning away from them.

"The wind has changed direction as well," George cried happily. "It's coming from behind us now? That's exactly what The Albion needs—an offshore wind."

Just as George finished speaking, the heavens opened. It was the rain which had been threatening all day, and with it, the moonlight was practically obliterated.

"Go and tell the others the good news." Katie pointed to where her siblings were waiting on the other side of the bonfire. "I want to watch the ship for a little longer. I can't explain it, but being here helping those sailors makes me feel closer to Mama and Papa somehow. I just feel sad that they will never know about any of this."

George squeezed her hand. "I truly believe that our loved ones who have already passed always know about the things that matter to us, Katie." He drew away respectfully to give her a few moments alone with her thoughts.

"Dearest Grandpapa," Katie whispered. "I hope you, Mama, and Papa can see how happy we all are in Stonehaven. We think of you and talk about you often, and I'm blessed to have George in my life, as well as many new friends—"

The words died in her throat as she saw a dark form separate itself from the shadows nearby.

It was a man...running directly towards her.

Before she even had a chance to scream, Carwyn Flanders sprang over the slippery rocks and seized her in a vice-like grip. He had the same menacing dark looks as John, and there was no mistaking who it was.

"You've ruined everything, Katie Anderson," he hissed in her ear. "I've waited years to return to Stonehaven and reclaim my rightful place as the man who strikes fear into everyone's hearts."

"Let...me...go." She tried to wriggle from his grasp, but all it did was make him even more determined, and he grabbed a handful of her hair, yanking it painfully and making her cry out. He clamped his hand over her mouth, his eyes glittering with pent-up rage.

"My brother John tried to stop me, and you know what happened to him," he grunted, panting heavily from trying to restrain her. "Why did you have to open the North Star Inn again? I had the perfect operation running, bringing all manner of stolen goods from abroad for my wealthy clients, without the Customs officers having a clue…and now I'll look like a fool…all because of a silly young woman sticking her nose in where it doesn't belong."

She aimed a well-placed kick, and he yelped as her boot made contact with his shin, loosening his grip on her slightly. "Th…the Customs officers are here," she stammered. "You'll go to jail for a very long time." She twisted to look over her shoulder. "George!" she screamed.

Everything turned into a blur.

She saw George charging back down the path from the woods towards her. Like some sort of miracle, the light from a dozen lanterns followed him, and she realised it was true—the Customs officers had indeed come to help.

"I'm not going to fail because of you," Carwyn snarled. He dragged her closer to the edge of the flat rocks they were on. Terror ran through her veins as Katie felt the waves crashing over the top. The swirling seawater sucked at their feet, making every step more treacherous.

"Let her go, Carwyn," George yelled. He held his arms wide to show that he had no weapon. "She's just an innocent young lady. This was my idea, so do the gentlemanly thing...let her go and take me instead."

Carwyn's cackling laugh held no humour, and he took another step backwards, dragging Katie with him. The ice-cold seawater was like a greedy beast clawing at the bottom of her dress, which felt like a lead weight even as the water receded between each wave. She risked a glance backwards and saw they were only inches from the edge. One false move, and they would both plunge to their deaths.

"I won't let you do this," she screamed, straining every sinew to pull him away from the precipice. "I've been through too much for it to end this way."

George strode closer, almost within her reach, but then stopped as Carwyn pulled a knife from his belt. The razor-sharp blade glinted in the firelight, and he laughed again. "If I go, she goes as well."

"Look out!" Katie screamed as she saw the largest wave yet rolling towards them. For a split second, Carwyn relaxed his grip, and she managed to spring out of his grasp.

"Why, you evil—"

Her captor's voice turned into an incredulous croak as Galahad streaked towards them, hackles up and a low growl rumbling in his chest. The hound launched himself at Carwyn, knocking him off balance. He staggered backwards, arms flailing, and then, in the blink of an eye, he vanished over the side of the rocks, howling with outrage at his inevitable fate.

George rushed forward and wrapped his arms around her, pulling her back to safety as Galahad trotted after them.

"I thought I'd lost you." His voice was thick with emotion.

"Nothing will part us." She swallowed the lump in her throat at how close they had come to a very different ending. "He's gone…can we save him?" Once the next wave had receded, she and George rushed to the edge, but it was impossible to see anything in the crashing, foaming waves beneath them.

"No." George shook his head. His expression was a mixture of relief tinged with shock. "He thought he could bend the sea to his will and make his fortune from others' loss, but in the end, the sea won."

Katie shivered against his chest, finally understanding. "Nobody deserves to die like that, but he chose it over jail." She looked deep into George's eyes. "Your pa might have suffered the same fate, taken by the sea, but he was a kind, honourable man. I know that because his son is the same."

The rain stopped as quickly as it had begun, and sparks drifted up from the bonfire behind them. George pulled her closer, and his eyes twinkled with amusement. "Are you flattering me, Miss Anderson?"

"Just saying what everyone knows is true." Out of the corner of her eye, she could see the Customs Officers approaching, flanked by Polly and Wilbur, who were talking animatedly and gesturing to where they had last glimpsed The Albion.

"I was trying to ask you something outside the inn last night when Beryl and Agatha interrupted us."

"Yes?" She rested her hands against his chest, feeling his strong heart beating beneath them. "I think we're about to be interrupted again," she chuckled.

"In that case, I'd better be quick." He brushed a sodden lock of hair from her face. "I know we're from different backgrounds, but I love you, Katie. Would you consider…"

"Courting?" She arched one eyebrow, and her pulse quickened.

"Courting…then a wedding…soon? I mean, I should ask Beryl and Wilbur first, I suppose, but—"

"I love you so much, my darling George. My answer is yes…and theirs will be, too." Their lips met in a tender kiss, then an awkward cough nearby made them spring apart again.

"Mr Oakley." George reached out and shook hands with the man standing in front of them. "Thank goodness you and your men arrived."

Eugene Oakley doffed his hat and broke into a broad smile. "Only thanks to your urgent message. We came from Bristol as fast as we could. We've arrested six men up by the lighthouse, and it will only be a matter of time until we find two more who slipped away into the night. The lighthouse keeper has a nasty bump on his head where they attacked him, but he'll be fine a day or two."

"What about The Albion? And all the stolen goods in the cave that we found." Katie's teeth chattered, and George hastily wrapped his coat around her shoulders.

"They're making safe passage and will moor up about an hour further along the coast. As for everything else the smugglers have hidden, once the storm subsides, we'll sail to the cave to collect everything. Hopefully, we can return the items to their rightful owners."

"So you think with Carwyn Flanders gone, that will be the end of the smugglers in these parts?" George sounded hopeful.

"I very much hope so. I shall be telling my superiors about your bravery. I wouldn't be surprised if you might get a letter from the palace to thank you for your services."

Katie blushed. "We just wanted to do our bit for the town, that's all." Another chill gripped her and she shivered again.

"If you'll excuse us, I need to get Katie back to the inn. Otherwise, Beryl will never let me marry her."

"A hot bath is all I need," she said, not wanting to make a fuss. "And then perhaps I can get back to the business of running a coaching inn in a quiet coastal town."

George grinned as Polly, Wilbur, and Tim crowded around, all chattering loudly about the night's events. "You might be surprised. I reckon the inn will be busier than ever."

"Why's that? I hope you'll be able to help when the sea is too rough for fishing." She leaned against his solid, comforting bulk with his arm around her shoulder and ruffled Galahad's ears as they made their way back to the cart.

"Once word gets out that you foiled the smugglers' plan, people will travel from far and wide to see the place for themselves."

"We'd better keep it a secret then." A sense of

peace washed over her, as though everything was right with the world again. "I just want a simple life, George. For us to be together, with friends and family nearby. And a business that keeps a roof over our heads and food on the table."

"That sounds perfect." His gaze softened as they shared a smile of understanding.

EPILOGUE

Three Months Later.

Katie felt a warm glow of belonging in her chest as she and Polly strolled down Long Street. It was a week before Christmas, their first one in Stonehaven, and there was a palpable sense of excitement among the townsfolk, which she had never experienced in quite the same way when they lived out on the moors at Castleford Hall.

The shop windows were decorated with extra candles and festive baubles, and the sweet sound of Christmas carols sung by the church choir drifted towards them from the town square where the vicar was rehearsing with them.

Ernie and Nora Waite waved from the other side of the road, then crossed to join them.

"Does the vicar normally rehearse carols?" Polly asked.

Nora gave them a beaming smile. "Oh no, my dear. It's for a special service he's doing this Christmas." She nudged her husband. "You tell them, Ernie."

The cobbler took his hat off, and Katie noticed his face had lost that haunted look she had assumed was his natural expression. Instead, he looked relaxed, even jovial. "The vicar decided he wanted to gather everyone together on Christmas Eve to celebrate our town's fresh start."

Katie glanced at Polly. "I'm not sure I understand, Ernie. Has something happened we don't know about? New businesses being set up, perhaps?"

He chuckled. "I told you they were humble, didn't I, Nora." His wife nodded, and Ernie leaned closer and lowered his voice. "It's to celebrate no longer being troubled by the Flanders brothers, Katie. Thanks in a large part to you and your family, as well as young George."

"Don't be silly." She felt herself blushing, especially as Gethin Cowley happened to pass just at that moment in his cart, taking barrels of ale up to the inn and gave them a knowing wink. "We just did what we thought was right at the time." Her heart pitter-pattered as she saw George hurrying towards them. She loved him more each day, and they had a very special week ahead.

"We're just telling Katie about the vicar's festive service on Christmas Eve." Ernie and Nora stood back to let two old ladies pass. "She doesn't understand the true impact of why this year is going to be so different for us in Stonehaven."

George linked arms with Katie, giving her a soft smile. "It turns out a good many of the business owners in town were being affected one way or another by John and Carwyn Flanders. Some were paying protection money. Others had years of debt still owing from shady dealings that Carwyn did before he fled to France, where he persuaded them to give him their savings to invest in fictional stocks. Not to mention the smuggling as well. But now the Flanders are gone, and the slate has been wiped clean."

"Folk were afraid to talk to each other about it, you see," Nora explained, looking embarrassed. "That's how they got away with it because none of us realised they had duped many of our friends and neighbours. It's been years of heartache and worry."

Ernie patted her hand reassuringly. "But now it's over, my sweet." They both looked at her and George with gratitude shining in their eyes. "This will be the first Christmas the townsfolk can sleep easy in their beds, free from John and Carwyn's evil ways. Of course, the vicar can't phrase it quite like that," he chuckled. "But we all know what he means by having this special service in the town square. It's a new start for us all."

"I'm happy we've made a difference."

As the Waites headed back to their workshop, Katie consulted her list. There was so much to do; her head was spinning with it all. "Now…should we go to the grocers next or see about your dress?"

Polly plucked the list from her hand and grinned. "You're doing neither of those things. George and I have decided you need the morning off doing chores."

"But what about preparing for everything? It's the busiest time of the year, and we don't want to let our customers down."

"Aren't you forgetting a little something?" George raised his eyebrows. "Our wedding…in two days."

"Of course not." Katie let out a long sigh of

contentment. "It's going to be a wonderful day. I think I just got caught up in all the planning for Christmas at the inn, wondering how many guests we might have staying with us and—" Her words trailed off as she spotted Robin clopping along the street at a brisk trot. Wilbur was holding the reins, and he was flanked by Beryl and Agatha, and Tim was in the back of the cart.

"I had no idea you were all coming into town this morning."

George helped Beryl and Agatha down, and Beryl straightened her bonnet, rolling her eyes. "Did you think we would let you do all the organising on your own? I know it's your name above the door of the pub, but we're family, Katie. Agatha and I are collecting all the supplies we need for your wedding meal from Alwyn Jones now."

"And Tim and I are going to mend your ma's roof while it's dry," Wilbur told George. "We had all those spare tiles from the derelict barn in the woods, and I promised her we would do the repairs before the next storm."

"I'm truly grateful. It's going to be strange for Ma when I'm not living at the cottage anymore after our wedding, but she insisted it was right for me to start married life with Katie at the inn."

"That's what brothers-in-law are for," Wilbur said cheerfully, picking up the reins again. "You and Catrin are part of our family now."

Tim blew on his hands to warm them up. "Also, I'm going to make her a new rocking chair after Christmas, as well. It will be the first piece in my new furniture making business."

"You and George should have a hot chocolate and cake from the teashop, Katie. I'm collecting our new gowns from Flora Craddock, the dressmaker," Polly said, wrapping her woolly scarf tighter in the cold wind. "After that, there's nothing left to do other than enjoy your wedding and our first Christmas here in Stonehaven. Ebenezer and Gabriel arrive tomorrow, so Agatha and I will prepare their rooms this afternoon." She waggled the list then tucked it in her reticule. "Let us take care of things for once."

Katie felt her worries start to melt away as she watched her loved ones go forth to do the various jobs she had been thinking about.

"Do you like the idea of a hot chocolate?" George asked her. They linked arms and strolled along the street. "I wouldn't be surprised if we get snow in the next few days. It's certainly cold enough."

"Actually, I think I'd rather take a walk on the jetty." She turned her face towards the pale winter sun and breathed in the salty air. Smoke curled up from the cottage chimneys, and frost still rimed the rooftops that faced north and would be in the shade all day. There was something about the crisp day and sparkling frost that felt invigorating after weeks of lashing rain and autumnal storms.

"That sounds like a good idea. Do you remember that night when we met again on the jetty?"

"How can I forget? I was so happy when I realised it was you. It was as if all those times I had dreamt about you over the years had suddenly become a reality."

He gave her a mischievous smile. "It wasn't a coincidence that we met in Pembrey Minster four years ago."

"Really?" She stopped walking and gave him a searching look. "I had a feeling you knew me, but it didn't make sense. I put it down to wishful thinking."

"I've never told anyone this. Many years ago, I went blackberry picking up in the woods by the inn. A well-dressed gentleman was looking around the property."

"Grandpa?"

"Yes. He said that one day his four grandchildren might come and return the coaching inn to its former glory, although you would be grownups by then. He gave me a few coins for the blackberries I'd picked. I think he could see times were hard for my family."

"That's the sort of kindhearted thing he often did."

"He said his eldest granddaughter was very special." George's eyes softened at the memory. "He said if our paths crossed, he hoped we would become good friends, and be happy together."

Katie felt close to tears. "It's as though he was giving us his blessing."

"I thought about that meeting many times, and one day, I overheard someone saying Sir William lived near Pembrey Minster. I went there for the day hoping to meet you. I wanted to see who this wonderful granddaughter was."

They carried on walking as she pondered how the different threads of her life had brought her and George together, against all odds. "If Uncle Norman had been nicer, we would never have come to Stonehaven." The thought seemed inconceivable now.

"It's funny how things worked out."

"Have you heard anything more from Constable Parry?" She didn't like to talk about that stormy night much, preferring to look to the future instead, but she knew the men had been awaiting trial.

"He came to visit me and Ma at the cottage this morning, as it happens. He wanted me to tell you that the trial went well, and the judge sentenced them to hard labour in Fremantle, Australia. The convict ship sails next week."

"I'm grateful that none of Carwyn's gang were from Stonehaven. I would have felt bad for their wives and families."

"He was shrewd enough to know that the local men would never be loyal to him. He picked men from France instead, with no ties to the area, and a handful from London."

"And still no news about him?" Katie shivered as she remembered Carwyn's cruel eyes and how his face contorted with rage as he dragged her to the cliff edge, with her life hanging in the balance.

"The sea hasn't given up his body. It probably never will after this length of time, but he must be dead. Nobody could have survived the sea that night."

She sighed, pushing away the thought that if anyone were going to defy the odds, it might be Carwyn Flanders. There would always be a tiny part of her that would worry they had no definitive proof he had died, but everyone had assured her he would have drowned within minutes in the towering waves or been smashed on the jagged rocks.

She changed the subject. "Are you sure your ma doesn't mind you living at the inn with us?" It had been bothering her, and she always wanted to be honest with George.

"Not in the slightest," he chuckled. "She will enjoy visiting us often. Also, she's relieved that I won't feel obliged to take the boat out fishing in bad weather. She knows I'm looking forward to working with you at the inn and just going fishing in the summer. It will certainly feel very different but in a good way. Who knows, we may have children of our own to look after very soon."

Katie felt a flutter of excitement in her chest as she thought about the future. Just as they were about to turn the corner to walk down to the harbour, she caught sight of two smart grey horses trotting towards them, pulling a gleaming black carriage. The coachman called a command, reining the horses sharply to a halt next to them, and a familiar figure threw open the door and jumped out of the carriage with a delighted smile.

"Cousin Max? What are you doing here? I thought you were stationed in India?" Once her surprise subsided, she remembered her manners and looked up at George. "This is my cousin Max, George. The one I told you about in Her Majesty's army. Max, this is George, my—"

"Fiancé," George finished for her. "Or should I say, husband in two days' time. It's very nice to meet you, Max. Katie talks about you often, and I know she's missed you."

After the two men shook hands, Max swept his hat off and hugged Katie. "A wedding in two days' time? In that case, it's lucky I came here today. How are you all? We have so much to catch up on."

"Yes, and of course, you must come to the wedding." She could hardly believe her eyes; it had been so long. The army had aged him. She'd noticed he limped as he walked towards them. "Were you injured? How long are you on leave for?"

"I was honourably discharged. We got caught in a skirmish, and I ended up being shot in my leg. They could only do a rudimentary operation, and the old leg won't ever be as good as it was." He shrugged, tapping his knee, seeming quite cheerful about the whole thing. "I never intended to be away for very long. To be honest, I missed home. And all of you," he added.

"How did you know where to find us?" She didn't

want to be cagey, but she still had no contact with Uncle Norman.

Regret and embarrassment flashed across Max's face, and he shook his head. "I'm sorry about what Papa tried to do to you when he inherited Castleford Hall. I found out about everything from Jacob and Mr Dryden, and although I'd like to say I'm shocked Papa could do such a thing, the truth is, I always suspected he would throw you out. I'm estranged from him because we had a huge row about what he did."

"Oh, Max, I'm so sorry." Katie patted her cousin's arm, feeling bad for him. "I assumed you would work with Uncle Norman managing Castleford and the estate when you retired from the army. That was surely what he wanted for you? Or a position in London, managing his affairs up there?"

Max screwed up his face, but more with anger than regret. "There's no chance of that. Papa was so cross I took your side that he told me I was no longer welcome at Castleford Hall. Mama cried, but you know how stubborn Papa can be. It doesn't matter. By good fortune, a mutual acquaintance introduced me to Lord Bevan, who was looking for a new estate manager, so that's what I do now." He gestured towards the smart carriage. "Life isn't too bad, as you can see," he chuckled. "Lord Bevan spends a lot of time in London. He said he's happy to leave me to get on with managing the estate, which will suit me very well. I only started last week and this is the first chance I had to come to Stonehaven."

"Grandpa bought the North Star Inn many years ago in case Uncle Norman didn't want us to live at Castleford." She tightened her winter cape against the cold wind. "I actually enjoy being a landlady, and as long as I know Polly, Wilbur, and Tim are safe, and we work hard, it's a good life. Beryl came to join us a week after we arrived here. In many ways, it's just like old times, but better," she smiled up at George as she added that last part. A thought occurred to her. "Does…does Uncle Norman know where we are?"

Max nodded. "Yes, he heard rumours, especially after Beryl left. But don't worry, he has no interest in taking any of this away from you."

"He'd better not try," George muttered protectively.

"Well, I have a few tenants to visit, but after that, my day is free." Max gazed up and down the street. "It's a charming town."

"You must go to the inn; Beryl will be so happy to see you. Just follow the road out of town and you'll see the sign on the turning for our lane. Everyone is running a few errands at the moment now, but I'm sure we'll all be home by the time you get there." She squeezed Max's hand, feeling a burst of relief that he was nothing like his father. "Honestly, having you back and living locally is the best news, Max. I'm sorry you've fallen out with Uncle Norman, but we've forgiven him if that helps. People have made us feel welcome, and we're settled here. I'm sure he'll come to his senses soon."

"Maybe, but life goes on." Max put his hat on and clambered back into the carriage. "See you later," he called cheerfully, knocking on the roof for the coachman to continue the journey. Katie watched the carriage roll away and suddenly gasped as she caught sight of the golden fleur-de-lis crest painted on the back.

"Look, George. Look at Lord Bevan's crest. It's the same as what I saw on those scraps of paper I pulled from the fire in our parlour." A horrifying thought slid into her mind. "Do you think Lord Bevan was involved with the smugglers?"

George rubbed his jaw, then shook his head decisively. "Surely not. A man of his social standing wouldn't want anything to do with smugglers. Think of the damage to his reputation if people found out."

They carried on walking, turning down the lane to the harbour.

"You're right. I'm making connections out of nothing." She pushed away a faint sense of unease as she remembered the fleur-de-lis on the scraps of paper. "We know the smugglers used our parlour as a meeting place. I suppose John Flanders had some of Lord Bevan's headed notepaper when he was his rent collector. He must have used it to write notes for Carwyn."

"Exactly." George gave her a reassuring smile. "It's all over now, and there's nothing more for us to worry about."

They strolled along the harbour wall, and Katie allowed herself to daydream about her future as George's wife. After a shaky start, the business was going well. Agatha and Beryl were already discussing which room to turn into a nursery and the delight of a growing family. She imagined her and George taking a picnic to the stream and their children's innocent giggles as they paddled on a warm summer's day.

"Are you happy, my love?" George asked softly. He had a way of knowing what she was thinking about that filled her with joy. "It's time to put troubling things from the past behind us, don't you think?"

Katie reached into her pocket and pulled out the farthing she had kept from that dreadful night when Norman had tried to send her and her siblings to the workhouse. She turned the coin over in her hand, thinking about everything it represented—how her uncle had thought so little of her. Then the way she had been forced to turn her back on her family home and everything she had grown up with.

"You're right, darling George. I thought I would keep this coin forever to remind me to be strong, but I don't need it anymore. I have you now... and our own children soon, I hope. That's more than enough blessings to be grateful for."

They had reached the end of the harbour wall, and she threw the farthing high into the air. It glinted in the low winter sun as it spun, then dropped into the white-tipped waves. For a brief moment, she could still see the coin in the grey-green water, then it slowly sank into the swaying seaweed.

"We have the rest of our lives to be together," George murmured. He wrapped his arms around her, and the gulls wheeled overhead, bright white against the clear blue sky.

Katie had never felt happier and could see now that without the tribulations she and George had been through, their paths might not have crossed again. Fate had brought them together, and she was meant to be with this kind-hearted man. It was almost as though it had been written in the stars.

READ MORE

If you enjoyed The Farthing Girl, you'll love Daisy Carter's other Victorian Romance Saga Stories:

Sophie's Secret

Torn between keeping secrets or revealing the truth, with the shadows of age-old wrongs hanging over her...can Sophie find the love and happiness she deserves?

Sophie Henderson's childhood changes in a heartbeat when she and her sister, Anne, are abandoned at Kingsley House, a charitable home for unwanted children.

As they grow up, Anne is full of restless ambition and sees marriage to a wealthy man as her way up in the world. But Sophie is happy to become a maid if it

READ MORE

means she can stay near Albert Granger, her childhood friend.

One day, everything changes when the wealthy businessman, Horace Smallwood invites them to sing at his hotel. And when Albert's parents, Dolly and Joe suggest she could also sing on their narrowboat, *The River Maid*, to entertain the well-to-do ladies and gentlemen staying at the hotel, the future looks rosy.

But as Sophie gains notoriety, she attracts the attention of unknown enemies.

And when she stumbles across something she shouldn't have, she gets sucked into a web of secrets and lies.

As much as she wants to do the right thing, too many peoples' fortunes rely on her staying silent.

Amid bitter rivalries and with the long shadows of age-old wrongs hanging over her, Sophie thinks her chance at love is lost forever.

And when a glittering future beckons, she is torn between old obligations and new opportunities.

Will letting go of her secrets be her salvation? And can Sophie ever find her way back home to the West Country and the happy family life she longs for?

Sophie's Secret is a heart-warming saga

READ MORE

romance that turns full circle with the narrowboat families of times gone by. Full of adventure, courage, heartache, and hope, this page-turner will linger in your mind long after you finish it.

*** * ***

Do you love FREE BOOKS? Download Daisy's FREE book now:

The May Blossom Orphan

Get your free copy here: https://dl.bookfunnel.com/iqx7g0u0s7

Clementine Morris thought life had finally dealt her a kinder hand when her aunt rescued her from the orphanage. But happiness quickly turns to fear when she realises her uncle has shocking plans for her to earn more money.

As the net draws in, a terrifying accident at the docks sparks an unlikely new friendship with kindly warehouse lad, Joe Sawbridge.

Follow Clemmie and Joe through the dangers of the London docks, to find out whether help comes in the nick of time, in this heart-warming Victorian romance story.